G000254365

Isle of Desire

Zara Devereux

LIBRIS

An *X Libris* Book

First published by X Libris in 1998

Copyright © Zara Devereux 1998

The moral right of the author has been asserted.

*All characters in this publication are
fictitious and any resemblance to real
persons, living or dead, is purely coincidental.*

All rights reserved.
No part of this publication may be reproduced,
stored in a retrieval system, or transmitted, in
any form or by any means, without the prior
permission in writing of the publisher, nor be
otherwise circulated in any form of binding or
cover other than that in which it is published and
without a similar condition including this condition
being imposed on the subsequent purchaser.

A CIP catalogue record for this book
is available from the British Library.

ISBN 0 7515 2311 9

Photoset in North Wales by
Derek Doyle & Associates, Mold, Flintshire
Printed and bound in Great Britain by
Clays Ltd, St Ives plc

X Libris
A Division of
Little, Brown and Company (UK)
Brettenham House
Lancaster Place
London WC2E 7EN

Isle of Desire

Chapter One

HER EARS WERE fine-tuned for the sound of the early morning post falling through the letter-box. No matter how late she had gone to bed or how deeply she had slept, she knew the moment the mail hit the mat. It was better than keeping a dog, and far less bother.

She woke fully and lay there for a moment, feeling Giles's body curled spoon-fashion against hers, his semi-erect penis nudging between her buttocks. She breathed deeply, inhaling the scent of his skin and the aroma of costly aftershave that mingled with his sweat.

Frustrated desire stirred within her, an unfulfilled yearning that warmed into anger. Giles muttered, feeling her move. He held her closer, his breath tickling her shoulder-blades as he grunted, 'What's the matter, Carla?'

'The post,' she answered, freeing herself and scrambling out of bed. She shrugged on a loose cotton robe, pushed back the tangle of light brown curls falling over her brow and flew down the carpeted stairs to the hall where her bare feet encountered mosaic tiles.

Even now, after several years of the Yo-Yo business of publishing, she still experienced that adrenaline buzz. The postman might have brought a contract, a proposal, a rejection. She disliked Sundays, bank holidays and Christmas Day, simply because they lacked this magical ingredient.

Several letters lay on the coconut mat set in its brass-edged well. Two had long brown envelopes with little windows signifying bills, and were addressed to Giles Davenport; two were white and important-looking, also addressed to him; the third was equally businesslike and bore her name, Carla Holt. She recognised it as coming from Toby Torrance, her agent.

Then, at the bottom of the heap, she found a mauve envelope with a flowery border, handwritten and impregnated with perfume: definitely a female sender. The writing sprawled, seeming to linger lasciviously over the curves and angles of Giles's name, as if the owner of this flamboyant hand wanted to trace round his body and explore his genitals in similar fashion.

Jealousy knifed through Carla's gut and her heart plummeted. Then she gave herself a severe talking-to.

Giles was famous, handsome, intellectual and charismatic, an acclaimed writer of science fiction novels, which had become something of a cult. Several of his books had already been adapted for TV, and there was talk of a major movie. The mauve missive had been sent by a fan. But hard on the heels of this came the niggling thought: fan mail usually arrived at his agent's office via his publishers, not his home address.

Feeling guilty, she held the letter to the light and scrutinised it. She could see nothing, so gave up and placed it with the rest on the hall-table, determined not to let her imagination run away with her. She carried her own letter into the kitchen where she delayed opening it, partly to tease herself, mostly because she liked this breathing space between knowing if the contents were something she should rejoice in or worry about.

It was a rainy morning, grey and dim. She flicked on the overhead spots. The kitchen sprang into shape, a superbly designed conversion from an Edwardian scullery. While Carla measured water into the green

2

cordless kettle, she ran her eye round the white units with gothic arched moulding and cupboards glazed in stained glass, the high-tech cooker, freezer, dishwasher, and William Morris-patterned wallpaper and tiles.

Le Creuset pans stood on shelves, along with brass ladles, sets of wickedly sharp knives, wooden spoons and recipe books. Giles was a gourmet chef and liked to cook when the mood took him. With an eye fixed firmly on the main chance, this usually happened when he wanted to impress dinner guests: actors, producers, bigwigs in the world of TV and films.

With her interest in history augmented by the research necessary for her work, Carla appreciated the skill that had transformed this detached villa in Richmond into a comfortable home with every modern convenience, while keeping the traditional features.

She sighed, hardly aware of doing so. The house belonged to Giles, not her.

'Come and live with me, darling,' he had insisted shortly after they had met at a seminar where he had been lecturing on creative writing.

Swept off her feet, bedazzled by his charm, magnificent good looks and formidable reputation, she had given up her tiny flat in Notting Hill and moved in. Two years ago, and a lot of water had flowed under the bridge since then. She thought about this as she deftly poured boiling water over the teabags in bright pottery mugs and folded back the wings of a milk carton. His career had really taken off during that time, while hers had declined. This did nothing to boost her self-esteem, and neither did Giles.

He was demanding, and liked to bounce ideas off her, so instead of concentrating on her own manuscripts, she often trailed around behind him, made sure he kept appointments, spent hours surfing the Net on his behalf, and acted like an unpaid secretary.

3

'Leave him,' Marie Abelson had advised brusquely with a flick of her mahogany bob. 'He's so goddamn selfish, honey. You've got more talent in your little finger than he has in the whole of his body, including his prick. It's just that he's been lucky.'

'I know,' Carla had replied, seated in Marie's luxurious apartment near Hyde Park, her home when she flew in from New York. 'Well, I suppose I do, though he must be brainier than me. He creates such wonderful twists to his plots. I only write romance novels.'

'So do I,' Marie had replied acerbically. 'And I'm on the bestseller list. You haven't been in the right place at the right time. You've got to learn to use your savvy, cultivate people, push yourself. That's what Giles does, and it pays off.'

'He looks down his nose at the kind of literature we write,' Carla had said, voicing her pent-up anger.

'He's a Grade One skunk!' Marie had retorted. 'How about the huge popularity of this genre? Does he think all women readers are stupid? I'll tell you this, hon, he doesn't patronise me. He wouldn't dare. I'd pulverise him. Sure, I've had him sneering at me when we've been on the same TV chat shows, but I always put him down. He can't win the argument. I'm successful on both sides of the Pond, and guys like Giles admire success above everything else. Trouble is, when you try to talk to him it's like paging the oracle. He knows everything and is never wrong.'

Marie's loyalty had brought tears to Carla's eyes. Last year she had attended a romance writers' convention in Florida, and had fallen in with this forthright American who had become her mentor and best friend.

'I don't know how you dare appear on the telly. I'd die. I simply can't sell myself,' she had said. 'Seems like I've always been in the background, the middle child, my sister an achiever, my brother the baby of the family.

Father adored her and mother doted on him. I buried myself in books, music and dreams.'

'That's fine. Isolation turned you into a writer, and a fine one, too. Leave the selling to your agent,' Marie had replied, stretching her sleek, exercise-honed body. She was glamorous, confident, all the things Carla longed to be. 'Giles is a self-opinionated bore and I wasn't surprised when you told me he was lousy in bed.'

'He says it's me,' Carla had murmured miserably.

'Of course he does. That shows what an asshole he is. Take a break. Try it with someone else and tell Giles to go stuff himself.'

It was fine to agree when she was with the strong, independent Marie, but Carla's courage failed when actually facing up to Giles. As now, for example. Marie would have ripped open the mauve envelope and demanded to know what the hell was going on.

Carla could not do this. She was too well brought up. Nice girls simply did not read other people's mail, even if they suspected betrayal.

She sipped her tea reflectively, then slid a knife under the flap and opened her letter from Toby. She had several synopses in the pipeline, but half expected another rejection. These had been piling up of late. Editors and publishers were getting exceedingly picky in the harsh financial climate of the late twentieth century.

Half a dozen historical romances under her belt and, despite favourable reviews and a modest, yearly cheque from library rights, she was still in a shaky position. So many people had jumped on the bandwagon, it was a struggle to keep a foothold. Most of her savings were gone and she hated having to ask Giles for money, and would never, ever confess to her family that she was not the success she pretended to be.

She concentrated on Toby's letter:

Dear Carla,

Sorry to be the bringer of bad news, but Julia Locke of Crown Publishers has finally decided that she can't use your new novel. They lost money on the last one, apparently – the libraries are no longer buying in so many books – the paperbackers aren't interested, etc. This is a bloody nuisance, especially as you have spent so much time and energy working on a rewrite for them.

However, don't despair – I have another proposition that may appeal to you.

Come and see me PDQ and we'll discuss it. Let me take you out to lunch. It's been some time since we had a cosy chat.

Yours, Toby

Carla read the letter again and then tucked it into the pocket of her robe. A cosy chat? What he really means is a fuck, she thought, the slow burn of lust smouldering in her epicentre.

She had only had one affair before Giles, and that had been a shambles. Toby was attractive and she recognised his signals, her own thwarted desires responding. He wanted her, but she had remained faithful to Giles, considering herself to be a one-man woman.

She heard footsteps above, then the lavatory flushing and, 'What are you doing down there, Carla? Milking the cow or something? Where's my cup of tea?' Giles shouted irritably from the landing.

'Coming,' she said, hastily placing the mugs on a tray and picking up his letters as she passed through the hall.

He was back in bed when she pushed open the door with her hip and entered the dimly lit room. Propped against frilled pillows under a lace-draped coronal, he was devastatingly sexy, his skin – darkly tanned from a recent trip to Los Angeles on a lecture tour – contrasting with the whiteness surrounding him. Carla had been left behind. 'It'll give you a chance to get on with your latest romantic outpouring,' he had said magnanimously. 'Not that it will take long – hardly a weighty opus.'

Now her heart flipped over in her breast at the sight of his classically handsome face, those steely, intelligent eyes, pronounced nose and square jaw. He always visited exclusive West End salons and his fair hair was appealingly tousled, curling at his nape. Her fingers tingled with the need to touch him. They had made love last night, and she was aware of the mingled scents of their arousal wafting up from the secret place between her thighs.

Her nipples crimped and her clitoris throbbed, unsatisfied by the encounter. As usual, she had been unable to reach the heights with his penis thrusting inside her. He spared little time on foreplay. Sometimes it seemed he wanted to get the act over and done with as quickly as possible, as if it was an irksome chore.

And this from the man over whom well-read members of the public raved, buying his novels as much for his photo inside the jacket as the contents. They would queue for hours in a bookstore where he was doing a signing session, looking 'all windswept and interesting', as Marie sarcastically commented. These personal appearances captivated them even more.

Now Carla watched him with a resurgence of sexual need, then flipped back the duvet and climbed into bed beside him. She had never lost the hope that someday, somehow, he would realise what she wanted to bring her to orgasm. Tentatively, she had tried to explain, but he had brushed it aside, convinced that he knew all there was to know about sex. She had avoided broaching the subject again.

'Where's my mail?' he said, as he sipped his tea. She handed it over. He examined the letters, remarking, 'Not much of interest here.'

'Nothing important?' she asked, setting her own mug on the bedside table, longing to ask about the mauve envelope, but not quite daring.

'An invitation to appear at a literary function. Another letter asking me to donate to a charity fund for ageing authors,' he replied, then added casually, 'and this fancy one's from Alicia Ashford. She's back in England and wants me to get in touch.'

Carla stilled, warning bells ringing in her brain. Alicia was a newscaster whose meteoric rise to fame had led her to hosting her own late-night slot where she interviewed celebrities. Giles had appeared several times and Carla's intuition had screamed that this boded no good. Alicia was reputed to be as hot-arsed and immoral as an alley cat.

'Will you do that ... get in touch?' she asked hesitantly.

'I might,' he said, a shade too quickly.

He shrugged his broad shoulders, and Carla reached over hesitantly and stroked the fuzz of hair coating his chest. He did not protest, merely continued to scan his correspondence, and she became bolder, trembling with desire as she let her fingertips circle the brown discs of his nipples.

He stirred then, and growled, 'Suck them.'

Carla lowered her face, breathing in the pungent male scent of him, opening her mouth and drawing one of the nubs between her lips, working her tongue over it. Her own nipples rose from their dark areolae, hard as stone, and fresh honeydew pooled at her vulva. Giles went on reading, but as Carla's hand drifted down to

his waist and beyond, she could feel his prick hardening.

Restraining the impulse to kneel above him and
impale herself on that upright bough of flesh, she
continued to lip his skin, her tongue flicking his small,
tight teats.

'You know what I like, don't you?' he said, his voice
husky.

Her palm closed over the long hot stalk of his penis,
and desire swirled in her loins. He reached down and
cupped one of her breasts, his thumb-pad brushing the
nipple. Voluptuous spasms racked her womb and made
her even more moist.

She lay with her cheek cushioned against his hard-
muscled abdomen and admired his beautiful cock. Her
senses were stimulated by its musky odour. He had
urinated but not showered since entering her love-
channel during the night hours, and she caught a trace of
her own piscine juices that had laved his manhood. The
entire bed reeked of coitus – salty, rich, marvellous.

The erect, thick, curving length of his phallus was
fully exposed, and she feasted her eyes on the swelling
veins and the soft, red, luxurious folds of skin where the
base of his shaft joined his balls. She touched them
gently, feeling them pulsating and moving in their wrin-
kled scrotal sac. Giles sighed and lifted his hips from the
mattress, pushing his prick towards her lips.

She leaned over him and, slowly and sensuously,
lowered her mouth till the tip of his rod rested against
it. He jerked upwards, impatiently. She parted her lips,
moistened them with her tongue and allowed the throbbing, smooth, twin-lobed glans to slide inside.

Now he was trapped – now she was in command.
She closed her mouth firmly round the globe, tasting
the bittersweet essence that escaped from the slit. The
skin was deliciously smooth, and she sucked him with

9

steady pulls, feeling him twitch in her mouth, feeling the head butting against the back of her throat, holding it there.

Employing a more subtle approach, she withdrew, letting her tongue play over the engorged helm. Leaving this quivering, she turned her attention to the shaft, burying her nose in his testicles, then licking all the way up his cock, round the retracted foreskin, and over the shining crimson head once more.

Giles gasped, locked his hands in her hair and thrust deeply into her mouth. She could not move, straddled across him, her bottom in the air. Her robe had ridden up and her sex valley was bare and vulnerable, wetness bedewing her swollen labia, eager lower mouth and pursed nether hole.

She wanted to move over him, to lower herself swiftly and plunge his weapon into the burgeoning flower of her vagina, writhe, pump, and angle her pubis so the root of his cock rubbed against her clitoris at every downward stroke.

But Giles was blind to everything except releasing the pressure in his groin, his phallus growing larger as he pulled Carla's head up and down fiercely. She knew he was about to climax, could feel the tension spiralling down his spine, gathering in his belly, the orgasmic explosion very near. She never minded receiving his libation in her mouth, but was desperate for relief.

She tried to say, 'I need to come, too,' but his huge cock prevented speech. Her jaw ached and his nails dug into her scalp.

He rocked her back and forth, impervious to anything save his own gratification. His chest was heaving, his hips rising and falling to meet the movements of her mouth. Then he came with unexpected violence, shooting out milky jets of semen that dribbled down her chin and smeared the curls falling forward over her breasts.

He slumped back, releasing his punishing grip on her head, his penis slipping from between her lips, limp but still partly erect. It glistened with her saliva and his own tribute.

Tears of disappointment burned behind Carla's lids. He pushed her away, then lay to one side, an arm over his eyes.

'Is that it?' she asked, her voice hard, almost hating him.

He removed his arm, turned his face towards her and said, 'What d'you mean?'

'You've finished, have you? You aren't going to fuck me?' Anger was making her reckless. Damn him! How dare he leave her with aching breasts and lust boiling inside her?

His eyes regarded her with a coldness she had learned to dread. 'I fucked you last night, didn't I?'

'Then what was this all about?'

He grinned unpleasantly. 'You started it. I was merely reading my letters.'

Carla bounced up into a sitting position, her breasts shaking, the nipples puckered with longing. 'All you were interested in was the letter from your tart, Alicia Ashford!' she exclaimed, violet-blue eyes flashing.

He eased down under the cover, so cruel, beautiful and indifferent that she wanted to kill him. 'Don't be silly, Carla. She's a business associate.'

'I'll tell her what a selfish lover you are, shall I? Or does she already know?' Carla blazed.

'Do what the hell you like,' he said nonchalantly. 'You're always moaning. What is it this time? PMT? Get a life, Carla.'

'I had one before I met you,' she shouted, appalled by her own words.

'Did you, darling?' he drawled mockingly. 'Ah, yes

... the lady novelist ... providing masturbation fantasies for bored housewives.'

'Whatever they were, they were mine ... my achievements, my books. I wasn't eclipsed by some arrogant bastard whose brains are in his balls!' she yelled, thinking: God, that's it. He'll ask me to leave.

His eyes sparkled maliciously, and he applauded, slowly and insultingly. 'Well done. I've never heard you so vocal. So, that's what you really think of me, is it?'

All the fight drained out of her suddenly. She was terrified. What would she do if he kicked her out? How to survive without him?

'No. I'm angry. I wanted more sex. I'm sorry, Giles, but you're so attractive,' she whispered, despising herself for her weakness.

He sank back, almost purring as he said, 'So that's the trouble, is it? You want more of me?'

'Yes,' she lied, thinking, I want an orgasm. I hoped you would give me one. Will you ever?

'We'll talk about this later,' he said, and got up. 'I can't hang around this morning. I've a script to finish.'

'I'll ring Toby. He has something he wants to talk over,' she muttered, realising that the problem was not going to be resolved. Giles would avoid anything that might hint at criticism.

'Maybe it'll mean some work.'

'Maybe. I'll try to see him today, then do a spot of shopping afterwards,' she added, following his lead and acting as if nothing had happened.

'Don't worry about me,' he returned airily. 'Lunch with Toby if you want. I'll get a pizza sent in.'

He sauntered into the en suite bathroom and Carla trailed off to use the other one along the passage. While soaking in the scented foamy water she managed to catch Toby on his mobile.

'Hi there. It's Carla. I can get in today, this morning,

if you want,' she began. 'What's all this about a proposal?'

'We'll discuss it when you get here. Eleven suit you?' he answered, the sound of his voice sending little pleasurable shocks across her shoulders, down her spine and into her loins.

'That'll be fine.'

'Everything OK?' he asked.

'Yes . . . no . . . I suppose so,' she replied, wanting him there, needing a shoulder to cry on.

'Is it Giles? He has all the subtlety of a ramraider. Cheer up, love. Worse things happen at sea.'

'Do they?'

'Of course. See you in a while.'

'OK. Bye, Toby.'

Carla flogged her rattling little Fiat into London with her foot on the floor, till slowed by traffic, then went straight to the municipal car park in D'Arblay Street. From there she walked the short distance through Soho to Toby's office.

It was still raining. Sooty splodges dropped from the leaden skies and greased the pavement. London at its most depressing, Carla thought gloomily, the weather doing nothing to lift her spirits. Giles had shut himself in his study before she left, armed with coffee and cigarettes, very cool and collected.

She was in a ferment of anxiety about their quarrel. Had she mortally offended him? Was his male ego irrevocably dented? She felt guilty and uneasy, and thoroughly miserable.

Worrying about what to wear for her meeting with Toby, she had settled for a calf-length brown wool skirt, a ribbed sweater and loose jacket, the whole livened by an orange silk scarf. Sensible brown shoes completed

13

the ensemble, and she had dragged a beret over her unruly hair.

Catching a glimpse of herself as she passed a shop window, she was in no way encouraged, hearing Marie's voice in her head, saying, 'You don't make the most of yourself, honey.'

Never had Carla felt this to be more true; her self-worth was at an all time low. Her depression lightened when she reached the narrow, crowded street where the old houses had been transformed into offices.

She paused before one of these, and pressed a button marked Torrance Literary Agency Ltd. A crackly voice answered, an outer door opened automatically and she climbed the stairs. On the third floor she was greeted by Toby's assistant, Sadie, a cheerful girl with green streaks in her short, spiky hair. She was wearing a petrol-blue PVC mini-skirt over a brief bodysuit and clumpy, stack-heeled shoes.

'He's expecting you,' she carolled, and Carla entered Toby's sanctum.

He leapt up and came towards her, hands extended. She took them gratefully, already soothed and calmed, responding to his warmth.

He was neatly built, slim and wiry, and his superbly tailored charcoal-grey suit had come from Milan. He selected clothes for comfort rather than sartorial elegance, yet this top-of-the-range gear was high fashion, as were his Gucci shoes and Zeitner watch. His glossy dark hair was slicked back and confined in a pony-tail.

He studied her for a second, his eyes wedges of sapphire in a thin, keen face, then bared even teeth in a smile and said, 'It's great to see you again. You're looking lovely.'

'I'm sure I'm not,' she returned, blushing, unable to accept compliments without embarrassment. 'But you look well.'

'I should do. No meat. No dairy products. I've kicked the two-pack-a-day cigarette habit, and eliminated coffee, sugar and alcohol from my diet. I'm becoming a macrobiotic bore,' he grinned. 'Don't know how long I can keep it up. It's all right to have sex, apparently – in fact this regime is supposed to increase one's libido.'

'And does it?'

She knew where this might be heading. Once she would have refused to take part in the game, but was no longer sure.

'I've not tried for a while,' he answered with a quirky smile. 'Keeping myself for you, Carla.'

There was something so light, humorous, yet caring about him that she lost her shyness, easy in his company as she never was with Giles. She began to feel better, aware of his hand on her shoulder as he drew her towards a chair.

He kissed her forehead, took off her beret and ran his fingers through her hair, following its flow from scalp to the tips. This caress was almost brotherly, yet Carla felt her nipples chafing against the lacy cups of her brassière, the heat gathering between her legs making her little bud throb.

'Oh, Toby,' she said with a sigh. 'I hope you've good news for me. I need a boost.'

He perched on the corner of his desk facing her, one leg swinging, the other braced on the forest-green carpet, casual and elegant and supremely sexy.

His eyebrows shot up quizzically as he said, 'If Giles is putting you down, remember that he hasn't your pizazz.'

'You must be joking!' she exclaimed, truly shocked by this extraordinary statement.

'I'm not. You've plenty of it, but you're not aware. And, frankly, you're a better writer.'

'Ha! Tell that to the publishers!' she cried scornfully,

though a tiny seed of hope took root in the region of her heart. Toby was always so supportive, fighting her battles, listening to her problems. She could not stop wondering what he would be like in bed, her imagination running riot.

'I try,' Toby replied, smiling as if he read her thoughts, 'but unfortunately he's big business ... for the moment.'

'And I'm not.'

'Things will change,' he promised, regarding her steadily with those searching blue eyes. 'Don't give up the ghost.'

'What do you suggest I do?' she said, every nerve responding to him. He was kind. He liked her. He was single. She wouldn't be hurting any other woman, and Marie had said it was time she tried a new lover.

'Have you heard of Angelo Lorenzo?' he asked, picking up a biro and fidgeting with it, as if he was missing the feel of a cigarette between his fingers.

'Who hasn't? Isn't he just the most amazing tenor in the world? The critics say he's the natural heir to the Big Three ... Pavarotti, Domingo and Carreras.'

He raised a hand placatingly. 'OK. I'm not questioning it, but he's not been around lately, or haven't you noticed? The press have gone dead on him.'

'That's right. I've wondered. No appearances at Covent Garden or the Met or anywhere for the last, what? Six months?'

Angelo Lorenzo, with a voice to die for, face and body to match. His stage presence was stunning, his acting superb. He held his audiences in the palm of his hand. Big and dark and golden-voiced, he exuded barely leashed sexuality. Carla had most of his CDs, and several performances on video. Whenever Giles upset her, she consoled herself by listening to that liquid tenor voice, and dreamed of meeting him –

16

talking with him – making love to him.

'Edward Connar – that's his manager – has been in touch with me,' Toby went on, eyeing her thoughtfully. 'Lorenzo has taken himself off to a Greek island and refuses to come out of hiding. Edward is doing his nut. He's trying to pacify furious theatre managers and record companies, to say nothing of excusing missed TV appearances. They're all threatening to sue. He faces crippling legal costs if Lorenzo doesn't get his finger out soon.'

'He's taking a holiday?' Carla leaned forward in her chair, aware of the seam of her tights working its way into her delta under her Lycra briefs. She was damp there. Talk of the tenor, coupled with Toby's nearness, was causing mayhem in her core.

'More than that. Seems he's become a recluse, refusing to see anyone. It's something to do with an episode in his past, which has returned to haunt him.' Toby shifted on the desk, his pelvis angled towards her, the generous bulge behind his fly pushed into prominence.

Carla swallowed, in an almost painful state of arousal. 'What has this to do with me?' she managed to blurt out.

'Lorenzo's shrink has come up with the idea that it will help him if he can get this out of his system by writing it all down, but he won't do it, says he has no skill in expressing himself on paper. He's scornful of the whole thing, is giving Edward a hard time. This is where you come in, Carla.'

'Me?' This was a morning of revelations, she thought – this rabid lust I feel for Toby, and now the news concerning Lorenzo.

Toby smiled and rose, coming to where she sat and lifting her up towards him, his hands cupping her elbows. 'Edward is looking for someone to ghost the reclusive Angelo's story. He asked me if I knew anyone

17

tactful, discreet and talented. Preferably a music lover. I suggested you.'

'I can't,' she squeaked, and tried to pull away. 'There's my new novel just started. And Giles. How would he get on without me?'

'Darling Carla. Stop people-pleasing, will you?'

'But Giles . . . my book . . .'

'Put your book on ice, and tell Giles that you're about to make a major career move,' Toby insisted, arm straining her to him, making her aware of the upward slanting length of his penis. She threw back her head, inviting him to kiss her throat, feeling the pulse hammering in the jugular.

'I'd have to go to Greece?' she panted, feeling herself melting and helpless, made warm and lubricious by the gentle touch of his lips as they descended to suck at her delicate flesh.

'That's right,' he murmured, straightening up and smiling at her. 'Zaminos, to be exact. Just think: a sun-drenched island, a famous tenor to work with, music, the sea . . . and a fat cheque at the end of it. No expense will be spared if I can find the right person.'

'You think it would be a good thing for me?'

'Ace,' he said decisively.

He touched her breasts through her sweater, and a frisson of excitement jagged along her nerves. Slowly, his hand dropped to her waist and found the knitted hem. She felt him lift it, sliding underneath, fondling her skin, walking upwards, till his fingers brushed over her nipples, slipped into the top of her bra and teased the aroused tips into ever more needful peaks.

'What about Giles?' she breathed, but was not sure if she was referring to this intimate touch or the Greek proposition.

'To hell with Giles,' he growled, bending his head and finding her mouth. Her lips softened and parted, welcoming the press of his fleshy tongue, her own answering with fierce little jabs and swirls.

She moaned, deep in her throat, and his free hand grasped her buttocks, pressing her hard against the stiff line of his penis. She closed her eyes, her tongue still tangling with his. Outside, she could hear the sounds of traffic heading towards Piccadilly and the statue of Eros, God of Love. But it was muted, like the sea pounding on some far-off shore – the golden shore of a Greek island.

She wrested her mouth away, her eyes staring up into his, as she said unsteadily, 'Toby, we can't. Sadie may come in.'

He chuckled and pushed his thigh between hers, making her even more aware of the hot, wet warmth of her labia. 'I've told her we're not to be disturbed,' he murmured, and licked one of her lobes, setting the earring swinging. 'Anyway, it's her lunch break. We're quite alone.'

'You organised this, didn't you?' she accused, but could not help gyrating her pubis against his hard, muscular leg.

'I live in hope,' he replied, his blue eyes glinting. 'I've always wanted you, Carla, but you've been so devoted to Giles. I knew that he wasn't right for you the first time I met him at that damned dinner party he threw. He spent the whole time wanking his ego. Remember?'

'Could I ever forget?' she groaned, wincing. 'I've never been more embarrassed in my life.'

'Yet you've kept on loving him. Why?'

'I don't know,' she whispered, and her arms came up to cling round his neck.

'He's never satisfied you, has he?' Toby's voice was thick with desire. 'I can tell. I'll bet you've never known what it's like to come off with a man. What do you do when he leaves you frustrated? Masturbate?'

19

'Sometimes,' she murmured very low, her face flaming. 'I have to. I can't stand it any more, but I feel ashamed.'

'Why? There's no need. It's fine that you've learned what your body needs.'

'Do you know what it needs?' she said, her breath quickening.

'I think so. Let me show you. Sit down over here.'

Silently, wonderingly, as if in a dream, she let him lead her to the chaise-longue near the window. She sank into its plush crimson upholstery while he took off his jacket, then undid his high-buttoned waistcoat and loosened his tie. He stood before her in his shirt sleeves, his cock distending the material of his trousers, and she reached out and clasped her hand round it, so big and hard, radiating energy.

He ran his tongue over her lips from corner to corner, then rolled up her sweater till it lay like a tight band across her chest. He nodded his approval as he saw her rose-pink nipples protruding through the lacy underwired bra. With adept fingers he pinched the swollen buds, holding them between finger and thumb in a compelling rolling motion that made her writhe and jerk.

He reached behind her and snapped open the clasp of her brassière, freeing her from the cups.

He sighed, smiled and admired her, then bent to touch her breasts again as if they were rare fruits. His fingers traced circles around the dark areolae, and he took each nipple into his mouth, nibbling and sucking, his tongue working over the ardent pink teats, drawing a soft moan of pleasure from her.

Her body was on fire, the blood rushing to her breasts and down to her thrumming clitoris. She thought of the times she had tried to stop indulging in self-relief, ashamed of the desire to complete the act after Giles had left her high, if not dry. Now Toby had put this right, telling her that masturbation was normal.

Her heart pounded like a drum at the notion that he was going to bring her to climax, the first she had experienced with anyone but herself. She watched him, mesmerised. His touch made her feel as though she had been put under a spell.

His hands roamed down her body, found the top of her tights and helped her remove them. Goose-pimples raised the down on her limbs. Now only the tiny white Lycra triangle of her panties protected her mound.

She felt him pause, lower his head to kiss her stomach, and run his slick wet tongue round her navel. Then a finger dipped past the top of her briefs, and every pubic hair seemed to have its own particular sensation as he rubbed over it softly.

He trailed his fingers back and forth across her swollen lower lips as he kissed her mouth again. Her tongue slid, wet and skimming, along the roof of his mouth, tasting him, wanting to absorb him, longing to give him pleasure. Her hand moved over the engorged penis straining against his fly. She found the button at the waistband of his trousers, then unzipped him and his cock shot out, thick and sturdy, the bulbous head fiery red and already wet. She palmed it, rubbed it, made it bigger, as he eased down her panties.

Impatiently, she kicked them away. Now she was open to him, her thighs wide apart, pink labia unfurled, the pearly head of her clitoris rearing from its hood. Crouching between her spread legs, he dipped a finger into the silvery juice he had created in her vulva, then stroked the silken-smooth, damp aisle.

The first deep tremor flowed along her thighs and into her loins as he carefully located her bud and began that wonderful slow massage which would bring her to orgasm. She cried out and clung to him, trembling,

21

moving into and around him, while he kissed her mouth, her ears, her neck, bringing her closer and closer to the edge.

Ecstasy flowed like liquid fire through every fibre of her being. Her body half rose from the couch as her orgasm swept over her in a surge of glorious pleasure. Toby gasped and held her, putting his other hand between her buttocks, widening the quivering crevice and sinking two fingers into her vagina. As the tension relaxed and she plunged down from those blissful heights, so he kissed her again, enclosing her warm, wet sex in his hand.

Carla heaved against it, pulling him closer, grasping his cock and guiding it into her depths, giving her spasming vaginal walls something round which to clench as the orgasmic ripples receded. He braced himself, his head thrown back, eyes closed as he came in a rush, groaning and shuddering.

He did not withdraw at once, cradling her in his arms and covering her eyelids, her hair, her lips, with tender kisses. 'You came beautifully,' he whispered softly. 'And you did it for me.'

His hands coasted over her breasts and moved downwards, tracing the line of her pubic wedge, dipping his fingers into her vulva, then lifting them to his nose and inhaling her fragrance.

'It was amazing, Toby,' she murmured, glowing inside, feeling shamelessly wanton, relaxed, almost boneless, as a woman will when she has been fucked to completion by an understanding lover.

'Better than Giles?'

'Giles hasn't a clue.'

He held her face between his hands and made love to the soft fullness of her lips. It was perfect and she applied the pressure of her agile, zestful tongue, staring up at him as they kissed, her eyes wide open.

22

'We've wasted so much time,' he said, sitting up and running his hands through his hair. 'Come back to my place and spend the night with me.'

'I can't . . . not tonight,' she said falteringly.

'Will you tell Giles?' he cast her a smiling look, challenging her to make the break.

'I don't know,' she said, guilt kicking in now that the madness of passion had faded a little. 'There are rules, aren't there? One shouldn't cheat on one's partner.'

'Does he cheat on you?' He was observing her closely with his bright blue eyes, as if he had secret information.

'I don't think so. Why? Have you heard anything?'

He tucked his penis away, zipped up and then buttoned his waistcoat, shaking his head and avoiding her gaze. 'Not exactly. He's popular with the ladies, but then so are any number of celebs.'

This served to fuel her suspicion that he was hiding something. Worries began to impinge. Now he had left her she missed his warm body, needed tactile contact most desperately. It made her realise just how sterile her relationship with Giles had become.

'I need to think, Toby. Give me a little time,' she begged, and fished around under the couch, retrieving her panties, tights and shoes.

He watched her in the mirror as he stood in front of it, knotting his tie. 'As long as you want on the personal side, darling, but I need to finalise this business with Edward. When can you give me an answer?'

Panic seized her by the throat. She fastened her brassière and rearranged her sweater before answering, 'In a couple of days.'

'OK. What are you going to do? Discuss it with Giles? He'll try to put you off.'

'I'll talk to Marie Abelson. She's shrewd.'

'And she shares my opinion of Giles,' he said crisply,

for he was Marie's agent as well as Carla's.

'I suppose you two have been discussing me?' Carla shot back. It annoyed her to think she might have been the object of their pity.

'We're both concerned.'

She combed her fingers through her hair and went into the adjoining cloakroom, feeling dazed, unreal, nothing like the sensible writer who sat at her PC for hours. Something momentous had happened and she would never again settle for lovemaking that was one-sided.

She stared at her reflection in the looking-glass over the basin. Her eyes were bright, her cheeks flushed. With trembling hands, she ran cold water over her wrists and face before adding hot. She lathered her fingers and washed her pudenda, aroused by the slippery white suds passing over her sensitive delta. Even the smell of perfumed soap could not disguise the piquant odour of sexual emissions that wetted her cleft and smeared her inner thighs.

After dabbing herself dry with tissues and dusting herself with Toby's body talc, Carla put on her underwear and shoes and adjusted her skirt.

Push it from your mind, she told herself firmly. Forget you ever shafted Toby. Get back to Giles and the familiar. Make another attempt to talk to him about improving your sex life. You can't possibly burn your boats, can you?

She came out to find Toby lounging in his steno-chair, feet propped high on the desk, telephone clamped to one ear. He kissed his fingertips to show that he loved her, talked a little more, then replaced the receiver in its cradle.

'That was Edward. I rang to tell him I've spoken with you.'

'Oh dear, did you? What did he say? You've not

committed me to anything, have you?' she stammered nervously.

'No. Stop getting in a panic. I've told him I'll get back to him later in the week.'

He sauntered across to take her in a last embrace. She lifted her face to his, and he held her breasts through her jacket as he said seriously, 'Look, Carla, that wasn't just a casual screw. What I feel for you is something special.'

'Is it?'

He gave her an exasperated little shake, saying, 'Why is it so hard for you to believe you're worth praise or compliments or love? Seems to me you choose to be with a bastard who'll hurt you, as if that's all you deserve.'

'Don't be angry,' she pleaded, suddenly riven with guilt and fear.

'I'm not. Lighten up,' he said, smiling down at her, slim and handsome and immensely attractive. 'Phone me as soon as you've decided. OK?'

'OK,' she promised and he kissed her again, a deep, explorative kiss that seemed to fill her mouth with honey.

'I don't want to let you go,' he said, holding her tightly, making her aware that he was hardening again. 'Unfortunately, I've a meeting with another author.'

'I must go anyway. Goodbye, Toby.'

'Be brave,' he said, walking her to the door with his arm looped round her shoulders. 'Giles is only human, not a prophet. He has flaws, like the rest of us.'

'I know,' she replied, and left him.

She dragged her feet as she walked towards the car park, every step she took leading her away from Toby and pleasure. Now she felt weighed down with a burden of shame that clouded the wonderful hour they had spent together.

Chapter Two.

I DON'T WANT to go home, Carla thought as she drove away from Soho. I can't face Giles yet.

There was Marie's apartment, of course. Then she remembered that her friend was out till evening. She could go shopping, but it would mean finding somewhere to park and using her credit card, spending money she did not have. In the end she drove to Richmond Park and sat in the car, while rain lashed the windows and she wished she was anywhere but there.

Every movement she made drew her attention to her secret lips. Far from dousing her fire, Toby's skilled attentions had served to stoke it into fiercer flame. Her skin felt softer, her breasts seemed larger, the nipples swelling as they rubbed against her bra. Her whole being quivered, sparklingly alive. She shivered in the driver's seat, thirsting to be back in Toby's arms, to feel his cock entering her vagina and his fingers stimulating her clitoris.

The tender sliver of flesh throbbed, hidden in her moist folds. She was tempted to caress herself through the thin barrier of tights and briefs, but was still inhibited. Although the park was deserted on such a dismal day, there just might be someone lurking in the bushes. How humiliating to be caught in the act.

She concentrated on Toby's proposal and Angelo Lorenzo. Such an opportunity couldn't possibly come her way, could it? Giles, maybe, though he would never consent to hiding his light under a bushel – he'd want his name emblazoned on the cover.

She cringed inside, doubting her abilities. She had never been a journalist, was hopeless at short stories, only good at dreaming up sagas set in bygone times, all frills and furbelows, noble heroes and dastardly villains, and beautiful heroines in need of rescue.

Giles is right, she decided wretchedly. It's historical hokum. I'm nothing but a hack turning out potboilers.

I'd better talk with Marie about this Greece trip, she concluded. I'll go home and cook something tasty for dinner. Then, perhaps, I'll ask Giles's opinion, and ring her later.

Starting the engine and slipping the car into gear, she moved out into the road. It was like driving through a monsoon, with the windscreen wipers making little impression on the deluge.

Carla bolted from the garage after putting the Fiat away. She was drenched by the time she had found her key, opened the front door and let herself into the hall. She had noticed the light shining from Giles's study. He'd be working. She wouldn't disturb him yet, just take up a cup of coffee in a while.

As she stood dripping on the tiles, the silence of the house pressed down on her. It was uncannily quiet. No music. This was odd, as he liked to work to music – particularly baroque, and he denigrated her love of sweeping strings and big orchestral scores. Was he in? He must be. His Jaguar was in the garage. He'd hardly be out walking in this weather.

If it were me, she thought, taking off her jacket and

hanging it on the branching antlers of the hall-stand, I'd be tucked under the duvet, snoozing. But that isn't Giles's style. He has a strict work routine. That's how he manages to produce such a turnover. Not like me, who gets writer's block and goes into intense gloom, for which the only solace is sleep.

She sensed that the house was occupied. It did not have that empty feel about it. Giles was there, some-where. In the old days, one would have heard the clack of a typewriter, but computers only hummed. In a way she was glad she did not have to face him at once. Not good at lying, she doubted her ability to play the adulteress.

Don't be stupid, she chided herself – you're not married to the guy. Coffee then. This would give her an excuse to put off the evil hour.

The kitchen surprised her. It looked positively unkempt. There were dirty plates on the table, a dish with bits of pizza welded to it, a half-empty bottle of Sauterne, used wine-glasses. Two of everything, she noted, and wondered. Maybe one of his mates had dropped in. Perhaps they were even now ensconced in the study discussing some erudite point concerning deep space, time-travel or black holes, way beyond her comprehension.

I'd better check, she thought. He'll want coffee, too, whoever he is. She was relieved. This way she would not be alone with Giles, and she'd have time to push the encounter with Toby further back in her memory, perhaps even manage to convince herself that it had never really happened. But I don't want to forget, she thought, desire coiling like red-hot wire in her womb. *I want to repeat it.*

She mounted the stairs, the thick carpet muffling her footsteps. Still wrestling with heated memories of Toby, she was almost past the bedroom door on her way to the study when she was suddenly arrested by sounds from within.

She stopped, rooted to the spot. What was going on in there?

The moans, groans and sighs were those associated with a couple in the throes of passion. And there was the definite creaking of bedsprings.

Hand on the doorknob, she hesitated for a moment only, then stepped inside. She froze, her eyes telling her what her slow wits refused to take in.

Giles lay on the bed, his head buried between the wide open thighs of Alicia Ashford as he nuzzled into her wet cleft. She was mouthing his cock, slurping and pulling, feasting on him like a greedy animal.

Carla gasped. Alicia looked across and saw her. She let Giles's engorged weapon drop, her dark eyes wide and wary. Then she relaxed and smiled, a feline, crimson smile smeared with his pre-come juice. She made a ring of her fingers and, tightening them around the base of his turgid weapon, prevented him from coming. Her manicured claws matched her lips.

'What's up?' he asked, his voice muffled as he foraged amongst the thick black bush coating her mound, his tongue exploring the nooks and crannies of her glistening pink-brown avenue.

'We have a visitor, darling,' she crooned in that husky, come-to-bed voice so familiar to the thousands of viewers who watched her nightly on their television screens.

Giles lifted his head and his face dropped. 'Carla,' he muttered. 'I wasn't expecting you back yet.'

'That's bloody obvious,' she snapped, borne on a wave of rage and indignation. 'How dare you have that woman here – in our bed? You scumbag! Unfaithful, conceited, manipulative bastard!'

'Take no notice of her, darling,' Alicia drawled,

unabashed, her hand holding his balls, one finger finding the area of skin near his anus and tickling it.

He dragged himself away from her crotch, disconcerted by Carla's sudden arrival, and pulled the sheet over his rapidly shrinking member. 'We don't want any trouble, Alicia.'

'Trouble?' Alicia feathered her fingers through her short hair – just like she did in a shampoo commercial, which had cost the manufacturer a fortune. 'She can't do anything to us. Can you Carla, dear?'

'Don't hold your breath,' Carla countered, encased in ice, too numb for tears. 'I can tell the press, have your names blasted all over the front pages of the dailies, get you featured in trashy magazines. It would ruin your image if I told them that Alicia Ashford, that warm, caring, oh-so-friendly presenter, is shafting every man in the studio, including the tea-boy – and Giles Davenport in particular. Oh, yes, there's a lot I can do.'

'But you won't, sweetheart,' Giles almost pleaded. 'It's nothing. A bit of fun, that's all.'

'You planned it, you piece of filth,' she retorted. 'Couldn't wait to phone her as soon as I was out of the door. She's welcome to you. Think he's the world's greatest lover, do you, Alicia? Wait till you know him better. He's never gone down on me, and I'm surprised to find him doing it to you.'

'I wouldn't tolerate anything less,' Alicia replied, her eyes cutting to Giles, forceful and dominating. 'Is this true?' she demanded.

'No, it isn't,' he blustered, flinching at her tone. 'She's so ordinary. Not like you. You're wonderful . . . exciting . . .'

'Don't forget "useful",' Carla put in acidly. 'He's a user, Alicia. He'd sell his grandmother to get his face on TV.'

She went to the wardrobe, hitched two cases from the

top shelf, flung back the lids and started to yank her clothes from hangers and thrust them inside. Drawers crashed open as she rooted through them, removing her belongings.

'What are you doing?' Giles said, watching her sulkily while Alicia merely shrugged and poured herself another gin from the bottle by the bed.

'I'm leaving you,' Carla replied through gritted teeth.

'You can't do that. Where will you go? How will you live?' He sounded genuinely concerned but she knew all he was bothered about was scandal.

'Don't worry, Giles. I'll manage. As for this leaking to the press, don't forget the old adage that bad publicity is better than no publicity.'

'But, Carla! Constellation Press are launching my new book next month. I'm due to go on a signing stint. I need you to help me.'

Carla stood facing him, arms akimbo. It was as if she saw him for the first time, his mean little soul displayed in his eyes, like a tiny, wizened walnut. She was in bits inside yet felt amazingly strong. It was as if she had shucked off a huge weight.

This light, airy feeling was intoxicating. She eyed Giles and Alicia with such blistering scorn that they should have withered where they lay. Thank you, Toby, she whispered inwardly. Thank you so much.

'I don't know how you'll cope, and I don't care,' she remarked, so cool and steady that she amazed herself. 'You should have thought about that before you screwed her.'

She clicked the cases shut and fastened the straps while he sat there stonily, his prick limp and lifeless in Alicia's fingers.

'I'll send round for the rest of my things,' Carla said. 'There's a lot needs sorting, books, papers, two years' collection of debris.' She leaned over and unplugged

31

her portable player, adding, 'I'll take this now, and my CDs and videos. Don't mess with my computer or I'll hire a heavy to break your knee-caps.'

'But . . .' Giles began.

'There's nothing more to be said,' she responded smartly.

'Where will you be?' he asked, sheepish and uncertain.

'At Marie's, but don't try to contact me. I don't want to see you again. I'm not the sort of person who believes in remaining on friendly terms with her ex, so don't even think about it.'

'How bitter, and what a bitch you are,' Alicia remarked, giving up on Giles's prick and refilling her glass.

'It takes one to know one,' Carla snarled, shaking off the last remaining shreds of civilised behaviour.

She upended her cases and wheeled them to the door. This galvanised Giles into action. He leapt up, somehow diminished, looking smaller and older, his cock tiny compared to Toby's.

'Let's talk about this. Don't do anything you'll regret,' he pleaded anxiously.

She paused, eyeing him contemptuously, her hard gaze lingering on his genitals. 'I'm regretting nothing,' she said. 'Least of all *that*,' and she reached out and flicked his penis, making it swing from side to side. 'Toby's is much, much bigger – a magnificent specimen. While you were grubbing about in Alicia's cunt, I was fucking him.'

'You were what?' he roared, blood suffusing his face, his eyes bulging.

'Bonking him brainless, *shagging* him, being given the most mind-blowing orgasm I've ever had!' she shouted back. 'Something you have never done. What's more, I'm going to Greece. I've been offered an important commission, working on the life-story of Angelo Lorenzo.'

'Under your own name?' he asked instantly, as she had known he would.

'No, but the fee is huge, and it'll set me on the road for even bigger things. Goodbye, Giles, and may your willy shrivel and drop off.'

'Let her go,' Alicia advised him, her voice slurred. She slumped across the bed, her big breasts pointing towards the ceiling, her legs spread, exposing her dark, hairy fork and the pouting lips of her sex.

They are well matched, was Carla's final thought as she left the room. Whores, in their individual ways – selling their talents, willing to sacrifice their integrity, their honour, their very souls on the altar of Mammon.

'Don't argue. I'm coming along,' Marie declared, proffering the Kleenex. 'Stop crying, Carla. The best thing you've ever done was walking out on Giles. You can stay here with me till you get your flight booked, and then watch your ass, Zaminos . . . here we come!'

Carla could not stop shivering, delayed shock hitting her like a sledge-hammer. Barely inside the door of the apartment, she had broken down, sobbing all over Marie's silk jersey T-shirt.

She had been pushed into a chair, handed a stiff brandy, and told to stay put while Marie rang the concierge and ordered him to bring up the rest of the luggage. This now littered the Persian carpet in the sumptuous drawing room of the high-ceilinged, turn-of-the-century maisonette.

'My cases are so shabby,' Carla wailed. 'I'm making a mess of your lovely home.'

'If you don't shut up, I'm going to throttle you,' Marie exclaimed, impressive in her snug-fitting designer jeans, that sexy space between the tops of her thighs clearly defined.

She always managed to look chic, whatever happened. Her build was statuesque, and she held her shoulders back so that her breasts were displayed, even though she was wearing a black, loose-fitting top. This finished at the apex of her thighs, focusing the attention on that fascinating gap which Carla envied so much.

There wasn't an ounce of fat or an inch of cellulite anywhere to be seen on Marie's lean flanks and boyish buttocks. Carla had seen her nude when Marie treated her to a sauna at a wildly expensive beauty centre in Knightsbridge. They had undressed together, with Marie flaunting her body and Carla trying to hide behind a bathsheet.

'It's all right for you,' she sobbed. 'Blokes queue up to take you out. I may never find another boyfriend.'

Marie heaved an exasperated sigh and came to rest beside her. 'And what's all this you've just been telling me about shafting Toby? Sounds like he's smitten.'

'He was probably passing the time, being kind, making me feel better,' Carla moaned, wishing she could cry gracefully, her face red and blotchy.

'Bullshit!' Marie protested. 'The guy's got the hots for you, has had for months. D'you think I didn't notice he had a hard-on every time we mentioned your name? I felt so sorry for him, I almost offered to give him a blow-job, but knew it was you he fancied.'

Carla sniffed, but her eyes were no longer wet. The dampness seemed to have settled in her crotch as she imagined Toby's cock fully erect and frustrated because of her.

'You really think he was sincere?' she ventured.

'I know so, hon,' Marie answered positively. 'Now, we've got a lot to plan. Put that tissue away and let's get down to it. I think we'll make a list. You need a makeover: new clothes, new hair-do, new cosmetics.'

'I've no money.'

'You will have. Just get your butt over to Toby's office and sign that contract, demand part of the cash upfront. Then we'll go spend, spend, spend!'

'Really?' Carla said.

'Really. Leave it to your ole Aunt Marie. We're going to turn you into a beauty. All the studs'll be slavering after you, wanting to lick out your fanny. They'll be so hard they won't be able to walk.'

Carla essayed a smile. 'And you'll really come to Zaminos?'

'Try stopping me. I've a friend who has a villa there. He and his significant other would love us to visit them.'

'But your work . . .'

'Work sucks. It can go on hold. I need a vacation. The publishers have given me a million dollar advance, and can wait for the manuscript. It'll stop them getting too high-handed. Show 'em who's boss. Where would they be without us authors, eh? Now, an early night. You look bushed.'

Carla was glad to relinquish her will to this forceful woman. She took a shower, then slipped under the sheets in the guestroom. Unpacking could wait till tomorrow, and so could all the other complications incumbent on breaking up a relationship.

The brandy had been strong and she was worn out. As she drifted to sleep, she heard the roar of London's traffic beyond the park and it somehow got mixed up with Marie's voice, speaking from the other room, a one-sided conversation that meant she was using the phone.

'She's OK, Toby. Don't worry. Yes, she's left him. You can tell Edward Connar that she accepts. I'm going along for the ride. We'll stay with Leandra. Where? Oh, she's shacked up with Rutger Eberhardt – kinky stuff. How does it grab you? What a turn-on! You coming over, too? Don't leave it too long, I'm about to work a miracle on our little duckling. I've a hunch she'll turn into a swan. You may lose her if you don't watch out. Especially if Rutger gets his hooks into her.'

After keeping an appointment at Toby's office and being introduced to Edward Connar, a persuasive individual with puffy eyes and once well-defined features now submerged in fat, Carla signed the contract and left the men to finalise details. Then she went to meet Marie at Elysian Fields, an exclusive beauty parlour in an equally smart street lined with boutiques and restaurants.

The name is apt, considering where I'm heading, she thought, pushing back the thick glass door and entering its clinical, almost stark interior. It smelled expensive, of steam and pampered female flesh, aromatherapy oils, tinting formulae and perm lotion.

Marie was waiting for her, seated on a white calf-skin couch as supple as satin, talking with the proprietess, who bore the single name, Chloe.

Carla, her earlier confidence fading, found her awe-inspiring. A former Miss World who had invested her winnings wisely, she was groomed to perfection, lissome and svelte, every hair in place, each finger- and toe-nail lacquered and shining. An artist in her own way, she could wave her magic wand and transform the plainest woman into a sex goddess, while those already blessed with good looks went to her when they needed to cut a spectacular dash.

It was only because Marie was her favourite author, a regular client and not above name-dropping, that they had been booked in at such short notice.

Chloe had barely noticed Carla on their former visit

to the sauna. But now she swept towards her, smooth, tanned legs bare beneath the skimpy white cotton nurse's uniform, smiling and saying, 'Ah, Miss Holt! So you're flying to Zaminos to meet Angelo Lorenzo! How thrilling!'

From that moment onwards, Carla relinquished control of her body, her power taken away. Marie abandoned her to go off with a sari-wrapped assistant, a petite Singhalese girl who was about to immerse her in the flotation tank.

Carla, feeling awkward and out of place, had not expected Marie to leave her, but Chloe intended to give her personal attention. 'Let's get started,' she invited, as she led Carla beyond the reception area, along a white-carpeted passage to where a series of doors connected with cubicles.

In for a penny, in for a pound, Carla thought. This is an everyday occurrence for women like Marie, but I've never even had a massage, and rarely go to a hairdresser's, and then only to a local salon to have my split-ends trimmed.

Chloe shut the door behind them and Carla was enveloped in the glowing peach decor, cunningly designed to promote an aura of well-being and peace. The bathtub was peach porcelain, the towels, shower-curtains and floor covering of the same warm shade. Even the couch was upholstered in it, and resembled a shrine dedicated to Venus rather than a plain old massage slab.

Chloe held out a towelling bathrobe, saying, 'Undress, please.'

Disconcerted, ashamed to show herself to this supremely fit and shapely woman, Carla reluctantly obeyed. She was momentarily embarrassed by her practical, chain-store underwear, but thankful that her mother had drummed in the instructions that she must

37

always make sure it was clean and mended, 'just in case you're involved in an accident'.

Oh, God – the parents. I'd better let them know I'm going abroad. It'll give Mother something to boast about at her WI meetings.

She wanted to fold the robe around her but Chloe would have none of this. She looked her over with the eye of an expert. 'You've a good body – not a stick-insect by any means. And what man really likes that? You've lovely breasts, a handspan waist, rounded hips and a firm bottom.'

'I'm too fat, aren't I?' Carla muttered self-consciously.

'No. It's only model girls who strive for these ridiculously thin, bordering-on-anorexic figures. Many of the dress designers are gay, and I'm convinced they make their gowns with willowy, lanky boys in mind.'

'You think so?' Carla said, brightening as she looked at herself in one of the many, gilt-edged mirrors.

'I know so,' Chloe smiled, running her fingers down Carla's spine. 'Men like something to grab hold of while they're screwing. As for tits? Aren't they all obsessed by breasts, longing to be suckled again?'

'I hadn't thought of it that way.'

'It's true,' Chloe said levelly. 'So stop fretting. No one is ever satisfied with their looks.'

'Aren't you?' Carla was amazed, considering her to be faultless.

'My nose is too big,' Chloe answered, leaning forward and studying the offending organ in the glass. 'Maybe I'll have plastic surgery one day.'

She helped Carla into the bath. The pink, scented water flowed over her skin like silk, and Carla tingled as Chloe's hands fluttered delicately as if measuring and assessing her, testing her reactions. Her body came alive under those tender ministrations, the lathered sponge teasing her nipples and dipping down between her legs, which parted slightly, hungry for more.

Those painful images of Giles in bed with Alicia that had tormented her for hours were fading, obscured by the new sensations, new awareness, new lusts coursing through her.

When she left the tub, Chloe towelled her. She continued to rub Carla's breasts lightly after they were dry, and a pleasant heat warmed Carla to the core. Lazily she leaned against Chloe, pictures of Toby and his lively prick forming in her imagination.

Chloe motioned her to the table, and she lay down, the cool air dancing across her naked buttocks, followed by Chloe's oiled fingers kneading and working, freeing the tension in every muscle of shoulders, spine, waist and thighs. In between the thighs – exploring, pinching, passing out again just as Carla sighed and raised her hips a little towards that tantalising touch.

Backs of thighs and knees, down the calves to the ankles, then working between each toe, stretching, easing, fondling. Heat rose wherever Chloe's fingers landed, spreading through Carla and knotting in her clitoris. She pressed down, trying to rub the insistent nubbin against the sheet beneath her, but to no avail. Her juices seeped from her love-tunnel, spreading towards that ardent little organ, the seat of sexual sensation.

Chloe continued the massage as if unaware, but as she leaned over, her breasts swung forward, the rounded curves swelling at the opened collar of her uniform. Carla caught a whiff of her essences breathing out between those breasts, the unmistakable scent of female arousal cutting through the French perfume. It matched her own, which wafted up from between her legs.

'Turn over,' Chloe said, her voice holding a commanding note impossible to disobey.

Feeling so relaxed it was as if every bone in her body had dissolved, Carla rolled on to her back, eagerly presenting her breasts and pubis, surrendering herself to the masseuse. For the first time ever, she wanted to lie naked in a woman's arms, to feel breasts against her nipples, a blunt and furry cleft instead of a crested penis rubbing against her clitoris, to be caressed and brought to glory by a twin spirit who would know precisely what she needed to attain the most exquisite orgasm.

Chloe's eyes were dreamy as she skimmed her palms over Carla's breasts, down to the plateau of her belly, the triangle of her mound, and the inner plains of her thighs. She moved swiftly, never delaying long enough for Carla to succeed in catching the rhythm necessary for climax. Chloe's fingers were adept and skilful. They shimmied across Carla's bush, making her cry out.

Chloe paused, eyebrows raised. 'You need waxing there, just to tidy it up. Then you'll be able to wear the tiniest bikini, the flimsiest panties without wisps of hair showing at either side. We'll see to that next.'

She moved away and returned with a little pot of depilation cream. Carla waited, breath sucked in, hardly daring to let it slide from her lips. Her clit swelled, protruding from her labia, aching for attention.

Chloe hovered at the foot of the couch and said, 'Ease down and spread your legs.'

Carla did so, her buttocks supported by the padded edge, her legs raised and bent at the knee. She jumped at the first touch of Chloe's fingers on her exposed labial groove. She could feel her inner self beginning to pulse. Warm, loose and lubricious, she waited for Chloe's next move.

Fingers wet with the fragrant, oily cream, Chloe worked across Carla's pubic hair with insistent, circular motions. She made whorls and patterns in the light brown plumes, and her every movement thrilled

40

Carla's clit. When she took up a small wooden spatula and started to scrape away the loosened hair, a new prickling sensation of urgency added to the build-up of tension in Carla's sex.

Her nipples firmed and, sensitive to her need, Chloe reached up and fondled them, passing her palm from one to the other till Carla gasped and lifted her hips from the couch, almost in supplication.

Chloe returned to the half-depilated curls, and the sensation of the scraper passing so close to her bud brought Carla to the edge. She longed to grind her clitoris against it, to rub up and down till she exploded in release.

More than this, she yearned to feel Chloe's fingers holding the little organ, lifting it from its hood, pressing down on each side of the stem till they found its root, then drawing it up, subjecting the head to fierce friction.

Chloe continued with her task, parting the pink furls, seeking out stray hairs, removing any trace of the delicate fluff remaining on Carla's lips and round her anus.

'That's better,' she remarked, admiring her work. 'You're smooth and pink and lovely. Good enough to eat. This will soothe the skin.' She took up another jar, and poured a little puddle of lotion into her cupped hand.

This time there was no doubting her intention. Her cream-smeared fingers slid over the flesh of Carla's inner thighs, then trailed along the eager, denuded labia, and, finally, caressed the swollen button of flesh standing up at the top of the cleft. She worked it, circled it, played with it, tormenting the hard, wet bud, but never leaving it entirely, inventive, imaginative, rousing it to an ever greater peak of sensation.

Carla moaned, filled with a gnawing, aching need that made her want to clutch at Chloe. The feeling grew in the wellspring of her being, deep, visceral,

41

unstoppable. Chloe increased the speed of her strokes, no longer playing, now intent on bringing this to a conclusion.

Up and up, Carla rose, struggling to scale the mountain-top, an electric charge shooting through her as she reached a crescendo that ended in a blur as she toppled over into orgasm, feeling Chloe's hand cupping her wet, throbbing mound and thrusting her fingers into her convulsing heartland.

Marie walked in just after. She looked as smug as a cat who has been at the cream. 'That new girl,' she said. 'What a find. She sure knows what to do to make the hormones zing.'

'She did her training in a temple devoted to bodily sensations and erotic delights,' Chloe replied. 'She's extremely popular among my clientele.'

Carla shrugged the robe around her, still dazed, aftershocks of pleasure rippling through her. She had no doubt that Marie had just gone through a similar experience and this no longer came as a surprise. She realised how little she knew of the world and the sexual preferences of those who inhabited it. It was as if she had been cocooned, first by her parents, then by Giles, who had been so afraid she might leave him to fend for himself. Not that he needed her as a person, simply as an adjunct to his writing empire.

But she was too content to dwell on negative things, willing to be passed over to beautiful Andy of the manicured hands, close-cropped head and single gold ring in the left eyebrow.

He clucked and fussed, head to one side as he considered her hair, remarking, 'Who has been cutting it? Looks as if they've used the garden shears.'

'I don't want it short,' she said, her voice acquiring a new strength.

'I promise not to do more to the length than remove

the merest whisper at the ends. It curls naturally, and we'll have you with a head full of coiling ringlets. Leave it to me. But first, highlights, I think. It's rich mouse at the moment. I want you to be tawny blonde. OK?'

'OK.'

When he had done with her, she shook her head, giving it a big whoosh as he ordered. Her reflection was astonishing, her hair transformed into a gold-streaked gypsyish mane.

Chloe went to work on her face, emphasising her cheekbones with blusher, applying brown mascara to thicken her lashes, deepening the colour of her eyes with shadow, outlining her lips and reshaping her brows by plucking out rogue hairs.

'Wow!' Marie said, awed when she saw the completed picture. 'Just wait till Toby gets a load of this. Now, we're going to buy clothes. Lots of 'em, and all expensive. You're done with high-street stores.'

'I won't see this writer,' the tall man declared, unfolding his long legs from the couch on which he had been lounging, and stalking across the marble floor towards the wide open doors that led to the terrace.

'But, Angelo, consider your position.' Edward Connar dragged a tissue from his pocket and wiped the sweat from his face. 'We're losing money . . . a great deal of money.'

'I have plenty,' Angelo answered indifferently, scowling blackly at the view hundreds of feet below the garden. Beyond the cypress trees, the sea sparkled, crested by bars of creamy waves, while boats bobbed at anchor in the bay.

'You *had* plenty – once,' Edward reminded heavily. He was a strong-willed man who could usually wheedle his way round the most temperamental star in his stable. 'But it won't last forever. You aren't exactly thrifty. Like to live in style, and who can blame you? So do I, but all of us are going to feel the pinch if you don't get back to work soon.'

'To hell with it,' Angelo responded, his voice thickly accented. He glowered at the bougainvillaea clinging to the walls and was unmoved by the display of pink and white oleanders in terracotta pots. 'I'll come back when I'm ready, and not before.'

Edward sighed, eased his balls into a more comfortable position inside his white linen slacks and decided the time had come for firmness. Opera singers sometimes behaved like spoilt children.

'Cut the crap, Angelo. What about the performance of Verdi's *Requiem* at the Albert Hall in September? Carlo Bianza is booked to conduct. Rehearsals must begin in two months or it'll fuck up everyone's schedule. It's all arranged. The London date is down in my planner. And then there's the new Scala production of *Turandot*.'

God, these prima donnas! he thought. Keeping them in any sort of balance is a thankless task. He found himself in the position of financial adviser, confidante, chief cook-and-bottle-washer and nanny combined. And all he wanted to do was make a half decent living. Well, he admitted to himself, maybe it wasn't as simple as that.

The truth was that he adored music. It thrilled, uplifted and inspired him, but he had no capacity for producing it, so had devoted his life to those who could. Working with difficult, moody musicians was meat and drink to him, exciting, rewarding and exasperating.

Much more of this and I'll wind up with a coronary, he thought gloomily. I'm overweight as it is, and how can I give up smoking with this bugger causing me so much grief? The local food won't help either.

He fumbled for the packet, lit up a cigarette and tried

44

another tack. 'Listen, Angelo. You like singing, don't you? You want to sing. Jesus Christ, it's your life. You have a God-given gift, man. Don't waste your exceptional talent.'

He paused, letting this flattery sink in, dubious as to its effect. Angelo was nobody's fool. He had fought his way up from the gutter, streetwise and tough. This was at the heart of his incredible appeal to women, this roughness coupled with a shrewd brain, animal magnetism and movie-star good looks.

Edward stared at the straight back turned stubbornly towards him, the blue-black hair curling around the wide shoulders. Angelo had left his bed not long before and was mother-naked. He had an all-over toast-brown tan. His shoulders tapered to a narrow waist, the buttocks were lean, tight-muscled, and the hips hollowed on either side. His legs were long and beautifully moulded, a sculptor's dream. He stood, balancing his weight easily, his torso upheld by those magnificent legs. He was in his mid-thirties, young to be at the top of the operatic tree, but there was a maturity about him. And his body was at the peak of perfection.

He turned towards Edward, who could not help gazing at his genitals. They drew the eye like steel to magnet. The size of his penis even in repose would have made an ordinary man proud in full erection. It was long and brown and thick, a bough of solid flesh, and the balls swinging beneath it were like sap-filled fruits. Edward felt a stirring in his groin, his phallus swelling under his silk boxer shorts.

He sighed. Angelo was the epitome of the heterosexual macho male who would probably punch him on the nose if he propositioned him. Ah, well, he'd just have to make do with the plethora of beautiful youths so readily available on the island. Thank God for the homoerotic Greeks.

'I asked Toby Torrance to find me an author,' he continued, grinding his stub in a soapstone ashtray and reaching for the pack again. 'She'll be landing shortly.'

'*She!*' Angelo thundered, his arms spread dramatically, his voice echoing through the luxuriously appointed, airy room. 'You expect me to tell my secrets to some bespectacled, middle-aged writer? I can't do it. I *won't* do it.'

Oh, Lord, there he goes again, throwing a tantrum, Edward thought, while he said, placatingly, 'She's not old. She's young, and a devoted fan of yours.'

Angelo stood spread-legged before him, hands on his hips, his peat-brown eyes flashing as he smiled and said, 'Pretty?'

Edward tried to recall her face. He had met her in Toby's office. Mousy, he remembered, and frightened of her own shadow. He had doubted at the time if she would be able to handle Angelo, but Toby had been insistent. Edward had had the feeling he was sleeping with her.

'I suppose so.'

'Has she got big tits? Is she attractive? Sexy?'

'Not to me.'

'You don't know what you're missing,' Angelo teased gaily, his mood changing with mercurial speed.

'I do,' Edward answered ruefully. 'I was married once upon a time. A horrible experience!' And he shuddered.

Angelo threw back his head and laughed, the sinews standing out like cords at his throat. Then he swung round towards the terrace.

'Where are you going?' Edward shouted, feeling defeated and suddenly old in the face of such virility.

'Swimming,' Angelo answered, heading for the pool.

'Damn you,' Edward growled under his breath, thoroughly nettled. 'All right, ruin your career. See if I care.'

He followed at a slower pace, Armani wire-framed sunglasses shielding his eyes. The light glittered on the expanse of water transformed into pure sapphire by the tiles lining the base and sides. It was rectangular, with curving stone steps at the shallow end where a fountain gushed from the mouth of a gilded dolphin. The villa had belonged to a shipping tycoon before Angelo bought it, and no expense had been spared in its construction.

It'll have to go if he keeps up this absurd nonsense, Edward grunted. He can't possibly be meaning to retire, can he? Even he must be aware of how pig-headed he's being.

Next time he looked, Angelo was in the pool with a raven-haired nymphet who was shrieking and giggling in his arms. He lifted her high and brought her down, wide-legged, piercing her with his iron-hard cock. A cascade of droplets shimmered like diamonds over her lithe, naked limbs. Her shrieks changed to moans, her giggles to mewling sounds of pleasure, as she slithered up and down on the enormous prong penetrating her vagina, the water sloshing in faster and faster motion.

Edward stumped off, leaving Angelo to his frolics. His prick was in urgent need of attention, the circumcised head rubbing against his pants, a thrill of anticipation tingling through the shaft.

I'll take a stroll on the beach, he decided, and soon, without doubt, I'll be in some secluded cave assuaging my hunger between the buttocks of a golden-skinned descendent of Apollo. No god this time, but an obliging rent-boy.

Chapter Three

THE COVE SPREAD out in a horseshoe. Sheltered by rocks, it was a private retreat reached only by a steep pathway from the Villa Artemis, whose ochre tiled roof and white-stucco walls contrasted strongly with the endless verdure.

The resinous aroma of fir scented the air, and blended with the salty tang of the turquoise sea, which piled up and broke on the beach in splinters of foam. The sun blazed from a cloudless expanse of blue.

This paradise could all be mine, if I play my cards right, mused the woman lounging on a bright, hand-woven rug. I think I could persuade Rutger to sign it over to me. That would be a coup. The master so besotted with his submissive slave that he would give her his secret hideaway.

She gurgled with laughter, languorously stretching her body, which was naked except for the tiny triangle of gold lurex covering her pubis. Small-boned, slender and firm breasted, with honey-coloured hair pulled back from her cat-shaped face. A face, moreover, instantly familiar to thousands of cinema-goers: Leandra Lafage, not only a sex-goddess, but a surprisingly competent actress.

She had her years with the RSC to thank for that,

when she was plain Maureen Davis struggling for recognition, pointedly ambitious, using anyone as a stepping stone to success. It wasn't playing a walk-on part in one of the Bard's tragedies that had got her where she was now – on a sandy beach in Zaminos – but taking her clothes off and posing for open crotch shots in a skin-mag.

She was not ashamed of displaying her attributes so brazenly. Unlike some stars, she did not become coy or indignant when this was brought up. She accepted it, was truthful about it, and fond of reminding pushy interviewers that if they had a problem with it, she didn't.

The only problem that bothered her at the moment was how soon she could seduce the young man walking up from the water's edge. He was her new driver and bodyguard, and she was hot to try him out.

She raised an evenly bronzed arm, the full globes of her breasts lifting as she waved and said, 'What's it like, Stefan?'

'Fine. No jelly-fish,' he shouted back, quickening his pace, his penis and balls bobbing gently, barely contained by a miniscule jock-strap.

Leandra could feel her labia swelling against the tight strip of fabric cutting into the groove. Her bud stirred, and a pulse quickened in her core. She was creaming the narrow gusset, wanting to escape the restricting fabric. She flexed her coppery-sheened legs and the thong tightened along the deep crease dividing her buttocks.

Yes, he was handsome, hand-picked from several applicants. Interviewing them had been entertaining, whipping up her passions, but he had fulfilled her requirements. His references were genuine, he was personable and clean and, above all, possessed a fine physique. Her fingers longed to smooth his biceps, run

49

over his pectorals and tweak those wine-red nipples. This would be only the beginning. Emboldened, she would slip her hand down to cup his cock.

He reached her, stood above her, broad and stocky, his silhouette blotting out the scalding rays of the sun. She shaded her eyes against the glare pulsing around his head. For an instant the past hung heavy as a cloak over her. He was the sea-god, Poseidon, surely? And she a helpless mortal about to be penetrated by his divine phallus?

Get a grip, she chided herself, her sense of humour bubbling up. Don't start living the role you're rehearsing. Bollocks to Stanislavski and method-acting.

But the idea was enthralling, none the less, and appealed to the romantic in her which, aeons ago, had been buried deep under cynicism.

'Sit down,' she encouraged, patting a place beside her.

'Madame?' he queried, not sure of his position as yet.

'It's OK, Stefan. You don't have to stand on ceremony here.'

He looked puzzled, his English not too good. The job was important to him and he did not want to blow it at the onset. He dropped to his hunkers, his thigh muscles knotting under tanned flesh scribbled all over with dark down.

Now she could see his face. He was extremely attractive, with clean-cut features and sepia hair twisted into rat-tails, dripping sea-water. His eyes admired her, deep blue, slightly oblique, like those of a saint in an ancient Byzantine fresco.

No saint, she guessed, her glance cutting to the bulge pushed to prominence between the solid thews directed towards her. He's accustomed to women tourists who've dropped their reserve along with their knickers, bewitched by the powerful, aphrodisiac spell of the island.

Men, too? This idea neither shocked nor astonished her. It added to her arousal. Her education had been thorough under Rutger's unconventional tutorage.

She passed her hand over Stefan's knee and up the inside of his thigh. The bulge grew bigger and his eyes alert. 'It's all right,' she murmured, lowering her voice to that sultry, intimate purr that had her audiences squirming in their seats. 'I have other duties for you, Stefan, ones that I didn't mention at your interview. Oil my back,' and she held out the bottle of sun-lotion.

He took it, sinking from his haunches to his knees, and the tip of his erect penis appeared at the top of his pouch, nudging his navel. It was fiery red, a single drop of dew glistened at the slit.

Leandra dipped a fingertip in the moisture and smeared it over the glans while Stefan knelt there as if carved in bronze, head bent as he watched. Then his hips began to rock back and forth in tiny movements, urged by the screaming need for release pounding through his testicles.

She teased him, clamping her hands on his firm, high buttocks and saying, 'Not so fast. There's no hurry. I want a slow, leisurely fuck. But first: the oil.'

He nodded, and she presented her shapely back to him. His hands glided over the sun-kissed skin. He lingered on that sensitive, erogenous zone at the nape of her neck, then slipped across her shoulders, tracing her spine, past the hollow below her waist and down to where a dimple marked the V at the division of her bottom cheeks.

'Mmm . . . that was yummy,' she sighed, slanting a glance at him.

'Thank you, madame. I do my best to serve you.'

'Oh, you will . . . you'll serve me all right. Lie down.'

He lay flat, a sacrificial victim of her lust. She mounted him, agile as a cat, her slim legs bridging his body. Her breasts hung over him and she leaned closer till one nipple brushed across his lips. His mouth opened at once, and he tongued the swelling, rose-brown teat, then sucked it avidly.

Leandra let her head rest back, face uplifted to the sun while waves of pleasure washed from her breasts to her clit. She dragged her nipple from him, and moved upwards till her crotch rested where her breast had been. The lurex was pulled tight, burrowing into the vertical line of her cleft. Fingers fumbling with impatience, she undid the narrow ties, raised herself a little to remove the impeding tanga and threw it to one side.

Now her pink slit was exposed, fringed by scant, fairish hair. The lips unfolded, twin petals of turgid flesh coated with silvery juice. Her clitoris stood proud like the pistil of a jungle orchid, and she flicked it, patted it, fondled it. Desire pulsed through her, heavy and demanding. She drove her fists into the small of her back, arching her pubis as Stefan's tongue darted out, licking her bud, sliding along her lower lips, into her entrance, delving and probing.

He supped on her ambrosial sweetness, buried his face between her sun-browned thighs, seeking out each plump fold and worshipping at the altar of her clitoris.

'That's it,' Leandra moaned, her voice soft and smoky. 'Work it ... yes, yes ... work it! Use your fingers, too. Stroke it, part it, open it ... not like that, like *this*.' And she drove her hands down to spread her labia majora, smearing her fingers with her juices and rubbing each side of her nubbin, avoiding its crown, pressing back, subjecting it to hard friction.

Her action gave Stefan greater access. He plied his tongue energetically, reaching up with his hands and pulling at her rock-hard nipples. The ecstasy mounted and she surrendered to it, screaming as the tidal wave of orgasm crashed over her.

She slid down his body, the hot hard lump of his confined penis pressing into her belly. Her lips met his and she tasted her honeydew on them, sweet and pungent. Her tongue ravaged his mouth, exploring his teeth, his gums, the soft, slippery inner lining. Then she lifted her head and he smiled into her eyes, and his penis jerked, reminding her of his need.

She shifted to one side, caressing him through the tight purse of black fabric, running a fingernail up the central seam that curved over his high, tumescent rod. Stefan groaned.

Leandra loosened the thongs. The pouch fell away and released his skyward pointing, ten-inch serpent. She knelt beside him, wound the crisp curls of his pubic hair round her fingers and then took his phallus between her lips, sucking gently.

She held back, running her tongue over the slit, relishing the flavour of lusting male garnished with sea salt. His shaft grew larger and more congested and his eyes narrowed, slightly out of focus as he observed her mouth and his cock joined together.

Leandra was well schooled, though looking back on her sex life pre-Rutger, she saw it as a series of unsatisfactory fumbles. Now she had acquired the skills of an Eastern houri and, when in the mood, could make her partner writhe in an extremity of almost unbearable bliss – begging her to stop, imploring her to continue.

Had Stefan yet experienced the dichotomy of pain/pleasure? she wondered. And her vagina contracted with a spasm of longing.

Removing her lips from his quivering phallus, she continued to caress it with her hands while drawing the crimped, silken skin of his balls into her mouth. She licked the scrotum, and allowed her tongue to explore more intimately, feathering across his perenium and tickling round the entrance to his rectum.

The tiny nether hole relaxed and she smiled inwardly. This, too, had been used as an instrument of satisfaction. I must tell Rutger, she noted, sketching the conversation behind closed eyes, as if on a memo pad.

She ventured the tip of one finger into his anus, not for a moment neglecting the penis that vibrated in her other hand. The puckered brown hole opened easily and she toured the rim then, abruptly, returned to gorge herself on his cock.

It pulsed more urgently under her lips as she moved forwards and back, sliding out to the end, then pushing strongly in, so deep that the helm passed her uvula. Holding it still, she slowly pumped it, while her hand massaged the shaft.

Stefan groaned and panted. She was driving him mad, refusing to let him guide her into the rhythm he needed to bring on his crisis.

'Surrender,' she whispered, intent on milking him of his semen, waiting to feel it spurt into her mouth.

'No. Wait. Let me enter you,' he gasped, fighting to hold on to the substance she was determined to draw from his loins.

'You want to bonk away at my pussy?' she chuckled, letting his prick slither from her mouth.

He did not answer, simply seized her in a vice-like grip and rolled her over on to her back. Then he clamped a thigh over hers, pinning her to the rug, rubbing his cock against her. She was surprised by her reaction to this roughness. She wanted him to do it, to take her forcefully, to possess her with his body and ravish her with his beauty.

She opened her sex for him with her fingers and guided that enormous prong so it could plunge into her. She hitched her legs high, resting her ankles on his shoulders, drawing him ever deeper into the very core of her. He was most generously endowed. She could feel his glans butting against her cervix, her vaginal walls stretched, the base of his cock grinding against her clitoris.

He jabbed at her violently with the full length and thickness of his weapon and she clung to him with her arms and embraced him with her legs, winding them round him. He should have his pleasure, as she had taken hers earlier. She threshed and winced and clawed at his back, her nails leaving bloody stripes, feeling that final swelling of his organ that signalled ejaculation. He gave a sharp bark, face contorted, then slumped across her.

Leandra lay there listening to his heartbeat gradually slowing. Seagulls drifted on the thermals and she watched them lazily, completely fulfilled – for the moment. Then she saw a prismatic flash high up among the rocks, and her lips curved in a smile.

So, someone had been watching them through binoculars. She knew who it was and hoped she had given an impressive performance.

He had been island-hopping, his yacht re-entering the harbour as dawn painted the sky with luminous green and orange fans.

He stood at the prow, his nostrils quivering as he inhaled the heavenly scent, a blend of dewy earth and pine, lemons perhaps, and something indefinable, like the memory of a herb garden. It was a combination even more potent than the piquant, oceanic fragrance of aroused cunt, and Rutger Eberhardt relished this above all else.

His gun-metal grey BMW had been waiting, but for a moment he had watched the frenzied activity, with fishing nets rising and falling against the ever lightening sky. A group of sailors, who had obviously been drinking *mastika* as if it was beer, were singing, shouting and brawling on the quayside.

It was a timeless scene. Ulysses could have marshalled his adventurers there or, centuries later, Venetians mustered seamen for their merchant ships or war galleys.

Now, standing on the cliff near his villa, he seemed to be surrounded by the spirit of the island, soaking it up, translating it into images. He would later convey these to Robin Channing, that unfortunate young author who, in his innocence, had not realised just how much license Rutger would take with his novel, on which the film was to be based. He had been summoned to Zaminos to work on the script.

But for the moment Rutger could forget the responsibilities of directorship, lifting his field-glasses and concentrating on the tableau below him, brought close by the powerful lenses.

Two lovers were mating, golden-brown against the white sand as they rolled from the rug in ecstatic delight.

Rutger stood motionless, a striking figure, his shaggy blond hair bleached to platinum by the sun. Above average in height and powerfully built, he had ice-blue eyes that blazed with cold fire as he watched his mistress reaching the zenith of passion.

His balls ached and the cobra-head of his phallus lifted beneath his form-hugging black Levis. His fingers tightened round the binoculars as he imagined their next meeting. Although they had staged the encounter, she would be punished. All part of those exciting lessons where he taught her the meaning of eroticism, freeing her from taboos, making her accept and enjoy the dark secrets of her innermost self.

The sun was strong, the breeze warm, and the setting perfect. Rutger owned several homes in various parts of the world, but it was here that he felt at one with the creative force – here among these islands where civilisation had been born.

He had chosen this spot on which to stage the major project of his career, a story of gods and humans, an allegory in one sense, an almost pornographic spectacle in another. It was ambitious and he was putting his reputation and wealth on the line, but Rutger throve on risks.

Leandra would draw in the crowds. He'd be very surprised if *Whom the Gods Love* wasn't a hit at next year's Cannes Film Festival. And as he focused on her nipples and that delicious fork magnified by the glasses, his need for satisfaction became urgent.

She was lying beside her lover, facing the point where Rutger was concealed. He knew she was aware of him.

He laid the binoculars down, his tanned hand moving to his fly. He let it rest for a moment, enjoying the sensation of the flesh swelling beneath the denim.

He conjured images of Leandra and a host of other women, picturing breasts like orbs or small and pert, nipples long and brown or tiny as miniature rosebuds. He thought of pink virginal deltas, and experienced avenues, red and hungry, and love-buds of varying size, some boldly protruding, others coyly hidden. The varieties of genitalia never ceased to amaze him.

He unzipped his jeans and slipped a hand inside to hold his erect penis, stroking it firmly. Now more heated visions floated in his brain, the deep divide between buttocks, the forbidden hole of either sex. Women's more generous rumps, or the tighter flanks of men? He had enjoyed them all.

His cock throbbed in his hand and his movements quickened. It was as if fingers other than his own fluttered over the bulging head, while impudent, unseen hands cradled his testicles and explored his fundament. Thoughts of nymphs and dryads, satyrs and fauns, Great Pan himself, blazed through his mind.

He held the spear of power in his fist, caressing it, massaging it, wishing it was Leandra who handled his swollen rod. His seed was surging, an irrepressible tide. It erupted forcibly, shooting out his libation. It spattered his hand, his thighs, and the fertile earth of the island.

When Carla set her feet on the tarmac and smelled the intoxicating odours wafting around her, she knew she had come home. Up in the eighties, the heat hit her, almost too much after the rainy spring she had left behind in England.

She was stiff from sitting, though the flight from Heathrow had passed in a flash. Excitement and anticipation energised her, and the effervescent Marie swept her along, across the baggage hall, through customs, till they stood in the glare outside the airport.

'There's the car. Come on,' she shouted, pushing her trolley piled high with luggage across the melting asphalt towards a hunter-green Range Rover.

They were accompanied by Marie's secretary, Ruth Barnes, a gawky girl wearing cutoffs and a crop-top. Her thin bare legs ended in DMs with brocade velvet uppers, and her dark hair was shaved over each ear, the multi-hued crest gelled. Several little plaits threaded with African beads hung down at the back. They clicked as she moved.

Despite her appearance, Ruth was amazingly efficient. She had the bags stowed in a trice, even while chatting up a stunningly handsome local Romeo who said his name was Stefan.

'What a hunk,' Marie muttered, settling in the back-seat with Carla and licking her lips as she eyed his wide shoulders and the crisp curls brushing his white collar.

'Leandra always surrounds herself with drop-dead gorgeous guys.'

'I thought she was with Rutger Eberhardt, the film director.'

Marie shot her an exasperated glance. 'That wouldn't stop her. Rutger would probably encourage her. He'd want to watch.'

'He would?'

'Sure.'

This is a crazy world I'm entering. Everything is happening too fast, Carla concluded. First the break-up, then moving in with Marie, who had gone with her to clear out what remained of her belongings from Richmond; together they had dumped most of them in charity shops. This had been traumatic – and so was the sight of the stranger who stared back every time she looked at herself in a mirror.

This new image was not entirely due to Andy's clever use of his scissors or Chloe's professional expertise, nor the clothes that had set Carla back hundreds of pounds – paid for from Edward Connar's generous advance. It had more to do with her self-confidence, which had taken an upward curve when Toby had made love to her, and continued even though she had been destroyed by Giles's betrayal. Signing the contract had forced her to believe in herself. She had to – or run away screaming.

Now her highlighted hair complemented her skin, her facial structure was emphasised by a warmer foundation and her eyes sparkled like amethysts under the darkened lashes. The lustre that now illuminated her came from within. She agreed with Marie that leaving Giles had been the best thing she had ever done.

There had been so little time and so much to do, and then they were on the plane heading for Zaminos, their final destination the Villa Artemis. Carla was relieved yet disappointed to know that she did not have to meet Angelo Lorenzo yet, having been given instructions to wait till Edward contacted her.

The town dropped behind as the FWD climbed steadily, passing groves of orange trees and hedges thick with smilax and quince. The sea lay on one side and corn-filled valleys on the other, rimmed by distant mountains where icing-sugar monasteries clung to precipitous crags.

All was lush, hot and fragrant. Carla felt as if she had never lived anywhere else – expanding under so much sunshine, she became free and wanton and incredibly randy.

The road ended; sensor-powered gates swung open and the Range Rover passed through, gravel crunching under its tyres. There lay the villa, single-storeyed and sprawling, set amidst cypresses and flowering shrubs.

'I expect they're sunning themselves,' Marie said, striding through the front door and across the wide tiled hall as if she owned the place.

The sound of water tinkled through a pillared opening. Light sliced across, dazzling white after the cool, purple-shadowed interior. Carla stepped out on to a paved terrace at the edge of a large pool circled by padded loungers, cane chairs and round cast-iron tables under striped umbrellas.

A man was sitting in the shade wearing horn-rimmed spectacles, with papers spread out before him. He looked up as Marie said, 'Hi, Robin. Long time no see. How you doing?'

'I'm OK,' he said, with a shy smile.

He took off his glasses, pushed back his chair and got to his feet awkwardly, as if ill at ease amidst such hedonistic luxury. He was shorter than Marie, slim-shouldered and bony. His arms and legs, bared by vest and baggy shorts, were thin, and he had stayed in the sun too long; his skin was reddened. He wore a white cotton hat with a floppy brim from beneath which his friendly eyes peered, each side of a ruddy, peeling nose.

Marie clapped herself on the brow theatrically. 'Oh, hell! Of course! It's your book Rutger's adapting. I heard about this. Nice one, Rob.'

'Thanks,' he stammered and his eyes switched to Carla.

'Carla Holt. She writes, too,' Marie explained. 'You two should get together.'

A nereid surfaced suddenly, shaking back her streaming hair and shouting, 'Marie! Thank God! I thought you'd been held up. Things are never on time out here . . . one day, two days . . . it doesn't matter. I've never come across any place that adopts the policy of *mañana* so completely and utterly.' She swam towards the stone steps at one end and rose from the water.

Carla thought of Venus born from the sea, and indeed this was a remarkably lovely woman. She recognised her from films and TV appearances, and had read that she was something of an *enfant terrible*, renowned for her outspokenness and total disregard for convention.

'Nice to meet you, Carla,' Leandra said, after they had been introduced. 'Marie's told me so much about you, been on the phone for hours lately. I don't read much except scripts. Have I heard of you, or do you use a pseudonym?' Without waiting for an answer, she rushed on, 'I've met Giles Davenport. He wanted to get me into bed.'

'And did he?' Carla asked. His unfaithfulness still hurt.

Leandra shrugged her shoulders and smiled, saying, 'No. He didn't rock my boat. Sorry to hear he upset you, though. Marie filled me in about his spreading it around. Alicia Ashford's an all-time bitch. Talk about wired.'

61

She was naked, except for a string of beads round her supple waist. Two strands dangled down in front, touching the top of her neatly trimmed pubic triangle. The sparseness of the hair revealed the split fig of her sex, and Carla could not help staring at it, so high and sharply etched.

Leandra turned and snapped her fingers at Robin. He leapt forward, holding out a towel, his eyes filled with cringing adoration as she snatched it from him.

'D'you want anything else, mistress?' he asked, an undeniable erection tenting the front of his garishly patterned shorts.

'Go and make sure Dorcas has laid out my evening gown,' she commanded, a loud crack resounding across the terrace as her hand slapped down hard on his shoulder.

'Ooh . . . that's so sore,' he complained, rubbing the fiery spot.

'You should have obeyed me and used screening lotion,' she answered, her voice cold and merciless. 'On your knees.'

'I'm sorry, mistress,' he whimpered, crouching at her feet, bending to place his lips on her high, delicately curving instep.

'You will be, by the time I'm finished with you,' she promised. 'Now get up!' And she stood with regally tilted head as he towelled her dry.

Carla was blushing with embarrassment, yet conscious of excitement darting along her nerves. Sweat was beading her body, putting her deodorant to the test. She wanted to tear off her clothes and leap into the pool.

This exchange between Leandra and Robin was unexpected. Marie had warned her that she would find life different there, but she had been unprepared for this. Robin Channing's book had caused a stir, a mid-list offering that had risen steadily to the top. Carla had read it, envying his gift for telling a fast-moving, adventurous, even erotic tale firmly founded on scholarly research. And here he was, acting like Leandra's slave and aroused by the humiliation. It was unbelievable.

Leandra turned, and Carla could not repress a start of surprise. Her hostess's back and thighs were evenly tanned, but her buttocks bore blotches like the imprint of an opened palm. These were visible for only an instant, then hidden as Robin draped her in a long cotton voile sarong. Carla thought for a second she had been mistaken, but no – the marks were clearly visible through the transparent fabric.

'Come inside, darlings,' Leandra carolled. 'I'll show you your rooms. Stefan will be on call. You can borrow him if you want. He's a great lay.'

'Where's Rutger?' Marie asked, grinning at Carla, an I-told-you-so expression on her face.

'Somewhere about,' Leandra answered casually. 'You'll meet him at dinner.'

'Looks like you've met him already today,' Marie remarked, glancing meaningfully at Leandra's backside.

'Ah, well . . . yes. Lunchtime, to be precise. He saw me fucking Stefan on the beach this morning. My behaviour warranted a severe paddling.'

'I see,' Marie said slowly, her eyes bright and challenging. 'D'you want to share this with us, Miss Lafarge?'

Leandra gave Carla a sidelong stare as they entered the first of the two large, marble-floored bedrooms prepared for them. 'Maybe not quite yet,' she murmured. 'Let the new girl get settled first. Don't want to scare her off, do we?'

Carla frowned, puzzled by these half statements and innuendoes. It made her feel left out, not one of the gang, someone too green and naïve to be let into their secrets. She voiced something to this effect when Leandra had drifted away to change for dinner.

'Honey, let it flow,' Marie advised. 'Rutger's the boss. He'll decide if and when.'

'If and when what?' Carla snapped, feeling suddenly enervated. She needed a shower and a nap. 'I came here to work. Nothing more than that. If there's some hidden agenda, then I want to know about it. It was kind of your friends to offer us somewhere to stay, but I can easily move into a hotel.'

'Come down off your high-horse, hon,' Marie soothed. She signalled to Ruth, who stopped unpacking Carla's suitcase and stood waiting instructions. 'Find Stefan or someone and get a tray of tea sent in.'

'Right,' Ruth said, and strolled to the door.

'Brits never feel happy until they've had a couple of cuppas, do they?' Marie added. 'Leandra should have realised that.'

'Leandra was too busy ordering Robin about,' Carla said indignantly. 'Why does he let her do it?'

Marie seated herself at the intricately carved dressing-table and took a brush to her hair. 'He likes it, I guess.'

'How can he possibly?' Carla sagged on the muslin-draped double bed, gnawing at her thumbnail, further annoyed to see that she had chipped the metallic mulberry polish.

'Some guys get off on it. Women, too,' Marie answered reflectively, unbuttoning the top of her beige silk blouse and blowing down it to cool herself.

'You're talking about masochism, I suppose,' Carla said, beginning to feel desirous, her juices wetting the gusset of her panties. 'Oh, don't worry, I'm not entirely ignorant of this, or sadism. I've read *Venus in Furs*.'

'And didn't understand it, I'll bet,' Marie put in shrewdly. She undid her blouse fully, exposing a pair of large breasts cradled in a coffee lace brassière, which did not conceal the darkness of the areolae beneath or the nipples that stood out firmly.

'That's right. I'd never submit myself to anyone,' Carla averred loudly, watching fascinated as Marie started to pinch her teats into ever more prominent peaks.

'There speaks a gal who's never experienced the thrill of being dominated by a master,' Marie said slowly, her breath catching in her throat. She pushed the lacy edge down, and her breasts rose over it, the nipples like staring eyes. She sighed, and rolled them between her fingertips, adding, 'It makes me horny just thinking about it.'

Carla was astounded, though there was an answering tingle in her own breasts and her clitoris pulsed between her wet lower lips. 'D'you mean to tell me that you've been a submissive?' she asked.

'Sure,' Marie answered, her bare legs splayed each side of the stool as she rucked up the hem of her smart linen skirt, higher and higher, till Carla could see her bush. Marie was not wearing any panties under that businesslike skirt.

'You've been – what was it Leandra called it – paddled?' she managed to stammer.

'Yep, and spanked and whipped.'

'Whipped?' Carla's blood ran cold.

'Whipped,' Marie replied, and her fingertips opened her cleft where clear moisture glistened. 'I'd wanted him for some time, and Leandra had worked me into a frenzy with talk about what they did together. There was a party at their London house one night. Well, more than a party. Everyone there expected something unusual in the way of sex. It was wild . . . everything and anything that consenting adults could possibly dream of. Fantasies fulfilled, weirdest needs catered for.'

'Go on,' Carla breathed, sitting up slowly. Of its own volition, her hand rested on her skirt just above her pubis, the heat of her body penetrating her palm.

'He put me into handcuffs, chained my ankles and spread my legs apart. I was stretched over a trestle, bare-naked, and his guests were watching. He roused my breasts, kissed and licked them, while Leandra took control of my cleft, stroking my clit, making it ache and burn.'

Marie worked her fingers into her fleshy delta as she spoke. Her nectar seeped out, scenting the air. Carla could no longer control herself. Opening her legs, she pushed aside the cotton panties and wetted a finger in her own copious juices.

'And the whipping? When did that happen?' she whispered, her clitoris throbbing against her middle digit. She did not want to come yet, and withdrew from its head, patting round the labial rim.

'It was sudden, unexpected, like a red-hot iron burning my butt,' Marie said breathily. 'I couldn't escape it, tied to the trestle. He struck me again, laying on the stripes cunningly, never touching the same spot twice. Then he smoothed balm into my stinging bottom and penetrated my asshole and rubbed my love button. He lashed me again while Leandra frigged me. I came in a rush, and it was the best orgasm I'd ever had.'

'Oh, God . . . go on! Tell me more,' Carla cried, hand kneading at her clit. It swelled beneath her fingers like a ripe berry.

'Not yet. I can't hold back,' Marie moaned, her fingers fluttering over her love-button. Her thighs opened violently, and she gave a long, shuddering groan. 'Yes . . . yes . . . that's it! Ah, what a great feeling,' she sighed.

'Who did this to you? What's his name?' Carla

demanded, rubbing herself frantically and reaching a dazzling orgasm.

'Can't you guess? It's Rutger, of course. Who else? He's our master,' Marie said, back to normal now, wiping her fingers on a tissue and tugging down her skirt.

Chapter Four

HE WAS LATE arriving for dinner.

Manipulative, Carla decided. Controlling people. Keeping them hanging about. What a wonderful way to demonstrate power. *I don't like the sound of Rutger Eberhardt.*

Showered, rested and refreshed, and coming to terms with her recent experience with Marie, she was feeling remarkably buoyant. It was one of those rare times when she was halfway satisfied with her appearance: the new hair-colour, the spiralling curls, the dramatic makeup.

Clothes, too. Marie had been lecturing her about their significance, saying, 'Wear what makes you feel charged and good about yourself. Have fun. Lingerie can give you a real buzz. Never skip on this. Buy the most luxurious, even if you have to starve for a week. Coloured satins, lacy teddies, camiknickers, French knickers, itsy-bitsy G-strings, tarty bustiers, garter-belts, naughty nighties. Who says you've got to keep them on? Stockings, of course, never tights. I like to run around without panties sometimes, it kind of keeps me on my toes, gets me off. Think like a high-priced hooker and you can't go wrong.'

She had made sure all these items were included

when they went shopping, but Carla was still unsure. Writing romance novels had given her the opportunity to play out her dressing-up fantasies. Her heroines, though Cinderellas to start with, usually ended up richly gowned, and the tart-with-the-heart, an essential subcharacter, was always seductive in racy underwear.

Real life? Now was the time to put herself to the test.

Her debut into Leandra's glamorous world, and she had spent a long time deliberating. Ruth had darted between Marie's room and Carla's, offering advice. A fashion barometer, she had a finger on the pulse of what was being worn on the streets.

Marie selected a pant-suit of poppy red silk, with wide trousers and a brief top, but Carla settled for something more unusual.

As she walked into the reception room, she was aware of her body beneath a loose robe of finest hand-spun raw silk. The gown was the colour of sand, its neck cut away deeply. Embroidered with seed pearls, it was sleeveless, diaphanous, almost obscene. Resisting the urge to fold her arms over her breasts, Carla stiffened her spine and held her head high. Her nipples jutted through the fragile material, and her hairless mons formed a shadow at the apex of her thighs. She'd never dared go out *sans* panties before.

The room was spacious, its sixty-foot plate glass window offering panoramic views. The villa stood on a promontory with a private beach on one side and on the other a marina which sheltered stately yachts and ocean-going cruisers, playthings for the rich.

Though supremely elegant, with Chinese silk rugs on the tessellated floor and black leather chairs and sofas, the salon was comfortable, the atmosphere informal. A grand piano stood in one corner near a curving, gilded concert harp, and a white Carrara marble bar streaked with pinkish veins occupied space in an alcove.

Several pieces of genuine Greek sculpture took pride of place on plinths, and one wall was adorned with a framed section of mosaic taken from a ruined temple dedicated to the gods who ruled winds and weather. It showed a sea nymph with linten tresses, round breasts and coral nipples. She rested in the arms of a bearded Titan, whose giant penis was pressed between her rosy, dimpled buttocks.

'Nothing's changed,' Marie remarked, slipping her bare arm through Carla's. 'Same old thing, over and over. You'd think they'd have invented a variation on the theme by now.'

'Virtual reality?' Carla suggested, though she had not yet had time to open the lap-top computer in which she had extravagantly invested at Marie's instigation before leaving London.

She was accustomed to her solid dinosaur of a CPM which a friend had given her, seeking a home for his machine when he emigrated to New Zealand years ago. She had mastered this, was comfortable with it – it was like wearing a pair of old slippers. This new thing now – would she ever be able to use it to take notes of Lorenzo's story – if she ever got anywhere near him, that is?

'Cyborgasms. Zyberfantasy. Synthetic sex. I'd give it a whirl,' Marie said, pursuing the theme.

'Would it mean that VR could advance to the point where relationships are obsolete?' Somehow, this idea saddened Carla.

Marie pulled a face, then grinned. 'You old romantic, you. If it did, we'd be out of business. Gals would just pop in their electrified vaginal plugs and away they'd go. It's just another option. There's always going to be the need for holding and hugging, but it makes me mad that there are females out there who've never come.'

70

'What are you talking about? It sounds intriguing,' Leandra said, materialising beside them, voluptuous in a simple white tissue-thin gown.

'Sex,' Marie said.

'What else is there, darling?' Leandra opined. The shoestring straps crossing her shoulders deepened her tan. The back of the gown was non-existent, cut to below the waist. The tight bodice accentuated her peaked nipples and the curves of her breasts. A long moonstone necklace intertwined with Cretan gold beads dipped into the dusky valley between.

The skirt was designed to titillate, opening halfway up the thigh with every step she took, giving alluring flashes of the hothouse flower of her sex. Her bare brown legs shimmered, and her feet were encased in high-heeled strappy sandals. A pair of dangling ruby earrings brushed against her flushed cheeks, and her hair fell from a centre parting in a smooth, unbroken, wheat-gold sweep.

'Drinks, Robin,' she snapped, and he slunk off to the bar, his white suit crumpled, his hair untidy.

'We were talking sex machines,' Marie said succinctly. 'And I don't mean men.'

'I'm happy with my vibrator,' Leandra answered, her hazel eyes resting on Carla speculatively. 'Do you use one, darling?'

Carla could feel her blood rising. It seemed to come from her core, bathing her whole body in molten heat. 'No, I don't,' she admitted, accepting a margarita from the tray Robin brought across. She took a sip; the cold crystal tumbler was rimmed with lime and salt, sharp to the tongue.

'Heavens, you've no idea what you're missing!' Leandra exclaimed.

'Better than a cucumber,' Marie put in, her eyes sparkling wickedly.

71

'Not in the same class. Neither is a banana,' Leandra agreed with a throaty chuckle.

Carla exchanged a look with Robin. He pushed back a lock of his untidy light brown hair, his watery blue eyes confused. It was comforting to realise that he was almost as uneasy as she was. His face was red, though this was mainly sunburn, and he shifted his lean body from one foot to the other.

'Stop fidgeting,' Leandra commanded sharply, then reached out a casual hand and pressed the long stalk of his phallus, hooking a finger under it and jiggling his balls. He gasped, but remained passive, enduring her teasing caress.

Tired of this game, Leandra wandered towards the patio doors. 'Rutger should be here by now,' she said petulantly.

Music stole across the room from slender speakers. It reminded Carla of Giles's favourite works, unemotional, cerebral, the precise notes of Renaissance madrigals. Altos were accompanied by a lute, and the sounds, originally sung by castrati – male singers who had been deprived of their testicles as boys in order to preserve their soprano voices – were pure and unearthly.

It did nothing for Carla. She longed for something more gutsy, expressing a full range of human passions. And soon she would hear it – soon she would listen to the golden voice of Lorenzo. Perhaps he would sing for her alone. Standing in that beautiful room, with the moon rising over the sea and the stars brighter than she had ever seen them, she dared open herself to hope, a great surge of joy filling every corner of her being.

She was actually in Zaminos, with the express purpose of aiding an opera singer to resume his career. *She* was the favoured one, not Marie or Leandra, or any of those sophisticated, self-assured women whom she had envied. Toby and Edward Connar had selected her for this important mission. They had faith in her. She could do it, she knew, if only she could have as much faith in herself. *I can't wait to meet him,* she thought, tingling with impatience. *I'd do it now, if I knew the exact location.*

Two more margaritas, and she turned to Leandra, her voice bright with tequila-induced confidence. 'Is Angelo Lorenzo's villa near here?'

Leandra slanted her a glance. 'He's not far away, but I haven't seen him. I've sent several invitations to dinner, but had no reply. The word is that he lives like a hermit.'

There was a stirring near the arched portico; not exactly a step, not even a voice, more of a presence. Carla looked across the softly lit room and drew in a breath.

Even from that distance he radiated louche sexuality. Power blazed through him, so tall and distinguished, arrogant and princely. Everything else shrank in size – the priceless antiquities, the elegant salon, the people within it: Robin became invisible.

My God, Carla thought admiringly, *what an entrance. He certainly thrives on the dramatic.* It reminded her of Baron Scarpia's first appearance on stage in Act I of Puccini's opera *Tosca*, heralded by dark, threatening chords. He was the sadistic villain of whom the soprano sings after she has stabbed him to death in Act II: 'And before this man, all Rome trembled.'

'Rutger, there you are at last!' Leandra trilled and sashayed over to him.

'I hope you didn't delay the meal,' he said, his deep voice ringing with measured calm underscored by menace.

'Just a tad,' she confessed, and he slid an arm round her, pulling her against his midnight-blue velvet jacket.

'Keeping our guests waiting?' he chided with that

cultured, faintly foreign intonation. 'So impolite.' And his hand closed over her left buttock, squeezing it, the long, strong fingers entering the deep channel between both cheeks.

'I'm sorry, master,' Leandra whimpered, giving her power into his keeping.

'We shall have to think of a suitable chastisement, shan't we?' he growled as he held her slim body against his groin.

'Yes, master,' she murmured, eyes half closed, like a cat having its fur rubbed.

He let her go abruptly. A white liveried footman announced that dinner was served, and Carla followed the strangely assorted company to the terrace. Under the light of a moon augmented by flares in floor-standing girandoles stood a plain wooden table, the kind of well-scrubbed board peasants might have used.

But no humble worker would have ever been able to afford such cuisine, served in silver dishes by staff of both sexes. They had the smooth skins and brilliant eyes of the locals, beautiful, full-breasted girls and slim, athletic men as readily available for sampling as the food.

The meal was mouth-wateringly presented, garnished with lettuce and cucumbers and beef tomatoes. The light glowed on cut glass and Sèvres porcelain, and Carla was guided by her hosts, for every dish was strange to her.

'Try swordfish with lemon sauce,' Leandra advised. 'Or *louza*, a kind of highly spiced smoked meat. And don't forget the roasted doves; they taste like quail.'

'She must start with the island's speciality,' Rutger declared. '*Langoustes*, firm-fleshed and succulent lobster.'

It was the first time he had included Carla in the conversation, though his rapier-sharp eyes had been boring into her ever since they were introduced. The scene was dreamlike, and she was lulled by the potent, almost narcotic atmosphere of the villa, where every appetite could be indulged.

The variety of exotic dishes was dizzying, each with its accompanying sauce and wine. Fish was much in evidence, tender flakes cooked in filo pastry, mullet served on a bed of greenery, squid fried in garlic and olive oil. Pyramids of fruit decorated the table, along with epergnes of madonna lilies and fern, the strong perfume wafting from the waxen blooms to blend with the wonderful aromas arising on wisps of steam as the cover was lifted on yet another course.

Rutger leaned closer to Carla, and rested his hand on her knee under the table. 'The red wine of Santorin is excellent. Would you care to sample it?'

'Yes,' she murmured, concentrating on those sinewy fingers sliding towards the division of her thighs, while Rutger smiled across at Leandra who was feeding Robin morsels from her plate as if he was a pet dog.

At Rutger's signal a waiter leaped to attention and filled a goblet for her. Meanwhile, Rutger's fingers advanced towards their goal. Carla was paralysed, unable to do anything but wait for them to find it, yet shocked by his presumption.

Rutger would not be denied his will, filled with a superabundance of sexual fire. And she admired him, was impressed by his films, recognising a talent tantamount to genius. As a man, he was everything she could have hoped for, strikingly handsome, worldly and self-possessed.

His finger entered the very top of her crease and lingered on her excited bud, gently flicking it with an almost imperceptible movement.

The dessert arrived, a rich concoction of almond sweetmeats and ice cream. 'Eat,' Rutger said, and little flames, jets of amber, burned in the inky pupils of his eyes.

Carla raised a spoonful of the confectionery to her lips. It was cold, sweet, laced with Cointreau. She sensed that her role was one of complete acquiescence. His finger on her nub, moving oh-so-slowly and secretly, robbed her of thought. Her juices seeped from her, soaking into the back of her robe. Her nipples puckered into cones raising the delicate fabric. Fire was gathering in her belly as he tormented the hard wet tip of her clitoris.

'Has Edward Connar said when he wants to see you?' Marie's voice broke into Carla's sensual trance.

'No . . . sorry. He'll phone,' she said, irritated by any interruption. In her daydream, she allowed her mind to dwell on the plot of her current novel. Rutger became the master of the house and she observed, yet became the heroine, a nobly born but poverty-stricken girl who had recently taken the post of governess to his children. Now it seemed he had caught her in the church, making her sit beside him in the pew and slipping his hand under her black crinoline skirt. There were petticoats, of course, and cambric knickers, but these had an open gusset. It had been easy for him to inveigle a finger inside, stroke her soft pubic hair and centre on her nubbin.

She would be a virgin, of course, who had never even masturbated. 'Oh, sir, don't,' Carla heard her brain-child saying, and she somehow shared her emotions.

'Hush. No one must know,' he whispered, and continued that seductive rubbing.

Carla came out of this hypnotic state, knowing she would climax if he did not stop. She dropped her hand down to cover his, warning him to desist. He looked into her face with those devilish, icy eyes and said, 'You can't leave the table without tasting retsina.'

He withdrew his hand, leaving her with swollen labial lips and an aching clit. I shan't forgive him for this, ever, she vowed.

'Ah, yes, the famous drink of the islands,' Leandra chipped in, lounging back in her chair while Robin parted her slit skirt and began to lap at her cleft.

'Do you know how to test a retsina?' Rutger asked, picking up the bottle. 'Pour a little in your glass, like so, then place your hand over the top and shake it.' He carried this out while speaking, then passed it under Carla's nose and said, 'A good retsina will retain its characteristic wine and pine scent. A bad retsina will smell like vinegar.'

She took a gulp. It burned her throat and made her cough. She was already intoxicated, as much with Rutger as the amount she had drunk. She rose, staggering a little. 'Excuse me. I shall be back in a while,' she blurted.

'Don't wander too far and get lost. We have unfinished business, you and I,' he said in a sultry tone that turned her vitals to jelly.

She reeled down the wide, shallow steps and lost one of her toe-post sandals. She fumbled for and found it, then slipped her foot into it and proceeded. 'Boys and girls, come out to play. The moon doth shine as bright as day,' she sang, thinking: this moon certainly doth. I've never seen such a night. The breeze was soft and warm, the cicadas a soothing orchestral accompaniment to the murmur and hiss of the sea. Carla headed towards it. The ground became rougher under her feet, the sky obscured by trees. She pressed on, borne on a cloud of alcohol, the shadows broken by discs of moonlight filtering through leaves.

A sound arrested her. She crept towards it, then stopped in the shadows, staring. Ruth and Stefan stood there, glued at the lips. Her crop-top was pushed above her small breasts, their nipples dark against the paler skin.

Carla made to withdraw, embarrassed at viewing this intimate moment. Then excitement darted down to her womb as she saw that his jeans were unzipped and Ruth's hand inside. She took her mouth from his and, smiling, drew out his cock and started to rub it.

It was stiff and large, the dimness making it look black in her hand. He muttered something in Greek, and lifted her skirt, finding the thin panties and pushing them to one side. Then, urging her back against a tree, he lifted her, spread her legs and thrust his weapon into the darkness of her sex.

Ruth squealed like a cat in season, her legs wrapped round his hips, as she moved up and down frantically.

Carla gasped, her body on fire, her clit demanding fulfilment. She clutched at her mons, feeling its heat through her thin gown, dragging the silk into her cleft and rubbing herself through it.

She could see Stefan's penis glistening with Ruth's juices as he pulled it out, paused for a split second, then rammed it back into her vagina. She could hear their rapid breathing, their groans of passion, and the sucking sound as he withdrew then re-entered Ruth's luscious wet sex.

Carla could not stand it any more, and she moved swiftly away, not caring if they heard her. They didn't, blind and deaf to anything but the rising tide of pleasure.

I want a man with me, Carla said to herself, as she plunged down the path to the sea. This night is too beautiful to be alone. Fortunate Ruth, to have scored so soon. What happened between Rutger and me just now was not proper lovemaking. How dared he touch me like that when we'd only just met? There's something perverted about him – Leandra, too, and I'm not at all sure if I want to become involved.

Perfume tinged the air: thyme, lavender and heady odours unknown to her. Here was the place where the gods had been worshipped: Zeus, Aphrodite, a whole pantheon of immortals. It was eerie, steeped in mystery, throbbing with the sexual energy of the earth.

Carla paused under a pine. The sea whispered below her, starred by the lamps of night fishermen. They whirled a little, blurring into a necklace fit to adorn a goddess.

'I should be going back,' she said aloud, pronouncing the words carefully, her tongue too big for her mouth. 'No good hanging around out here. You won't find a Stefan, though you might get raped by a lobster and produce some prawns of your loins.' She started to giggle, and could not stop, hiccuping with near hysterical laughter. 'Fuck. That retsina. Fire-water or what? I wish Toby was here ... or even Giles, God help me! He'd handle everything. I can't bloody cope.'

The tears welled up, spilled over and rolled down her cheeks, big, salty tears that dripped off her chin and trickled into her cleavage. She wiped them away with the back of her hand.

'Can I help?' said a voice from the shadows.

Her entrails drew together with superstitious shock. She was suddenly cold stone sober.

A man's voice. Who? The phantom rapist? Monsieur *Langouste* in disguise? She didn't think so. There was something vaguely familiar about those rich, heavily accented tones. Their timbre vibrated in her inner ear and sent shivers right down to her G-spot.

'Thank you, but no. I've had a little bit too much to drink. The homemade brew is potent stuff. I'll stick to cocktails in the future,' she said, playing it light. She had taken a Self-Defence for Women course, and he'd get her knee in his balls if he tried anything.

'One should treat it with respect,' he replied, moving into the moonlight and her field of vision.

A big man, the silver light running over his features, planing the high cheekbones, the aquiline nose, the deep eyesockets, and his shiny black hair. She glimpsed him in that strange lightning-blast blue flung by planet Earth's satellite, whose influence was vital to its tides, its rhythms, the female cycle and the behaviour of those sensitive to the lunar pull.

She saw him for a second, but it was enough. Her knees weakened and her heart pounded. It was *him*. She was as certain of it as she was that day would follow night. She gripped the rough bark behind her waist, drawing strength from the rock-solid pine.

He was silent, too, looking down at her. She saw the red glow of the cigar held between his fingers and smelled Havana's finest tobacco. She wanted to say, 'But surely you shouldn't smoke? Your voice . . .' But the words remained locked in her throat.

Her mind was scrambling fast. He sought anonymity. If she confessed that she knew who he was, then he would storm off. More than anything else, she wanted him to stay.

'It's lovely here,' she said.

'It is. My favourite spot.' He came closer, leaning his broad shoulder against the tree, the red spark near his lips now. 'You've come up from the port?'

'I'm staying in a villa on the cliffs.'

'On vacation?'

'Yes.' There's no harm in bending the truth, she thought. I am enjoying a holiday, sort of. I can pretend, can't I? Does everything always have to be so prosaic? This is wonderful. Marvellous. A dream come true. I'm with Angelo Lorenzo, at last.

'You're very beautiful,' he said, in a slow, considering way. And he started to sing, softly but perfectly, as only a native Italian can, '*O dolce viso di mite circonfuso alba lunar . . .*'

Carla melted, lost, disoriented. 'O sweet face in the light of the moon,' she whispered. 'It's from *La Bohème*, when Mimi wanders into Rodolfo's garret in Paris and they fall in love.'

'*Brava!*' he said, his teeth forming a wedge of white in his dark face. 'You like opera, no?'

Careful, warned her guardian angel. Don't give yourself away.

'I know what I like. Not all opera, some. I happen to have a CD of *Bohème*, with Domingo.'

'Ah, the *maestro*,' Angelo replied, voice hushed in awe. 'What an artiste!'

The time for talk was running out. Carla could feel an irresistible current drawing them together, the influence of the moon on two people who needed to mate. Fate had ordained it. It didn't matter who they were or why they were there.

He threw away his cigar and ground it under his heel. His hand reached out for her, drawing her against his hard, warm body, and she was powerless to resist. Her sexual drive was running high, roused but not satisfied by Rutger, further inflamed by seeing Ruth and Stefan, and now she had met the star she revered, the man whom she had never thought to be with in a million years.

He smelled of the sun, the sea, Calvin Klein's *Eternity* and his own personal body odour. His white linen shirt was crisp under her cheek, and she locked her arms round his waist, the metal button of his 501s biting into her ribs. He was so tall that her head did not reach the pit of his throat, making her feel small and fragile and of incalculable value. His hands travelled over her very carefully, as if he, too, was aware of how easily he could snap her bones.

81

He bent his head, his face shadowed, then captured her lips with his. His kiss was sweet, dusky with smoke, and just for a moment he did not attempt anything further than that delicate meeting of lips. It was Carla who made the first move, opening her mouth to him, her tongue tangling with his in welcome and celebration.

The heat of his erection seared through his denims and her silk robe, and his hands cupped her breasts, the thumbs rolling over the stiff nipples. His kiss deepened, exploring her mouth, and her tongue danced, touching, retreating, touching again, till he jabbed his forcefully in and out, imitating the movement of coitus.

The tree bole was at his back, and he drew her close so that she leaned against him. The air played over her thighs and buttocks as he raised the robe, grunting in delight as he discovered her nudity beneath. He held each rounded cheek, then probed between, fingertips touching her wet sex and the tight mouth of her anus. His hands were so large and his reach so deep that one finger succeeded in reaching her clitoris, stroking it with an upward motion that nearly brought her to climax.

She moaned and felt for his cock, rubbing across the thick bar of flesh imprisoned in his jeans. His mouth slackened with the pleasure of it, lips wet as they fed on hers hungrily.

'*Mia amore*,' he breathed into her mouth.

Carla's fire flared up, invited by his words as much as his touch. No one, but no one, had ever spoken to her in such a thrilling way. It heightened her ecstasy, made her eager to pleasure him. Never had she been embraced by so big a man, never been so aware of the power of a male body, or so conscious of her own weak muscles.

He released her for a moment, spread his jacket on

the ground and then lifted her effortlessly, one arm under her shoulders and the other cradling her bottom. She slipped her arms up round his neck, fingers coiling in his crisp hair, releasing him when he bent to lay her on the improvised bed.

It was darker there, the moon hidden from view, its halo visible among the tree-tops. The crushed grass and flowers enveloped them in perfume and Carla made to take off her robe, but he prevented her.

'Let me do that.'

She sighed and handed herself over to him, this great dark man with the golden voice. He slipped the robe over her head and his large hands came down on the fleshy orbs of her breasts as she arched her back and pushed up against them, nipples begging for his fingers.

Her senses were reduced to sound, touch, taste and smell – and these were in overload. She had no need of sight, the longing for their union aching in her vagina, throbbing in her clitoris and spreading waves of desire through her whole body.

The moon sailed past the trees, and now she could see as well as feel and smell him. He lay beside her, his jeans gaping. Resting on one elbow, looking at her, he lifted out his phallus and rubbed the length of it. Carla could not resist touching it, her fingers taking the place of his, massaging the hot stalk and tracing round the rolled-back foreskin.

He eased down, resting her head on his shoulder, one hand reaching over to cup her breast and fondle its swelling tip, the other trailing slowly over her ribs and belly to her lower lips. His fingers deftly parted the engorged wings.

'You're so wet,' he said, his voice no more than a thick whisper. 'Ready for me. You want me? Say it.'

'I want you,' she gasped, pleasure shooting through

83

her as he plunged a finger deep into her vagina, withdrew it slippery with her juices, and spread this over her clitoris.

'Is this right?' he whispered, and his organ jerked as it moved between the ring of her thumb and forefinger. 'Tell me what you like. Your pearl is so hard, so big, bursting with desire . . . just like my cock, eh?'

'I love what you're doing . . .' she stuttered. 'Don't stop. I need to come so much.'

'I will help you. There, is that nice? Your slit is so smooth and high and lovely. I want to eat it.'

Never stopping that steady, slippery rubbing, he lowered his head and sucked one of her nipples into his mouth, winding his tongue round the pleasure-hungry teat, then moved to the other. Squeezing her breasts together, he succeeded in mouthing both nipples at once.

Carla whimpered her pleasure, sensation darting from her breasts to her clitoris, rampant beneath his artful finger. His penis wept tears from its single eye, and she used the liquid to coat his glans, subjecting the head to a firm motion, but always aware that she must not bring him to completion yet. There was so much of him she needed to experience.

He moved round, kneeling between her thighs, then lowering his face to her open, glistening crotch and breathing on it. Carla made mewing sounds, her clit quivering under the exhalation, and he did it again, teasing her.

'Oh . . . oh!' she cried.

'What is it?' he said huskily. 'Tell me what you want.'

'Your tongue . . . your mouth sucking me,' she urged, any shyness swallowed up in lust.

She could hear his pleased chuckle, and see his cock jutting from his fly, but this was her moment, and hers alone.

He put his lips to her vulva and kissed it as if he were kissing her mouth. She could feel the roughness of his stubbly chin chafing her most tender parts, but this added to the sensations. He settled close, holding her petals with his fingers, opening her to him, burrowing deeply, sucking strongly, drawing her bud between his teeth, working it with his tongue.

Her climax was coming, starting in her toes, running like liquid fire through her legs, her thighs, rising and rising till it exploded in a firework display in her brain. She lost herself in the little death, wiped out in blissful ecstasy.

He kept his finger on her quivering clit, and buried another in her vagina so that she could spasm round it. He stroked her face, and touched the sensual fullness of her lips with his own, then turned her on her stomach and massaged the swell of her buttocks. He ran a finger down the dark rift, going in deeper and deeper. Carla trembled and ached for his cock.

Then he took her, as she lay prone, guiding the heavy head of his weapon between the hemispheres of her backside and pushing it into her sex. His hands came round her belly, lifting her to her knees, and she crouched there while he thrust violently.

She yelled as her inner muscles closed round his massive shaft, the head driving against her cervix, almost too big for her. He was beyond caring now, intent on his own release. He hung on to her dangling breasts, seeking a purchase, pounding harder and harder. They rocked together, and the carpet of pine needles pricked her knees and jabbed into her bunched fists as she braced herself on stiff arms.

He grunted with effort, driving into her furiously, his wiry haired pubis scraping against her bottom, his taut, seed-heavy balls tapping the backs of her thighs with each thrust. Her breath rushed out at each jolting

85

movement and she was sure he couldn't go any harder. But he did, his fingers bruising her breasts, his hips bumping her bottom, his iron prick pumping with a savage strength that brought tears to her eyes.

Then he suddenly shuddered, gave a great cry, and she exalted with the last throb of his mighty cock as he came in her depths. He did not withdraw immediately, trying to prolong the sensation. She sank down slowly, and he lay over her body, his phallus still buried between her buttocks.

He shifted to one side and Carla rolled over, half expecting he would leave her now that he had emptied himself of sperm. He did not, holding her hand, kissing her cheek, making her feel special, not just a partner in a transitory sex encounter, soon over and even more quickly forgotten.

His touch was soothing and she wanted to sleep in his arms, safe and warm, with the night sounds like a lullaby and the wind breathing the scent of flowers. His smell, too, and hers: the heady, feral odour of sex.

But it could not be. She didn't want to push her luck, so disentangled her limbs from his, sat up and fumbled for her dress and sandals.

He looked up, arms crossed behind his head. 'Where are you going?'

'Home,' she replied, her voice muffled as she pulled the robe on.

'But I thought, hoped, you might come back with me. I have a villa too.'

'I can't,' she said, though everything inside her wanted to accept.

'Why?' He sounded angry, his movements quick and impatient as he tucked his penis away and fastened his jeans.

'My friends are waiting,' she lied.

'Men friends?' His voice was so angry that she shivered. This man could be jealous and possessive. It was part of his ego, his myth, which gave him the ability to express those violent emotions in the musical dramas.

'No one in particular.'

She kept her distance, well out of arm's reach. This had gone far enough. She thrust her toes into her sandals and turned to flee.

'Come back!' he shouted after her as she raced up the path to the Villa Artemis. 'I don't even know your name!'

She did not pause, but ran as if hounded by demons till she reached the garden and slumped against the wall edging the terrace, gasping for breath, a stitch clawing at her side.

Chapter Five

RUTGER EMERGED FROM the shadows at the top of the steps. 'Where have you been?' he said coldly.

'Walking. Is that a crime?' Carla retorted, thinking: bloody cheek! She made to brush past but he grabbed her by the arm, his fingers like talons. She would wear his brand for days to come.

'Walking?' he sneered, and his hand shot down to her fork, pushing in so hard and far that the fabric cut into her tender membranes. He lifted his fingers to his nose and sniffed. 'I think not, my dear! You're wet. You've been having sex. I can smell it. Slut! You need to be taught a lesson.'

'Get real!' she snapped. 'Who the hell d'you think you are, telling me what to do?'

But she was secretly aroused by the harsh note in his voice, the cruel smile lifting his sensual mouth, and the glitter in his chilling eyes. He was dangerous, and everything dark and reckless in her responded to him. This wanton self had been imprisoned too long. Now it was stirring in its bonds, freshly empowered every time she enjoyed a new sexual experience. Soon it would burst out into the light, no longer ashamed.

'You like it,' he said quietly. 'In time you'll be begging me to command your obedience. I know you, Carla, better than you know yourself.'

He did not relinquish his grip on her upper arm, and his free hand grazed her silk-covered breast, then came to rest under the curve of her backside. His breath was laced with brandy and cigars, an instant reminder of Angelo, who had left this hot, wet, smouldering sensation of pleasure in her cunt.

Before she realised his intention, Rutger rucked her robe up round her waist, thrust his knee between her legs and pushed three fingers inside her. Unable to resist, she bore down on his hand and he began to explore her pulsing, velvety-lined vagina. His thumb manipulated her clitoris, stroking and rubbing till she cried out, on the verge of climax.

Immediately he withdrew, wound an arm round her waist and turned her so that she stood with her back against his chest. She could feel his penis, exposed and erect, as he bent at the knees and shoved it into the cleft of her buttocks, moving in a lewd rhythm.

'May I watch, master?' Leandra asked, materialising like a white wraith, her diaphanous gown fallen to the waist, her glorious brown breasts glistening in the wavering light of the flares.

He smiled at her without ceasing to plunder Carla's most private parts. 'You may do more than that,' he said graciously. 'You can help. She needs discipline.'

In an instant he was frog-marching Carla into the villa, across a vast expanse of marble flooring to a large room set apart from the rest.

The decor favoured an idealised, Hollywood concept of the legendary city of Troy. It was sybaritic, and the colour predominantly scarlet. The overblown hangings, drapes, carpets and pillows looked as if they had been steeped in blood. A collection of rare, erotic statuettes and murals of couples straining in ecstasy were arranged against a crimson background. A central, bolster-strewn divan stood four-square under a red canopy, and the flickering candlelight, the strong perfume rising from brass incense-burners, the decadent luxury and brooding atmosphere made it seem like a pagan temple, not a place for relaxation and slumber.

'Welcome to my private apartment,' Rutger said, pushing Carla before him. 'Here you will learn many things, and when you leave it, you'll never be quite the same again.' There was triumph in his voice, and when Carla turned to look at him, she was riveted by the decadent, age-old wisdom in his eyes. A bolt of terror shot through her, but the curiosity that had been Mother Eve's downfall itched in her mind. What did he mean? What was he going to do to her?

Whatever he had planned, there was no doubt that he roused her lust. Maybe this would be less hurtful in the long run. The emotion she had felt for Angelo was even more alarming, for it involved her heart as well as her body.

She became aware that they were not alone. Leandra lay on a deeply cushioned couch with a zebra-striped throw. Her white skirt was lifted high, her long golden legs splayed, giving an uninterrupted view of her thinly furred pubis, and those alluring, dark pink lower lips, crowned by the swollen clitoris at the top. She was toying with it, gold fingernails glinting.

Robin stood by her side. His scrawny body was naked, save for a black spiked collar round his neck, a leather strap girding his waist, and chains running across his belly to wind round his short, thick prick. They were fastened in such a way that his balls were yanked high and his penis lifted. It was hard and swollen, the glans glistening with pre-come juice.

Carla's eyes went to Marie. She straddled Stefan where he sat in a thronelike chair, wriggling her hips to push his engorged cock deeper into her body. He wore a studded black leather jerkin and jeans, though the latter were wide open in the front, displaying his hairy belly and the root of his weapon. The rest of it was sheathed to the hilt in her vagina.

'Marie,' Carla exclaimed, unsure whether to be pleased or sorry that she was present. 'Tell Rutger to let me go.'

'We're Rutger's slaves,' she murmured, her head tipped towards Stefan's mouth, her slack lips seeking his. 'We do as he commands.'

Stefan lurched upwards with his hips and she cried out in intense pleasure as he forced his massive cock against her cervix. She was partly dressed, bare below her poppy-red top, and this had been pushed to her chest, her luscious breasts swelling under Stefan's hands, the nipples standing out like cob nuts.

Where was Ruth? Carla wondered. Had he left her after they had screwed, and scuttled back here at Leandra's orders?

Leandra rose to her feet and drifted across to Carla, a sweet fragrance breathing out from the secret garden of her sex. 'Don't be afraid,' she said. 'Life has so much to offer. There are infinite possibilities. The master opens us to them. We like you, darling, and want to share them with you.'

'Tonight I'll introduce you to a new kind of pleasure,' Rutger said, leading Carla towards the bed. 'Marie tells me that you haven't yet experienced it. Almost a virgin,' he added with a deep-throated chuckle.

Poised on her toes, Carla wondered whether to run for it. But what was the use? Rutger's servants would be well trained and in his pay. No one would come if she screamed.

The blissful encounter in the woods was fading fast, no more than a distant dream. All she could hope was that Angelo would not recognise her when they met formally. There she was, ready to tumble head-over-heels in love again, and it was an emotion that ruined her peace of mind and battered her self-esteem. She was better off without it.

'Very well, Rutger,' she said slowly. 'Teach me. I'm willing to learn.'

He motioned to Leandra, who said persuasively, 'Take off your gown and lie on your stomach.'

Carla removed her sandals and glanced down at her dress ruefully. She had paid a fortune for it in a Bond Street boutique, but now it looked like a rag, ripped in places, with dry leaves and earth clinging to the hem.

She trembled a little as she mounted the shallow steps surrounding the bed on all sides, uneasy at the turn events were taking. She regretted that the alcohol had worn off. It would be better to be drunk at such a moment. It's a joke, surely? she tried to assure herself. But one glance at Rutger's intense face convinced her otherwise.

'The blindfold,' he said, snapping imperious fingers at Leandra.

'Hey, wait a minute,' Carla protested, trying to wriggle away.

'Trust me,' he insisted, holding her gaze almost hypnotically before everything went black.

Velvet pressed against her eyelids, a scarf perhaps, and someone was fastening it securely at the back of her head. The knot caught in a strand of her hair, tugged painfully, then was untangled. The bed lifted as the person's weight was withdrawn. Carla tested her sensations. The quilt was satin, slippery and cold under her bare body, and there were parts that prickled: gilt embroidery, maybe.

All around was silence and stillness. Even Marie had stifled her moans of pleasure. With a wildly beating heart and a slow burn in her sex, Carla waited.

Without warning her arms were seized, stretched out wide and cords slipped over the wrists. She thrashed and cursed and struggled to no avail, trussed like a fowl, the cords pulling tighter as the ends were tied to the bedhead.

'Let me go!' Carla shouted, kicking out.

Iron hands gripped her ankles, forcing her legs apart. 'Be quiet,' Rutger said, his breath warming her bare backside. 'You must be bound to obtain full benefit from what I'm about to do.'

Now she was helpless, unable to move, ankles tethered to the footposts.

'It's OK, honey,' Marie murmured, somewhere near her face.

'Let us be your guides,' Leandra added, and cool fingers played down Carla's back, lingering between her fleshy valley, hovering over the opened lips of her sex.

Carla gasped and lifted her hips as much as she was able, straining to reach that tickling touch and have it press on the erectile tissue of her clitoris. Waves of excitement flowed through her, and her nipples rose against the satin. She stirred restlessly within her bonds to further increase the friction on those needy teats.

Leandra's hands were replaced by rougher, larger ones, and Rutger whispered into Carla's ear, 'Pain and pleasure. You will appreciate this after tonight. Ying and yang, dark and light, heat and its opposite.'

Carla yelled as something freezing landed in the exact centre of her spine. At first it burned, then pooled as the ice cube melted, droplets trickling across her ribs and down the avenue that gave access to her womanhood.

'You bastard!' she hissed, adrenaline running high. She was angry and aroused and ashamed of this lustful urgency.

'That's an insult. I don't like it.' His voice was as cold as the ice.

Carla's body bucked violently as something hit her bare rump. She yelled, and heard the upward whistle of a whip. Numbness was followed by warmth – warmth replaced by a searing heat that exploded into pain. It spread up and around, quivering along her nerves, till every part of her seemed possessed by agony.

'Oh ... oh ...' she sobbed, the tears soaking into the blindfold. 'Why did you do that? It's not fair! I can't defend myself.'

'Do you want to? You can tell me, Carla. Tell me that you want me to lash you again,' Rutger's sibilant voice caressed her ear, like that of a confessor dragging her darkest, most intimate secrets from her unwilling lips.

'No, I don't ... Leave me alone!' she wailed.

To her horror, she felt her juices trickling across her pudenda. It was humiliating to realise that he would have seen it glistening on her exposed labia. The pain was now reduced to a dull throbbing that echoed through her loins. Fingers touched her lower lips and squeezed her love-bud, filling her with licentious longing.

Then, as a tongue started to lap at her clitoris, her mind ceased to function properly. Hands reached under her, finding her breasts, pinching the nipples, drawing anguished moans from her. Hands oiled her bruised and fiery buttocks, slipping round and probing into her vulva, then going higher.

She had no time to register shame as an object was poked against her anal ring, hard and cool and alien. It vibrated gently, sending tremors into her bowels, making her inner walls clench. It was removed, then pushed into her vagina, its continual oscillation making her gasp. Lecherous visions filled her mind: she wanted it pressed to her clit, rubbing the stalk, buzzing on the sensitive tip.

Without warning, the whip seared her bottom again. Harder this time, while the vibrator hummed against

94

her bud. The leather strip rose and fell, landing in different places, and the circular movement on her clitoris was relentless.

She was defeated, soaking wet and open, and could do nothing but yield to the extreme lust she was experiencing. Rutger lashed her once more, then knelt behind her and snatched the mock phallus away. He held her mons in his palm and rubbed her over-stimulated clit with his fingers. At the same time he drove forward, ramming his cock into her.

She responded with unrestrained wildness, her yoked hands clutching at the quilt, her arms and legs shuddering, her head twisting and turning. She screamed and convulsed as a shattering orgasm clawed at her, and Rutger came with a final, savage thrust.

Carla sank into the darkness, lost amongst billowing waves that lapped against her bruised buttocks and tingled along her love-tunnel. Somewhere out of the far reaches of time and space, she was aware of being freed from bondage. Her eyes were unbound but she could not see for a moment. Then the room righted itself.

Marie's face hung over her. 'All right, hon?'

It was impossible to answer. Carla was not sure what she was feeling. Marie rolled her on to her side and settled her comfortably against the pillows. Leandra knelt beside her and spread cool, herb-scented cream into her burning weals. Then Marie brought over a glass of iced tea.

Carla sat up gingerly, wincing. There was no sign of Stefan or Robin, and Rutger had disappeared.

'Let's swim,' Leandra suggested. 'It'll take away your stiffness.'

Headlights swept across the drive. With a screech of tyres and a juddering rattle, a battered pick-up truck ground to a halt.

'It's Josh!' Leandra cried, and ran towards the man who jumped down from the cab.

'Oh, lordy! Indiana Jones has arrived,' Marie remarked sarcastically, following at a more leisurely pace.

'Who?' Carla asked, a beach towel draping her body, another wound turbanwise round her wet hair. They had just finished swimming.

'Josh Osbourne. Haven't you heard of him? He's hit the headlines from time to time. A deep-sea diver, a treasure hunter. He looks for wrecks of old ships, hoping for a part of the loot.' Marie hooked an arm round Carla's waist and walked her down to the truck. 'You must have heard of him. He's been on TV and written a couple of books.'

Carla shook her head, dredging through the backlog of information in her memory bank. The name had a familiar ring. 'Maybe I have,' she agreed.

But when she met him she knew that she would never forget again. He had an arm about Leandra, one hand disappearing into her robe, while she squeaked in mock protest and nestled against him.

He was a sinewy streak of a man, around six feet tall, with the build of an athlete. Rangy, long-limbed, he wore a sleeveless vest that emphasised an all-year tan, and his blue jeans were ragged, bleached white over the thigh and round the promising bulge at the fly area. His feet were bare.

Carla lifted her eyes to his face and was arrested by a wide smile, friendly but lopsided, as if he did not trust anyone on sight. Handsome in a craggy way, with a thin nose, hard mouth and a strong jaw, he wore a two-day growth of stubble, and his hair was tawny, long but tied with a leather thong.

He was a man with a mission, and vitality streamed from him, communicating with Carla's central core. It

96

was cerebral, yet at the same time extremely sensual.

'What are you doing here? Why didn't you let me know you were coming?' Leandra fired at him, her robe falling back as she lifted one leg and wound it round his hip, her cleft exposed.

'Thought I'd give you a surprise,' he answered, his accent English public school, but with an edge to it. 'Cover your pussy up for God's sake. D'you want to be thrown down and bonked? You'd get gravel-rash. I've been at sea for days – not a quim in sight.'

'I wouldn't say no,' she gurgled, but lowered her thigh, caressing his bare midriff instead.

'Do you ever?' he mocked. 'Who's your friend?' he added, and his eyes speared Carla's with a shock she felt in her bones. They were the most remarkable eyes, peridot green flecked with amber under thick, curling, gold-tipped lashes.

'Hello, Josh,' Marie said, smiling at him as if he was a long-lost mate. 'This is Carla Holt, the writer.'

'Hi,' Carla managed to get out.

'Hi, indeed,' he answered, with his crooked smile that reminded her of Toby's. 'You on holiday?'

'A working holiday,' she corrected, wishing her bottom would stop stinging. She wanted to forget Rutger's treatment and concentrate on this interesting individual.

'She's over here to make contact with a singer who's gone to ground,' Leandra put in, determined not to forfeit his attention.

'Ah, a reporter. And which particular example of the gutter press do you work for?' Josh replied, and Carla could almost hear shutters clanging.

'I'm not a reporter. I've been commissioned to ghost his life-story,' she corrected hurriedly, though lecturing herself for needing this man's respect.

'And you? What are you doing in this neck of the

woods?' Marie asked, accepting a cigarette from the pack he handed round.

'Oh, my usual thing. Let's go inside and I'll tell you all about it,' he answered, and sliding an arm round the waists of both Marie and Leandra, he led the way.

Carla fought with resentment. She would have liked to feel that brown, furry arm clasping her. She trailed behind them, pretending to herself that she did not care.

'*Sea Jade* is moored in the harbour,' he explained as they sat on the terrace and ate crusty bread, olives, and goats' cheese, washed down with *ouzo*. The women took theirs with ice, but he drank his neat, in true sailor style.

'Why didn't you use the marina?' Leandra asked. The cane chair creaked slightly as she crossed one leg over the other, her shiny bare knee protruding.

He laughed. '*Sea Jade* is my beloved mistress, but I doubt she'd be welcomed there, any more than an old whore. She's knocked about a bit, seen the seamy side of life. No, she's happier moored alongside fishing trawlers and ketches.'

'No need to ask if you're on to something,' Marie said, puffing smoke rings into the balmy air.

'A wreck, maybe even a very ancient one,' he replied, using his hands expressively. 'She must have foundered on the rocks in a storm, centuries ago.'

'Where?' Marie sat up sharply, eyes alight, the novelist within her seizing on this crumb of information. 'There might be a book in it. I haven't yet tackled a romance set in Ancient Greece.'

'It's not far. Outside the bay, but if there's any book, it'll be mine,' he returned sharply. He pushed the bottle her way, saying, 'Have a drink.'

'I'm talking novels,' she said, refilling her glass. 'Not the exploits of Elephant Bill.'

Josh ignored this and his vivid eyes alighted on Carla. 'Are you like her, always on the lookout for stories?' he asked, and though he had not moved, it was as if he had come closer.

'I think all authors do this,' she heard herself saying. 'It goes with the territory.'

'Tell us more about the treasure,' Leandra said, leaning her elbow on the table, the high curves of her breasts exposed as her robe opened. 'Will you find a piece of jewellery for me? Maybe a necklace worn by Helen of Troy?'

'You'll be lucky,' he scoffed. 'Heinrich Schliemann took all that when he excavated the site in 1873. The closest you'll get to relics is in a museum.'

'Then what drives you? Why do you risk your life in search of something so elusive?' Marie asked, looking at him with drunken solemnity.

He shrugged, and Carla yearned to run her hand down his unshaven jaw, to kiss the tiny scar that marked his sun-browned cheekbone like a crooked white thread, and taste the potent, anise flavoured *ouzo* on his lips.

'Because it's there,' he said, and did not stop looking at her. 'Because my ancestors were seamen . . . There's a story that one of 'em was actually a pirate. And because I love ships and everything to do with history.'

'Because you stand to make a great deal of money if you succeed in raising treasure from the deep,' was Marie's caustic reminder.

'I understand the thrill it must give you,' Carla ventured, her tongue loosened, her body, too. 'To handle an object that no one else has touched for hundreds of years . . .'

'Come sailing with me,' he urged, and suddenly and quite naturally he was holding her hand. 'Have you ever visited Crete, seen the remains of the Minoan civilisation? No? You haven't lived. We'll sail into the Bay of Messara, and then drive to Phaistos, a site more moving even than Knossos. The palace, built on tiers, overlooks a beautiful plain. Have you any idea of Minoan architecture? It's remarkable.'

'Shut up, Josh. This is turning into a boring lecture,' Leandra complained.

'Philistine,' he mocked. 'Of course, I forgot, one has to have aesthetic sensibilities to appreciate it.'

'I'd like to sail with you,' Carla said, returning the pressure of his fingers.

'Great. When?' he demanded, half rising as if to whisk her away then and there.

'I'm not sure. I'm awaiting a phone call from Angelo Lorenzo's manager. I must be here in case he wants me. It's a tricky one ... Lorenzo doesn't like being disturbed. It may take time to coax him into talking, even if he consents to a preliminary interview.'

'He obviously hasn't met you,' Josh said, and his thigh pressed against hers on the bench. There was a hole in his jeans and she could see part of his muscular thigh, darkly tanned and shaded with fairish hair.

'Watch that silver tongue,' Marie warned, quoting, 'Once aboard the lugger and the girl is mine.'

'Ignore her. She's a spoilsport,' Josh grinned. 'You can come, too, if you want, but I thought you got seasick.'

'I do. Thanks, but no thanks. I want to work on my tan. Make everybody jealous as hell when I get back.'

Leandra flexed her limbs and stood up, yawning. 'I'm going to bed,' she announced. 'Anyone coming?'

'Where's Rutger?' Maria asked, and she got up, too.

'Deep in a conflab with Robin. He's sounding out some new ideas for when the crew arrive.'

'Poor Robin. He looks as if he's been hit by a steamroller.'

'Don't be sorry for him. He loves it,' Leandra said coolly, then bent to kiss Josh full on the lips. 'You know where my room is, don't you, darling? I'm always ready to comfort a sailor home from the seas.'

'I know,' he said, and slapped her on the bottom.

There was an almost imperceptible lightening of the sky in the east, and that mystic hush which heralds the dawn. Carla was content to sit there with Josh, glad they were alone.

'You don't have to stay,' she said.

'I want to,' he answered. 'They aren't really interested in what I do, only in the secondhand thrill they get in hearing about danger. I think you're genuinely keen.'

'I want to find out all I can about the islands,' she said truthfully, but did not add that she was equally eager to know *him* – heart, body and mind.

She liked him, thought they had much in common, but could not deny the attraction she felt, that warm loosening in her sex, the need to go to bed with him.

Not yet though, not now, when her backside was bruised and her vagina sore from Rutger's penetration. She wanted to proceed slowly with this man, carving out a deeper relationship.

'There's a simple way to understand the Mediterranean,' Josh said seriously, and drew the dish of black olives towards him. He lifted one to her mouth, his fingers brushing her full lips as he said, 'Bite into it, Carla. That's right, bite deep. Everything to do with the islands since time immemorial seems contained in that sour, pungent taste, the history, the wars, the gods, the myths, the hot sun, the *sirocco*. It's a taste older than blood or wine, a taste as old as sex.'

She let the juice run over her tongue and understood.

Then they shared a last cigarette, and he walked her to the door of her room, kissed her lightly on the mouth and left her.

They decided to play on the beach all day.

Stefan and Ruth lugged down a picnic hamper,

bottles of wine and mineral water, rugs, cushions, towels, and an awning. Leandra and Carla brought up the rear with tote-bags full of sun-lotion and insect repellent, dark glasses and, in Carla's case, a paperback to read. Marie insisted on carrying a notepad and biro, ready for any sudden flashes of inspiration, but as the day drifted on and the heat increased, this remained at the bottom of her hold-all.

'I can't believe that it's only yesterday we flew from Heathrow,' Carla said, having just turned over after timing her session on her back – ten minutes and no more to begin with and a layer of high-factor oil, as Leandra, an expert on sunbathing, had instructed.

'I know. Isn't it just glorious?' Marie answered sleepily.

'I love Zaminos,' Ruth remarked, dripping salt water as she flung herself down on a towel. Stefan was with her, posing for the benefit of all, his body a joy to behold.

'Only Zaminos?' Marie hinted, and grinned up into his blue eyes. 'The inhabitants are wonderful, too.' And she lifted a lazy hand and lightly caressed the front of his leopard-skin posing pouch.

'I know,' Ruth replied, dreadlocks tumbling around her neck as she leaned forward to rub lotion into her shins. 'But I've had girl friends who went to Greece on package holidays and never came back, not for years, that is, when they flew home with a couple of kids, fed up with living with the bloke's parents. Don't marry 'em seems to be the rule.'

'Doesn't that apply everywhere?' murmured Leandra, soaking up the sun with the unrestrained enjoyment of a cat on a hot garden wall.

'Oh, I don't know. I wouldn't mind being married one day, if the right man came along,' Carla put in, wondering if she dared take off her bikini bottom. She envied Leandra her perfect, seamless tan.

Ruth, it seemed, had no such inhibitions, and was already bare as the day she was born. On first sight, her bush had been startling, the crisp hair dyed blue and red to match the streaks in her hair. Marie's was an entirely different colour to her mahogany bob, mid-brown and thick.

And my pussy is depilated, Carla thought. And I shall keep it that way, using the cream I bought from Chloe, though it does make me very conscious of my cleft.

'Get 'em off,' Leandra the mindreader said. 'We're all chums here. I'm sure Stefan won't object.' She raised herself up to include him. 'And you can discard that ridiculous jock-strap. Come on, let's see what you've got.'

'You all know,' he said, colouring under his tan, and pressing his thighs together in an attempt to control his wayward phallus.

'Carla doesn't,' Leandra reminded. 'Do you want to try it, Carla? It's big, but I've known bigger.'

Afraid of appearing prudish, though this was nigh impossible given last night's demonstration, Carla untied the thongs at her hip-bones and whipped her tanga away. Stefan looked – he couldn't help himself – and then smiled, pleased as he saw her bare mound. She sank back on her towel, adjusted her sunglasses and wide-brimmed straw hat, and tried to think of things other than sex.

Josh, for instance, though he and sex were inextricably linked. 'Where's your friend who arrived so late?' she murmured to Leandra, as casually as if he had not made enough impact for her to recall his name.

'Out in *Sea Jade*, I expect. He'd gone by the time I surfaced. He'll be back, don't worry. He has you in his sights.'

'I don't know what you mean,' Carla said sternly, though her clitoris stirred in its little cowl.

'He wants you,' Leandra replied, flicking sand at Stefan to make him look at her. 'And what Josh wants he usually gets.'

Does he indeed, Carla thought, annoyed. We'll see about that.

She leapt up and ran down to the water's edge, taking her first step into the sea. It was like entering a warm bath, and so clear that she could see the bottom.

How would it be to go diving? She wondered as she struck out, the water gliding over her and dipping inquisitive fingers between her thighs. And how would I feel if Josh showed me a wreck half buried in the sandy sea bottom?

She floated on her back, bouyed up by the gentle waves, and dreamed of weed-encrusted amphorae and of finding a rare object with Josh, which would set the archaeological world on fire. It was a glorious dream and lasted throughout the hot afternoon when, too somnolent to even talk, the picnic party dozed.

She was about to change for dinner, smoothing *après soleil* into her skin, when a call was put through to her room.

'Carla Holt?' asked Edward Connar when she picked up the receiver.

'Speaking.'

'Can you come over?'

Her heart did a crazy lurch, and she almost dropped the towel wound loosely around her. 'Now?' she quavered.

'Yes, you're invited to dinner. He's agreed to see you, but the trouble I've had! You'd never believe it. We'll have to go slowly. It'll be like treading on eggshells. He's the most awkward, bloody-minded sod I've ever had to manage, pardon my French.'

'Don't apologise. I think I understand,' she said, wondering how in hell's name she was going to face Angelo.

She'd screwed him. He'd be bound to remember, wouldn't he? If he didn't, she'd never forgive him. It would prove he was a callous son-of-a-bitch who simply shafted anything that breathed and then promptly put it from his mind.

'I'll send a car. Don't bring anything, no notebook or laptop, nothing to frighten him off. And do be careful what you say.'

'I will.'

Dear God, she thought as she replaced the brass and porcelain phone in its cradle. What on earth have I let myself in for!

Chapter Six

'*YOU WILL BE* polite to her, won't you, Angelo?'
Edward almost pleaded. 'I've asked her to dinner, nothing formal, just to give you a chance to get to know her.'

Seated at the black Steinway grand, Angelo kept his
back turned, and picked out passages from the score
lying open on the music rack.

'Umm?' he murmured. 'Sorry, Edward, *uno momento*.
This is a fascinating passage, don't you agree? So lyrical.
Listen.' His hands caressed the keys and sound flooded
the room, a full-bodied, inspiring passage depicting
heroic love.

'What is that?' Edward said, coming over to stand at
his shoulder. Then he recognised the composer.
'Wagner?' he went on, astonished. 'You're not seriously
considering singing *Siegfried*, are you? You're an Italian
tenor, not a German one.'

'So?' Angelo murmured. He was absorbed in the
score, a skilled pianist, and usually learned roles this
way before working with a répétiteur. 'Placido
Domingo has been singing Wagnerian leads for some
time and he's Spanish. Why shouldn't I consider them?'

Why, indeed? Edward thought dourly. Anything to
add to my troubles. 'But he is older than you, his voice
is mature now . . .' he began.

'And mine will be also one day, if I decide to return to the stage,' Angelo remarked casually.

'Ah, so you may be making a comeback? Nice of you to let me know,' Edward said acidly.

'I may, and then again, I may not,' Angelo prevaricated, and Edward fought the urge to strangle him.

But then Angelo started to sing. Not at full volume, but softly, as singers will when they are rehearsing. The room slowly and sensually filled up with the sublime climax of *Siegfried*, the love duet. Angelo's German pronunciation was perfect, and Edward listened enthralled. Was there no end to the talent of this enigmatic, infuriating man? Up soared the music, rising ever higher, like the climb towards the very peak of orgasm. Edward was moved to tears. He forgave Angelo, excused his egocentric, selfish behaviour, was prepared to put up with it, if only that divine voice would continue to seduce him, and not only him, but audiences worldwide.

'What do you think?' Angelo asked, as the final chords vibrated into nothingness and he lifted his hands from the keyboard and rested them on his knees.

'Wonderful,' Edward said, as dazed as a sleeper awakened. 'But not yet, Angelo. It's a huge, taxing part. You're not yet ready to tackle Wagner. He's something else. And don't get any ideas about *Otello* either. No tenor should sing this until he's fifty. Other Verdi roles, fine, but not the Moor.'

'You're right,' Angelo conceded, always serious and sensible when it concerned his voice. 'But at least if I sang Siegfried, she'd leave me alone. There's no way *she* could sing Brünnhilde.'

Edward chose his next words with care. Angelo was in a receptive mood and this was to be cherished. Was he about to divulge a revelation about his past?

'And who exactly are we talking about here?' he questioned cautiously.

Angelo's face sombered and his eyes flashed, hands as expressive as his voice. 'Genevra. Who else? My *bête noire*. The author of all my woes. The woman who hounds me.'

Drama, drama, Edward thought. Not only was Angelo an opera singer, but a Continental to boot, a combustible mix. But, Heaven be praised, he was opening up. This situation had to be handled with kid gloves.

Edward was sweating under his cream dinner jacket. He longed for a drink, to be out there, with the evening's meeting successfully concluded, leaving him free to roam the downtown bars in search of a congenial companion. One of those beautiful, sleek-hipped young men with skin like olive velvet and no qualms about offering their delectable arses for his enjoyment.

'I suppose you're referring to Genevra Scoville,' he said tentatively.

He had hit the nail slapbang on the head.

'That bitch! *Vipera*! *Strega*!' Angelo shouted, leaping up and gesticulating wildly.

'She was beautiful once,' Edward reflected, remembering the diva whom he had first met twenty years before. 'A gorgeous woman, and there was a superb soprano voice behind her magnificent tits.'

'I know,' Angelo said glumly, the fire draining out of him.

'But she's retired, hasn't she? After a series of farewell concerts, if my memory serves me?'

'Yes, and every time her performance was worse.'

'Then what has this got to do with you?' Daylight was beginning to dawn in Edward's agile brain. Angelo had been Genevra's protégé, and unkind gossip had suggested there was more to it; he'd even been called her toyboy. But this was at least five years ago. Nothing had been heard of her for a long time.

108

Angelo sighed heavily, and ran his big hands through his mop of curly black hair. 'I don't want to talk about it,' he said darkly.

Bugger, thought Edward, recognising that closed-down look. Then he realised that he had been conned. Angelo had cunningly diverted the attention from Carla Holt. Now he wouldn't know until too late whether the troublesome tenor would be rude to her or not.

Carla went through her wardrobe twice, asked Marie's advice, then Ruth's, and finally went back to the first thing she had thought of. She must look businesslike, and in no way resemble the woman Angelo had fucked in the woods last night. Even her choice of perfume must be less seductive – a fresh, floral scent would be appropriate.

Yet it was impossible to revert to how she had been with Giles. The subdued doormat had gone, never to return. The mirror reflected a lithe body blooming with health and sexual awareness, the skin already golden brown from one day in the sun. Twisting round, she looked over her shoulder at her backside. There was a faint line of stripes. The marks on her arm, bruises from Rutger's fingers, were more noticeable. And her lips were curled in a smug little smile.

She was shocked. So, deep down, she had not minded his cavalier treatment of her – had in fact gained shameful pleasure from it. Oh dear, she mourned, it would have been better had I remained in ignorance of this darker side of myself. It will surely influence my work. I'll find it hard to write romance after this.

Just thinking about it made her excited. She remembered the power of Rutger's penis, and the sensation of heat just before he entered her sex. Get dressed, she told herself sternly. You've an important interview. But the tender flesh at her secret opening was wet, her body denying her mind.

Attempting to ignore this, she pulled on a pair of black, lace-trimmed panties and settled her full breasts into the cups of a matching strapless bra. Despite herself, her nipples rose as her palms brushed across them and a dart of desire penetrated her womb.

Angelo! In an hour she would be with him. She dreaded it, panted for it, tried to hand it over to destiny, and failed. Surrendering to carnal lust, she caressed her nipples through the slippery satin, feeling them bunch. Then, baring one and keeping it primed, she dropped a hand down to the triangle of her mons. That, too, was silky smooth, the outline of her groove wantonly defined. She passed her finger up and down it, stimulating the bud partly hidden by the rapidly swelling lips.

Her eyelids closed as she allowed the feeling to rise within her. All afternoon she had been aware of the naked Leandra, and Stefan, whose cock was in an almost permanent state of arousal, surrounded as he was by four nude women.

At one point, Leandra had led him down to the sea, and Carla had observed them, waist deep in the water, clasped so close that she had known his penis was buried deep in Leandra's vagina. Ruth and Marie had lain on the rugs, playing with each other's nipples and then, quite shamelessly, they had assumed position sixty-nine, delving into one another's fissures. Only Carla had kept herself withdrawn from these sexual romps, still reticent.

But being a voyeur had roused her hunger and she needed satisfaction; she doubted that she would get it from Angelo. She must hurry. The car would be arriving to pick her up soon. She flicked her nipples once more, then held aside the leg of her panties. Her bare pubis shone forth, inviting, already moist. Once again she

110

experienced the thrill of the watcher, seeing herself in the mirror as she finger-fucked.

The need grew more uncontrolled. The tip of her tongue peeped from between her teeth as she gloated on that fragrant, wet slit with the black fabric pulled tightly into the crease at one side. Her clitoris stood out, the head pearly pink, almost transparent in its swollen state, the stem flushed with scarlet. She gave a low, melodious moan as she increased speed, finger flying. Then a shudder racked her from head to toe as she reached her apogee.

Slowing the movement of her fingers, she gently caressed that wonderful little organ that never let her down, satisfaction guaranteed, then rearranged her knickers and continued with her preparations for dinner with Angelo.

A cocoa-brown cotton dress, sprigged with white flowers, seemed to be the order of the day. It buttoned all the way down the front, had spaghetti straps, a sweetheart neckline, and fitted closely to the hips where it flared out, reaching almost to her ankles. Neat sandals, she decided, not those hippy-type thongs. The ones she chose were thick-soled and sporty, designed to support one if walking over rough terrain. She took up a natural leather shoulder bag containing a few essentials, and she was nearly ready.

She had been sparing with makeup, since her skin was glowing from sea and sun. She brushed her long, corkscrew curls back from her face and secured them with a white scrunchie; wispy tendrils escaped to frame her face and tickle the nape of her neck. As a final attempt at respectability, she took her glasses from their case and perched them on her nose. Needed only when working at the monitor, they were rather too showy, with red frames slanting upwards. But no matter, it was the overall impression that counted.

She had scarcely reached the terrace, wondering if she could down a margarita before leaving, when a footman announced that Mr Connar's car was outside. This is it, Carla thought, and drew herself up as if about to face a firing-squad. It's now or never.

The sunset blazed in full glory, and the trees stood out black against it, leaves filigreed like lace. Long purple shadows enveloped the landscape and touched the bottle-green Mercedes. A chauffeur opened the rear door for her and Carla sank into the luxury of leather, arranged her skirt and wondered if she should bother with the seat-belt. Did the rules apply in Zaminos?

She wanted to ask the driver, but was intimidated by the peaked cap canted jauntily over his eyes and the smart military-style uniform. The jacket was trimmed with brass buttons and the breeches, like those of a cavalry officer, ended in polished knee-high boots. Her interest stirred, supplementing that shiver of apprehension. He was an exceedingly dashing figure.

The car purred into life. Will it change back into a pumpkin at midnight? Carla mused, light-headed with nerves. Will that good-looking stud become a frog? If so, would he revert to a prince if I kissed him, or is it vice versa?

You're losing it, she thought. Get a grip!

The darkening skies, the white road glistening like snow ... And then electronic gates, massive, iron-spiked walls, a semi-circular drive, and a villa even more impressive than Rutger's ...

Edward came to meet her, hands outstretched, helping her to alight from the Merc. 'Miss Holt – Carla, if I may?' he said eagerly, and his warm smile enveloped her like a baby blanket. He looked rather like a large, plump baby, too, with mild blue eyes, floppy, silvery hair; yet she had heard he was tough as old boots. 'Come in,' he urged, taking her by the arm. 'He's waiting to see you. We've had a talk about it, and I think it's going to be all right.'

He sounded unsure, and Carla's heart lurched. She put up a hand to make sure her glasses were straight. They entered a hall the size of a ballroom. It had a glass cupola and an intricately tiled floor. Arches and pillars led off in several directions. The architecture was of epic proportion, the ornamentation harking back to Mycenae, with much use of azure, white and gold.

Then she heard music, and thrilled to the violently erotic splendour of the sound – decadent, sensual and barbaric. It cast a spell over her and she followed it to its source.

Angelo stood in the salon, hands clasped in the small of his back, head flung back as he stared at the rapidly darkening garden.

Then, without turning, he said, '*Salomé*, Strauss's masterpiece, and this is the Dance of the Seven Veils, when Princess Salome strips for her dirty-minded old stepfather, King Herod, in order to get the severed head of John the Baptist.'

'I suppose you'd like to sing John,' Edward said, trying to joke, though Angelo's sudden interest in entirely unsuitable roles stuck in his craw. He decided to add a downer: 'Unfortunately, it's a part for a baritone.'

The music reached a crescendo, then ended. Angelo suddenly spun round. His eyes went to Carla and widened.

'This is the young lady I've been telling you about,' Edward said, fighting his way through the thickening atmosphere. 'Carla Holt.'

Angelo stood before her and she felt herself die, lost for all eternity. She knew his face from photos, had glimpsed it by moonlight, but to see it clearly in all its beauty blew her away.

It was unfair that one man could look like that and have the added bonus of a marvellous voice. He had not bothered to change for dinner. His clothes were casual: black and white check cotton trousers belted at his narrow waist – baggy, yet drawing attention to the thick bough of his penis brushing the inside of his left thigh. He'd topped those with a black V-neck polo shirt, wore no socks, and slip-on loafers, hand-tooled by a Milanese craftsman.

Their eyes locked, and she knew her pitiful disguise was worthless.

'I know you,' he said crisply.

'Yes.' She did not waste her breath on lies, removing the useless spectacles.

'In the woods last night.'

'Yes.'

He paced nearer, like a panther closing in on its kill. 'You're a spy,' he grated, and never before had she seen a man possessed of such thunderous rage. It paralysed her.

'No,' she stammered, hands held before her as if to ward off a blow. 'That's not true. I was speaking the truth . . . just taking a walk.'

'Leave us, Edward,' Angelo commanded, without taking his burning eyes from Carla.

'But I don't understand. Are you two already acquainted?' Edward said, bewildered, exasperated and ready to throw in the towel.

'Just go.' Angelo's tone brooked no argument, and in a second, Carla was alone with him.

'Now,' he said, looming over her. 'The truth. You're working for a paper, no? Your paparazzi pals are lurking. They have the villa under surveillance.'

'It's not like that. I've been hired by Edward to help you write. No one knows, only my agent and the friends I'm staying with. Last night was a fluke.'

His scowl deepened, the black bar of his brows drawing together at the top of his Roman nose. 'Fluke?' he shouted, his accent more marked. 'I not understand. What is this "fluke"?'

'It means chance . . . accident . . . it wasn't planned.' This was awful, the worst possible scenario she could have imagined in her darkest nightmare.

'I don't believe you,' he snarled, and his eyes narrowed to slits.

'I don't give a fuck what you believe!' she cried furiously into his face, her temper rising to boiling point. 'I flew in from London to do a job. That's all. I went for a walk, met you and we made love . . . At least that's what I thought it was. Silly me!'

'I, too, thought that,' he said, and there was a hint of disappointment in his voice. 'But now I find I was mistaken. You're an opportunist. You hope to sell your story, get a lot of money, make me look a fool.'

'Oh, shut up!' she flared and swung round on her heel. 'You're paranoid. There's no more to say. I'll tell Edward it's off, go back to England, forget I ever met you.' She was almost at the entrance when she felt him behind her. He caught hold of her by the hair, yanked her round to face him and drove his mouth down on hers in a punishing kiss.

The breath was knocked out of her, as his arm prevented her lungs from expanding. She struggled, managed to gasp in air, beating at his back with her fists, but his tongue, bruising and possessive, penetrated her lips. She hated him in that moment, yet her body responded, remembering the powerful thrust of his hips as he entered her, the tenderness of his touch, the promise which, in spite of herself, she had believed lay at the heart of their brief, nocturnal encounter.

Now that was gone, and yet nothing had changed as far as she was concerned. It was all in his head.

He was treating her as if she was a slut, jerking at the buttons of her dress, opening her to his mouth, and he grunted as he saw her breasts swelling in the fragile brassière. He pounced on one nipple, sucking it through the satin, rammed a hand into her lower back and ground her pelvis into his groin, making her aware of the erect phallus trapped in his chinos.

He tore at the lower buttons, ripping the fabric, and driving his thigh against her pubis. She tried to keep her legs closed, but his knee parted them with vicious force, almost lifting her from her feet. The crotch of her panties was drawn tightly, dragged between the lips of her cleft, chafing her clitoris. As he moved his knee in regular motion, so the frottage became unbearably exciting.

He bit her nipple, gnawed at its swollen tip poking through the black silk. She cried out in frantic pleasure and jagged her nails down his cheek.

'Filthy little bitch!' he muttered, and flung her away from him. She hit the wall with a force that made stars dance before her eyes. She stood there, her breath rasping harshly in her throat, her ears ringing, while Angelo strode to the patio and shouted, 'Krista! Come here!'

A girl slid round the door, a lissom brunette with wavy hair tumbling around her shoulders. Her full breasts and rounded hips strained against her short skirt and skimpy top.

'Sir,' she murmured, adoring him with her smouldering eyes.

Angelo seized her and forced her to her knees in front of him. 'Suck me,' he ordered.

He stood with his legs spread and his knuckles on his hips, watching her as she deftly unzipped his fly and drew out the dark pillar of his erect penis. Her mouth closed round the helm, and he pushed his pelvis upwards, driving it fully into her mouth.

Carla gasped, disgusted, yet with jealous desire knotting her vitals. She was powerless to move as his eyes pierced hers across the room, and he smiled, an unpleasant, taunting smile.

'You see, Miss Holt,' he said in those dark tones that wrapped themselves around her like velvet, 'last night meant no more to me than this ... a bodily function needing release. She is devoted to me and will do anything I ask, won't you, Krista? She'll even let me piss in her mouth.'

Krista withdrew from his cock for a moment, looking up at him with fawning, spaniel eyes. Angelo held his penis and rubbed the shiny glans over her lips. 'Lick it around the hole. You know how to please me.'

The girl stretched out her tongue and worried at the sloping head, lapping at the crystal drops appearing at the slit. 'Ah, that's good,' Angelo whispered, burying his hands in the mass of her hair. He thrust hard, until the whole of his lengthy shaft was buried in her mouth, as her face pressed into the wiry black thatch that coated his lower belly.

Carla tried to turn away. She did not want to watch the girl performing fellatio, but could not help herself. Fascinated yet repelled by the tableau, she felt her vagina contracting with need.

Angelo was getting into the rhythm of it now, thrusting and withdrawing, then thrusting again into Krista's wet and willing mouth. He was breathing rapidly, his eyes half closed, his face tense. Faster and faster he rode Krista, heedless of her choking moans, using her mouth as he would have used her womanhood, slamming against her face.

Then he cried out in his native tongue and, at the moment of ejaculation, pulled out, his cock spurting jets of creamy white spunk. They fell on Krista's chin, her eyes, her cheeks and into her hair, droplets glistening like pearls against the dark tresses. It seemed to go on forever, and she reached out her tongue and caught the warm essence, drawing it into her mouth like nectar and swallowing it.

Carla could stand no more. She flung herself out of the room and left the villa. Edward was waiting by the car, leaning on the bonnet with the chauffeur, smoking a cigarette.

'Take me back,' she shouted.

'What's happened?'

'Just take me back,' she repeated, her face flushed and her eyes bright with tears.

'Carla, calm down,' Edward soothed, signalling to the driver. 'Don't cry, my dear. That bastard, Angelo. Will he never learn? Get in the car. I'll come with you, shall I?'

'Please yourself. I don't care, and I never want to set eyes on him again. I shall throw all my CDs away, take them down to the rubbish-dump – and tape over every single video with him on it,' she stormed irrationally.

Edward put his arm around her on the back seat, and she cried on his shoulder, wetting his immaculate jacket. Somehow, between sobs, she blurted out the whole story.

'I see,' he said patting her, his touch avuncular. Yet his mind was working overtime: this situation might be advantageous.

The last thing he wanted was to lose this girl who could be his salvation. Angelo might throw a wobbly and behave like an overindulged toddler, but he always harboured a soft spot for any woman whose body he had possessed, were it ever so briefly.

Edward had seen them queueing up at his dressing-room door after a show. Some people considered opera elitist, highbrow, only for snobbish squares. But Edward had seen how available the stars were and how ready to

118

screw their fans. They loved to be loved, and had their groupies just the same as any coked-up pop idol. And no one was more in need of this adulation than Angelo Lorenzo.

Josh sat in a dark taverna situated in a little side alley close to the harbour. It was crowded with local men; their women were not permitted to frequent cafes. Greek songs wailed from a battered radio, and the smell of coffee mingled with that of cigarette smoke. There was a charcoal grill, great pots of beans and trays of stuffed tomatoes. While he waited, Josh dipped into a plate of *meze* and had a glass of wine.

There was nothing he liked more than living among the inhabitants of whichever country he found himself in, learning their languages, their customs, absorbing the atmosphere. He had been lucky, born into money, given the best education, then allowed to follow his own goals. There had been no pressure to join the family business; his oldest brother was keen to do that, so Josh was given his freedom. A curiously tolerant lot, his family. Proud of his success, too, likening him to that rascally ancestor, scourge of the Spanish Main.

'Josh, my friend,' shouted a large, shambling bear of a man who now came in, filling the place with his genial presence. He made towards Josh's table, but progress was slow as he stopped to greet this person and that, exchange kisses and handshakes, pass the time of day with the old men, and pat the young boys on the head.

'Ah, at last,' he puffed, fanning himself with his Panama hat, thinning, grizzled hair sticking damply to his forehead. 'I couldn't get away. That new woman of mine . . . so demanding. She's only eighteen, thighs like a wild mare. I think I'm in love. I may have to marry her.'

He spoke in English, though Josh had picked up a

smattering of Greek. It was a matter of courtesy on the newcomer's part, and he liked to show off his linguistic skills.

'Can she cook?' Josh grinned as he lifted the wine bottle.

'Cook? Like a dream! You must eat with us soon!' And the massive man lowered his bulk on to a stool as he kissed his fingertips and rolled his eyes heavenwards to demonstrate the delights of his young mistress's cuisine.

Josh poured him a glass of the rough red wine, and toasted him: George Pavlos, curator of the local museum and expert on Greek history, passionate about this subject to which he had given the best years of his life.

They ordered, and were soon eating fresh sardines, boned, mashed flat and fried like fritters in olive oil, followed by herb omelettes and kebabs, thin slices of seasoned lamb grilled on a spit and eaten in a split piece of unleavened bread.

Josh knew it would be impolite to get to the crux of their meeting until their stomachs were full. At last George belched, wiped his hands with a lemon-scented sachet, and fixed Josh across the table with a pair of twinkling eyes set deep amidst fleshy folds.

'Now, tell about this find of yours,' he said. 'I must inform the authorities before you go any further.'

'Of course,' Josh said, holding out his cigarettes. George took one in fingers like sausages and bent his head to the lighter flame.

'I'm a professional,' Josh averred. 'I know that marine archaeology necessitates wooing the appropriate people. I've no time for idiots who plunder artifacts, risking damaging them and breaking the law into the bargain. But I've already investigated the wreck. It lies fathoms deep just outside the bay below the Villa Artemis.'

'Oh, yes. The villa belongs to a foreigner who's making a film. Some of our people are getting work as extras,' George said, then he leaned a little closer, winking lecherously. 'The star is staying there, Leandra Lafage. What a body! Perfection!'

'I know Leandra,' Josh returned, amused by the way his old friend's hand had dropped below his corpulent belly and was nestling in his crotch.

'You do? Could you get her autograph? Not for me, you understand, but my Desma would be so happy.'

'I'll do more than that,' Josh promised. 'I'll bring her to the museum. She needs to study the period and its ambience.' It was as well to keep in with the natives, Josh had found, and these islanders were particularly obliging. He went on to tell George what he had done so far.

'I've already followed the routine of marking the site with a buoy. We've gone down and surveyed the wreck, taken notes, made sketches and used still cameras and camcorders.'

'Good. And you've marked each drawing and photo with an arrow pointing North?'

'Naturally.'

The smoky taverna faded, and Josh was beneath the sea, surrounded by multicoloured fish and strange-shaped rocks with weeds clinging to them like mermaids' hair: his first dive to what he was convinced was a wreck. It was clear down there, and warm at first, though getting colder the deeper he went. His body was relaxed but he did not forget to be wary. Luke, his diving buddy, swam not too far away, and both of them were in direct contact with the *Sea Jade* by signal lines.

Then he saw it, and his heart started to pound despite his training. Almost invisible to an unskilled eye, the remains of a ship lay upended in the silt and sand, very old, covered in barnacles and concretions. He hand-signalled to Luke and checked the luminous face of his dive watch, adjusting the bezel to set the minute-hand.

The wreck called him like the sirens who lured sailors to their deaths. He stared through his mask, bubbles rising as he moved the fins on his feet and swam closer to it. Then excitement and a frisson of fear stabbed through him. He thought he saw something move, not a fish or weed. He stared harder. Could he really see a female form, or was it nitrogen narcosis? Had he been down longer than he realised? Was he running out of air?

He lost all sense of reality, hearing her singing, seeing her unearthly beauty as she swam in and out amidst the wreckage. Her body was deathly white, her tiny breasts tipped with rose, her hair long, floating. It, too, was white as bleached bone – and her eyes were like shards of ice.

Josh fumbled with his Nikonos RS. He had to capture her on camera. He forgot the cardinal rule that he should maintain good buddy diving procedure and let Luke know he wanted to shoot. Nothing mattered but his obsession with this naked creature with her little breasts, pitiless eyes and the dark pink cleft that opened like the mouth of a sea anemone as she moved her long, corpse-white legs.

Josh felt himself hardening under the shortie wet suit. His penis throbbed as he swam closer and closer to that beckoning opening. He aimed the camera, took shot after shot, getting ever closer, consumed with the madness of lust until the tension was released in an explosive orgasm. It was impossible, yet he seemed to see his semen jetting from the eye of his phallus, mingling with the sea and then sucked into the orifice of that icy predator.

Luke was there, making frantic hand movements. Josh lifted his wrist and glanced at his watch. The hands had not moved. No time had passed at all, as humans measure it.

'Are you all right, my friend?' George asked, and Josh saw his craggy face appearing through the smoke haze.

'Oh, yes . . . just thinking about the wreck,' he said, passing a hand over his eyes. 'One needs to be so careful down there.'

'You are brave, you divers. I couldn't do it, wonderful though it must be. I will wait on dry land and see these marvels when you salvage them.'

'And I can begin to do this?' Josh said, reaching for a cigarette. 'You'll give me the go-ahead?' He was not given to fantasies, yet it seemed as if the clammy chill of that watery phantom clung to him whenever he thought of her. Oddly, nothing had come out when the film was developed – only bits of the wreck and a drift of weed. He had dived several times since, but she had never returned.

'Yes. Certainly. Don't worry. I will get permission and handle the paperwork. My dear friend, this is most exciting. When will you start? When can I feast my eyes on these treasures?' George was as excited as a boy, his broad chest heaving under the soiled, collarless shirt whose lower buttons strained across the massive belly hanging over his belt.

'We don't know they exist yet,' Josh said, but he accepted when George pledged the expedition in a glass of retsina.

'They do. I can feel it in my water,' George said solemnly. 'And you will bring the photos and drawings to my office in the morning?'

'Yes. We must guard them. They shouldn't fall into the wrong hands,' Josh warned.

'I shall keep them in my safe,' George assured him, then stretched like a big tomcat and added, 'I go home to Desma now. After such a meal and so exciting news, I need to go to bed with her. I've never felt so virile. Her pretty little cunt is a better aphrodisiac than Spanish fly or two dozen oysters.' He cast an enquiring eye at Josh. 'There's nothing like it, is there? The taste and feel of warm, wet pussy. How are you fixed? Why don't you come back to my house? Desma has a sister, almost as lovely, and certainly as willing.'

'No, thanks. Not tonight. I have plans of my own,' Josh answered.

'You are embarking on a love-affair? The best of luck, my friend. You are a brave man and need a lovely woman in your life. Is it the heavenly Leandra, by any chance?'

Josh laughed and said, 'No, though I've had her in the past, and could again, if I wanted.'

'You have?' George's eyes goggled.

'Yes,' Josh nodded, and settled back on the bench, glass in hand. 'I knew her before she was famous.' He did not add 'corrupted', but smiled inwardly.

'And the lady you want now?' George hinted heavily, lumbering to his feet.

'She's English, too, but very different to Leandra, who's capable of looking after herself. This one needs care, I think.'

'Good luck with her, and I'll see you tomorrow,' George said and, extricating himself from the friends who wished to delay him, disappeared out of the door into the noisy alley.

Josh looked after him for a moment, then drained his glass and got up. He left the taverna, walked to the quay and got into his truck. He could see the lights bobbing on *Sea Jade*, and wanted to show her to Carla Holt. He turned over the engine, and headed up the hill towards the Villa Artemis.

Chapter 7

'*ARE YOU SURE* you don't want me to come in with you?' Edward asked anxiously as the Merc pulled up below the wide, sweeping steps.

'Yes,' Carla said. She could not get out of the car quickly enough, wanted to lock herself in her room, ring Toby and give him an earful, and then cry herself to sleep.

'Don't do anything in a hurry,' Edward advised, his face waxen in the car's dim interior. 'Sleep on it, Carla. I'll phone in the morning.'

The Merc purred off in the direction of the town, and Carla stormed into the villa, praying she would not see anyone. She felt a hopeless failure, and had so much wanted to be successful in this venture, proving to herself (and Giles?) that she could do it. She couldn't face the thought of going home with her tail between her legs.

The villa was quiet, but Marie was on the terrace, lying back in a basket chair, her feet propped high, a martini to hand as she dictated to Ruth. She waved when she spotted Carla. 'How'd you get on with Lorenzo?'

'Don't ask,' Carla snapped, dragging over to the table where the laptop stood humming and active, its monitor aglow.

She was consumed with envy. Marie, though vowing otherwise, had come prepared to work, and she seemed capable of concentrating no matter what. She's a professional, Carla thought. I wanted to be like her, imagined coming back after a day with Angelo, punching in my notes, burning the midnight oil and producing an entertaining, polished, witty autobiography in his name. I was prepared for him to take all the limelight, happy to sit in the wings. Edward had even promised that I should get a mention in the preface – briefly, of course, simply saying I had been Angelo's research assistant. That would have suited me just fine.

Pain welled like an open wound inside her. She had not quite realised the extent of her need to do this work. Now all her hopes and dreams were as bitter as grave-dust in her mouth.

'Sweet Jesus! What's wrong?' Marie asked, sitting up. Ruth paused, and clicked SAVE.

'The man's impossible! A pig! No, it didn't go well and no, I don't wish to discuss it,' Carla shouted and stalked off.

'You need something to lighten you up,' Marie called after her. 'Go see Rutger. Leandra's with him, and Robin. He's always good for working out your frustrations.'

Carla pretended she had not heard. She made a beeline for her room, but when she got there her restlessness increased. She put off phoning Toby, unwilling to admit even to him that the whole thing had been a fiasco. Her head throbbed and her eyes were sore with crying. The beauty of the evening seemed to mock her, the serene moon and the stars dusting the indigo sky a reminder of her own foolish illusions. Not only was she miserable, but her body cried out for release. Vivid mental pictures of Krista sucking Angelo's penis tortured her. Jealousy stabbed her sickeningly in the gut every time she remembered the milky stream arcing from its tip and falling on the girl's face like warm rain.

It should have been *her*! If it weren't for that damned commission, it *would* have been her.

This was totally irrational. She wouldn't have been in Zaminos at all were it not for the job. But she didn't feel rational – she felt angry, upset and, most of all, gravid with the need to be penetrated by a penis. Her own fingers weren't enough. She hungered for a thick, long male organ, as stiff and solid as a spear, plunging into her and using her to the limit.

Damn! She swore, and raced out of the room, her feet taking her towards Rutger's apartment, almost of their own volition.

The strains of a string quartet drifted through the partly open door, its controlled elegance in shocking contrast to the scene being played out as Carla entered.

Leandra lay across a high bench, her skirt pushed up, raised haunches bare. Her ankles were restrained by mink-lined metal cuffs and, like her legs, tethered in such a position that they were stretched wide. Her hair streamed down, almost brushing the cool marble. Rutger was leaning over her, and the gentleness with which he smoothed her face and trailed his hands over her shoulders sent chills down Carla's spine and made her vulva spasm.

He looked across at her. 'Come in, my dear,' he said softly. 'Leandra is about to be disciplined.'

He wore a white toga with a purple border. It was draped across his chest and back, but did not cover his rampant cock, arrogantly pointing to the ceiling. His linten hair shone, his tanned skin almost black by comparison, and his eyes had a peculiar, mesmeric glitter.

Carla crept towards him, her sex-valley moist. There was something compelling about the sight of this man dominating Leandra, and she could feel herself becoming more aroused as she looked at the woman's exposed sex-lips protruding from between her legs. The pink flesh was pursed, the sharp dividing line fringed with fair fluff that did not hide the dew seeping from that fascinating slit. Carla wanted to run her fingers up and down the ridge, explore Leandra's nether hole, and massage the enlarged clitoris protruding between the labial folds. Never before had the sight of another woman's sex organs aroused her so sharply, filling her with this desire to fondle them.

Following the direction of her eyes, Rutger rubbed a finger along Leandra's delta till it was coated with honeydew, then held it to Carla's lips. 'Taste,' he whispered, and his phallus quivered.

Carla put out her tongue and licked it. Her nostrils were filled with rich, warm fragrance, and her mouth enjoyed Leandra's juices, salty and flavoursome, so like her own.

She gasped and swayed towards him and Rutger caught her in one arm. His penis prodded her and he unfastened her dress and cupped her mound, his fingers sliding on the black silk gusset. His thumb found the hard point of her erect nodule and flicked it. The hot feeling spiralled through her, and she jerked as he pressed her love-lips together and then withdrew his hand.

'It is time you dressed for your part,' he said, with a snap of his fingers.

Robin appeared from the shadows, wearing a leather codpiece. His back was zigzagged with stripes. He bowed, lowering his gaze to the floor. 'Yes, master,' he said humbly.

'Carla is to wear something more suitable. It's time she examined her passions, desires and anger, all needing urgent release. Help her,' Rutger commanded, and paced towards Leandra.

He picked up an object like a badminton-racket, springy and pliable and covered in white leather. His penis swelled, larger and harder as he stood behind Leandra. 'I shan't mark you this time. We're too near those first shoots. It wouldn't do for your fans to see that you're a naughty girl who has been punished. The paddle won't bruise you, as soft as a love's kiss – but with a bite, none the less.'

'Thank you, master,' she said fervently. 'Whatever you say.' Then her body bucked against her bonds as he struck a resounding whack on her rounded golden buttocks.

Carla's heart was thumping, and her bowels churned. The paddle swished down again, and Leandra howled, then sobbed her thanks to Rutger.

'I don't want to watch this. You can't make me,' Carla protested, distraught to find her lower self getting wetter, and trembling on the edge of orgasm at the sight of the hot pink flush spreading over Leandra's rump.

Rutger smiled sardonically. 'No one is using force. You are free to leave whenever you wish.' He was challenging her, and she accepted.

'Come along, Robin,' she said, her voice trembling with apprehension and excitement. 'Show me what I'm to wear.'

He ducked, his manner subservient, and her latent desire for revenge rose in a blood-red tide. She itched to hold the stock of a whip like a phallus in her hand, and then crack it through the air and bring it down on Robin's hide. Not because he was Robin – that harmless, self-effacing writer – but because he was male, with a cock and balls dangling between his legs.

He darted into an adjoining room, and she followed, the impact of paddle on flesh and Leandra's moans ringing in her ears.

The room was candlelit, hung with mirrors and hooks holding various implements: whips, riding crops, canes, birches, and an assortment of chains, blindfolds, cufflinks and gags.

A crosspiece stood centre stage. A bondage couch was nearby. It had a hole in the padding for the face and another lower down to give easy access from below to the genitals of whoever might be tied to it. There was a wooden structure resembling the stocks once set up in market-places so the populace could pelt criminals with garbage.

Robin showed Carla a whole range of leather, rubber and PVC skirts, corsets and catsuits, along with high-heeled shoes and boots, all over the top, hinting at decadence beyond Carla's imaginings. The writer within her took notes; the woman quailed and thrilled and wanted to come.

She picked a red leather bustier, wickedly curved and uncompromisingly tarty. She stripped and slipped it on. Her breath rushed out in a gasp as Robin strained at the front lacing, pulling it as tight as he could before tying the ends. Her waist was reduced to doll size, her breasts tumbling over the top, the nipples plum-red and aroused. It was too hot for stockings, but she put them on anyway, sitting on a stool and rolling them up her legs, black and shiny and alluring, with suspenders clipped to their lace tops.

When she jumped up and screwed round to see her backview, she was aroused by the lewd sight of her bare bottom below the basque's edge, which ended at her hip-bones. The crease of her arse was exaggerated by the satin and elastic straps upholding the stockings. The straight seams marked the backs of her thighs, the swell of her calves and the slimness of her ankles, and the impossibly high heels altered her stance, making her buttocks jut out.

'No panties,' Robin said, from where he knelt fastening the buckles of her fetishly spiked black shoes. 'But these . . .' And he proffered a pair of elbow-length, close-fitting satin gloves.

Carla pulled them on. The tips were cut away and her coppery gold nails emerged like claws. Metal rings gleamed on the backs, adding to the threatening allure of her outfit. Robin lifted a crop from among the other instruments of correction and, almost reverently, placed it in her hands.

'I am ordered to do your make-up,' he said with a kind of cringing eagerness, and the codpiece stretched even tighter over his thickening prick.

Carla sat at one of the mirrors while her transformation took place. Robin was good at it. 'I always do my own, when I'm in drag,' he confided shyly.

The mask went on. Behind it she could do or say anything, no longer Carla. She could hide behind the purple eyeshadow and thickly coated lashes, dark foundation, hectic blusher and gash of an aggressive crimson mouth. Robin backbrushed her hair till it stood out in a barbaric Medusa mane, fixed with lacquer.

Is this me? Possibly the *real* me? She contemplated her image as she strutted in front of the glass. Walking in six-inch stilettos was difficult, but she persevered. They did so much for the legs, making them seem longer, sexier, leading the eye to her bare mons veneris framed in red suspenders.

She wished Giles were there to see her – but wanted Angelo even more. That would teach them, the chauvinistic pigs. And she stiffened her spine and held her head high, striding around and slashing the crop against the wall. It made a gut-satisfying noise. How much better it would sound on vulnerable flesh.

Dear God, she thought, and for a moment her heart bled. What is happening to me? But I like my new image: a warrior princess, an Amazon no man can hurt again. I'm the one who'll mete out justice now.

131

Robin, tasks complete, waited.

'Into the other room, slave,' Carla said, brandishing the crop.

'Ah, perfect . . . a dominatrix in the making!' Rutger said admiringly. He pulled Leandra's head back by the hair. 'Look at her, darling. Isn't she beautiful?'

He released Leandra's bonds and took her into his embrace, her silk skirt slithering down to cover her flaming red bottom. She leaned into him, the lash serving to make her adore him more.

'She is very beautiful,' she agreed, and wound her fingers in his blond chest hair, playing with the brown nubs of his nipples. Then she looked up into his eyes and said, 'May we beat him together, master?'

He nodded graciously, 'You may.'

'Thank you, master. I shall use the tawse,' and she picked up a bundle of thongs woven into a short handle, and thrust it into Robin's face. 'Kiss it,' she ordered.

He obediently placed his lips to it.

'And Mistress Carla's,' Leandra reminded, supplementing her command with a flick of the tawse across his belly.

Carla offered the crop to his mouth and he kissed it.

'I shan't bind you,' Leandra went on, pacing slowly round him, examining him from every angle, kicking his ankles apart so she could tease his bulge. 'You must prove your submission by staying still.'

'Yes, mistress.'

'And no coming! If you spurt before I tell you, then you'll get a dozen more blows.' She pushed the tawse handle under his chin, lifting his face towards hers as she asked, 'What are you?'

'A disgusting worm, mistress.'

'And what happens to disgusting little worms?'

'They get beaten, mistress.'

'What did you say? Speak louder, worm.'

'They get beaten, mistress.'

'So they do. Especially horrible, filthy worms who jerk off. Isn't this so?'

'Yes, mistress.'

Do they mean it, or is this part of the game? Carla wondered, and the hot, tingling feeling increased in her kernel.

Leandra slapped the tawse against her palm, testing it, then hit him across the back. Carla saw his body bend as he crouched over, head down, hands clutching at his penis. Fresh marks scored his flesh. He remained silent, and Leandra hit him again, and again. She inserted a finger under the ties of his codpiece. It fell away. His cock uncoiled, the shaft upright, the head fiery and wet.

Leandra ran her fingers over the tip, and Robin groaned. 'You're making my hand sticky,' she complained, and wiped it in his hair. 'What do you say?'

'I'm sorry, mistress.'

'And I'm being so lenient, too,' Leandra said, her red lips curling in enjoyment. 'Aren't you a lucky slave? Here's another beautiful mistress ready to beat you . . .' And she nodded to Carla.

Carla sneaked a glance at Rutger. He was watching Leandra tormenting Robin, his tapering, aristocratic fingers caressing his cock in rhythmical strokes. Carla wanted it inside her and was furious with him for coolly and deliberately stirring up her basic, carnal lust. If only it were he who cringed before her as Robin now did.

She brought the crop down on his rump hesitantly.

'Harder,' Leandra urged.

She demonstrated for Carla, using the tawse to lash him firmly, Carla took fire from this, her strokes alternating with Leandra's, falling into a pattern. Heat dragged at her entrails, her sex was juicy, her throat parched. She shared Robin's pain, watched the red

133

stripes appearing on his thighs, buttocks and shoulders, and was amazed that this was so exciting. The state of his phallus betrayed his arousal, and her miniature organ throbbed in sympathy.

The tawse bit home again and Robin gave a strangled yelp and climaxed in a spurt of white semen. Leandra kicked him, shouting, 'Disobedient muck-worm! Didn't I tell you not to come? Ugh! Messy! What shall I do with you?'

He was on his knees now, clasping her legs, burying his face in her skirt, his voice muffled as he said, 'Anything, mistress. I'm yours.'

She narrowed her eyes and considered, one foot tapping the floor. Carla waited, her body running with sweat. Her breasts throbbed and her nipples ached. Her juices bedewed her thighs and the tightness of the corset seemed to force the blood into her loins.

Rutger's cock was huge now, swaying slightly as he moved, the mushroom-like head glistening. 'He must pleasure his new mistress while we watch,' he said, and drew Leandra to the bed.

'Do it, slave,' Leandra ordered, then loosened her waistband. The skirt fell in a silken puddle and she tossed it aside, then lay across the bed, legs splayed, her deep pink cleft naked and open, eager for Rutger.

Carla's need for completion was so compelling that she froze as Robin crawled across to her, his tongue stretched out. She tensed and whimpered as it flicked the bulging head of her clit. He parted her wet lower lips with his fingers, holding them back and inserting his mouth over her valley, sucking at her vulva, dipping his tongue into it, then withdrawing to lap gently at the turgid bud.

She cupped her breasts and pinched her nipples, tripling her sensations, and thrust herself against the warm, willing tongue that was masturbating her so skilfully. It was not the same as when Angelo went down on her. Then, she was concerned about giving him satisfaction, too. But Robin was her slave. This was for her enjoyment alone. She was selfishly, gloriously free and pleasure-bent, and could understand how powerful a man must feel when he pays for the services of a whore.

She plunged her fingers into Robin's hair, visualising Angelo doing the same to Krista, and she growled, 'Do it! Go on! Suck me . . . suck me!'

As the pre-orgasmic waves started to gather and roll through her, she feasted on the sight of Leandra and Rutger copulating. He had flung aside his toga, his strong body rippling with muscles. He put his hands under Leandra's buttocks and yanked her down till her thighs were supported by the bed, the legs bent at the knees, the feet placed flat on the floor. He stood between her fork, his tightly muscled buttocks driving his cock home as he plunged it into her.

She gave vent to throaty cries, and he leaned forwards, legs spread, his sinewy arms taking his weight, gyrating his hips, grinding into her. He had positioned her so that he would see Carla being tongued. And Carla watched him, saw his glistening shaft appear momentarily at the upward stroke, saw Leandra's wet, red sex, the lips folded back like a carnivorous jungle flower, eagerly sucking it back in again. Sight and sensation became inexorably mixed as Carla felt Robin licking her, heard Rutger's panting breath as he neared his climax, and felt her forces gathering to hurl her over the abyss in a shattering orgasm.

She yelled when it came, shuddered, knees weak, and her voice was joined by Leandra's shrill scream of release and Rutger's deep growl of intense satisfaction.

Though it was early, the port was already buzzing. The trawlers had been unloading their catches since

135

daybreak and gulls circled and wheeled, scavenging for fishy scraps.

Carla clung to the inside of the passenger door as the truck careered down the hill. Paxia rose from the seafront in a series of terraces, steep alleys and white houses. Women in rusty black were shaking out mats, scrubbing steps and sweeping pavements.

Josh had not spoken to her since knocking on her bedroom door with a cup of strong, bittersweet Turkish coffee. 'I'm kidnapping you. Drink this, get up and jump into some shorts. Oh, and bring a sweater. You may need it later.'

He was like a breath of fresh air, and Carla had grinned up at him and done what he ordered with hardly a protest. She did not ask any questions. He was there, he wanted her company, and she needed to get away. If Edward phoned, then he would have to wait.

Now Josh parked and walked her to a dark, cave-like taverna where the smell of freshly baked bread competed with that of roasting coffee beans. An old man sat at the bar, passing his time over a cup of water and a necklace of amber beads.

'I'll buy you a string,' Josh said, guiding her to a woven rush chair near a table with a red and white checked cloth. 'They click all over Greece. It's nothing to do with rosaries. A legacy from the Turks, worry beads, much cheaper than cigarettes. Speaking of which, I need to stock up.'

He went to the counter and she picked up a two-day old newspaper from Athens. He came back and sat beside her, his legs in those holey jeans stretched out, shabby deck shoes on his bare feet. He was in desperate need of a shave, yet Carla liked that rough, adventurer kind of look. Where she hailed from, trendy young men cultivated designer stubble, but it came naturally to Josh.

'Why are we here?' she asked as coffee arrived, with crusty bread and herb-flavoured grilled sausages.

'Why not?' he said, glancing at her with amused, tigerish eyes.

'I can think of several reasons.'

'Name one.'

'I don't know you very well.'

Josh gave a sharp bark of laughter. 'And you do Rutger and Robin and the rest of the motley crew, I suppose?'

She pointed her legs away from him, knees demurely together. Her white shorts were very brief, cutting into her central cleft, constantly reminding her of past pleasures. She blushed as she thought about her behaviour in Rutger's apartment, and was thankful that Josh was ignorant of this. As far as she was aware, he had turned up that morning.

'I got talking with Marie last night,' he said, as if picking up on her thoughts. 'I had intended to take you moonlight sailing, but by the time we'd stopped chewing the fat, everyone else had gone to bed.'

'And where did you sleep?' she asked, the words out before she knew it.

He laughed, little lines, sharp as incisors, fanning out at the corners of his eyes. 'Not with her, if that's what you're wondering.'

'I'm not,' she returned frostily.

He chuckled again, and added meat to his hunk of bread. Then he deliberately slid closer, till she could go no further, pressed against a whitewashed wall. 'Liar. You were wondering, all right,' he said, in that pleasant, drawling voice. 'Don't be coy. We're going to be lovers, you and I.'

This shocked her, and she finished her breakfast in silence. Of course, what he had just said was the truth and nothing but the truth, but she would have liked to

137

prevaricate a little, string out the final confrontation in order to convince herself that she was not turning into a sex-mad lunatic.

'Ready?' he said, holding out his hand. She nodded, a chill raising the down on her limbs as his fingers contacted hers. Then he picked up the tab.

The temperature was rising as they strolled through the market. It was noisy and exhilarating, traders haggling, housewives arguing, and chickens crowing loudly in wooden pens. A few pale-skinned, bemused-looking strangers wandered along, but not many, for Zaminos had not yet fallen prey to the package tour holiday.

Carla stopped at a stall run by Moroccans, attracted by skirts and shawls of peasant weave in raw colours and simple patterns.

'You want one? Never pay the asking price. Haggling is expected. They'd be insulted if you didn't. Here, let me have a go,' said Josh, taking over when she would have preferred to test out her skill at bargaining.

When they left, she was carrying an incongruous Harrods' bag containing a skirt. Josh held out his fist, saying, 'Open your hand.'

'Why?' she asked suspiciously, hating anyone to do this after a childhood incident when a spotty male cousin had dropped a large housespider into her shocked and shrinking palm.

His eyes pierced hers, so green against his strong-boned, bronzed face. 'Trust me,' he insisted.

He took her hand in his and turned it upwards. His fist hovered over it for an instant, no more, then she felt something cool and smooth. It was a long necklace of clear brownish yellow beads, each one a perfect drop of fossil resin from trees millions of years dead.

'I said I'd have you clicking. You'll be worse than a dolphin,' he said. 'It's a talisman, too, brings good luck

... especially if it's a gift. Stronger still if the giver desires you.' He took it from her and slipped it over her head, then arranged it, the backs of his hands brushing over her nipples. She was speechless. 'That's kind of you,' she managed to say, and her fingers went to it almost automatically, touching the cool amber, moving from bead to bead.

'Very nunlike,' he observed, and his eyes darkened. 'I've always fancied having sex with a convent novice. I'm thinking about it now. Feel,' and he angled his body so they were hidden by a stall, then gently seized her wrist and guided her hand down to the fullness behind his fly.

Carla felt as if every fibre in her being had melted, leaving nothing but a lubricious pool. Her hand closed over the powerfully throbbing rod in his jeans. He followed the downward drift of her gaze, and whispered, 'I want to fuck you.'

They stood together for a second before she broke away, and his hand came across to touch her back lightly in a protective gesture as they walked on.

The stalls were golden with lemons, and green with cucumbers, olives and lettuces. A cool scent lifted off them, a combination of night dew and sunshine.

'Supplies,' Josh said. 'We're going to need some on the boat.'

'And how long do you propose keeping me there?' she asked, shivering as she thought of long, sunfilled days and purple, moonlit nights where, on a deck or in a little cabin below, he would fulfil his desire and hers.

'Depends,' he responded maddeningly. 'It's not only for you. The crew will be hungry. There's a lot of work to be done today.'

He bought fruit and fish and breadsticks. Without a by-your-leave, he piled plastic bags into her arms and proceeded to the butchers' stalls – all scrubbed slabs

139

and razor-sharp cleavers. Carcasses drooped from large hooks, adding the smell of fresh blood to the conglomeration of other odours. He placed his order in a swift spate of Greek, and came away with a bunch of skewers twined with heavily spiced slices of lamb.

'I can't carry any more,' Carla declared, already hot and certainly bothered, more by the proximity of this man who was riding over her roughshod than by the sun blazing like a molten disc in a cloudless blue sky.

'You won't have to. We're nearly through.'

'I'd like to buy some postcards ... haven't had the opportunity to get down here,' she said, wondering if passers by took them for a married couple shopping for food. Certainly, she felt like that in some respects.

'Writing home?'

'Yes, the parents. So far I've only phoned them to let them know I arrived.'

'Proud of you, are they?'

'Not especially.'

'So you're always trying to prove yourself?'

'I guess so,' she conceded. He asked far too many questions, and all of them to the point.

He found her a giftshop, saying, 'I'll take the bags. Meet me on the quay,' and then loped off.

She watched him go, wide shoulders under a blue cotton shirt narrowing to a slim waist, lean hips and a perfectly formed tight arse under those tatty stonewashed jeans. His hair snaked into an untidy ponytail and she wanted to see it loosened, brushing across her belly as he advanced his mouth towards her clit. Pulling herself together and trying to ignore the seam of her shorts chafing her moist secret lips, she headed towards the postcard stand.

Later, she found Josh on the jetty in the company of a loose-limbed giant with the physique of his African warrior ancestors. He was wearing khaki trousers slung low on his hips, and a backward facing baseball cap.

'This is Luke, my diving buddy. Luke, meet Carla,' Josh said, and then he pointed to a schooner riding at anchor beyond a jumble of spars and masts. 'And that's *Sea Jade*.'

'It sure is, and she's jealous as hell. So you better watch out if you're planning on coming aboard,' Luke warned, grinning down at Carla. His features were broad and handsome, though his nose had been broken at some time.

An American, she decided, not a West Indian. 'You have to have a buddy when you dive?' she asked Josh.

'We always go in pairs.'

'Safer that way,' added Luke, undisguised in his admiration of her, his liquid brown eyes going over her breasts and down to the apex of her thighs. 'I'd sure like to be your buddy.'

'I've never done it . . . diving, I mean.'

'And you won't be learning today,' Josh said crisply. 'I'll start you in a pool.'

So, this was not to be a one-off meeting? He was charismatic, appealing, and the heat of his cock through the denim had made her wet. But let's see how it goes, she thought. Once I didn't understand Marie when she said, 'Hon, if you don't reach forty without becoming a cynic, then you've never been in love,' but now I do.

She shaded her eyes with one hand and stared at *Sea Jade*. It was painted white, with an old-fashioned figure-head above the bowsprit, and looked like a toy on that vast expanse of blue.

A dinghy powered by an outboard motor took them to the ship. Luke steered, while Carla clung on like grim death. The only boat she had ever ventured into had been a punt on the lake in the park.

Sea Jade grew bigger, her sides towering over the dinghy. Luke swarmed up a dangling rope-ladder and

Josh helped Carla negotiate the tricky bit between the swaying dinghy and the schooner's deck. This over, she began to enjoy it.

The view was spectacular: Paxia and its terraces, and groves of gnarled olive trees against a backdrop of misty blue mountains. She met the skipper, the mate, six other sailors and the diving crew, and smiled inwardly. Marie, Ruth and Leandra would have been in their element, surrounded by such hunks, all bursting with virility. The air quivered with testosterone.

The deck was neatly stacked with equipment necessary for underwater exploration. Everything was in its place; lives might be lost through carelessness. It became very apparent that Josh was an exacting taskmaster when it came to diving. After the first introductions, Carla was left very much to her own devices.

The ship could be powered by canvas or engine. The bay was not far enough to warrant manning the sails, so after weighing anchor, they chugged in that direction. The anchor was dropped again near a marker buoy, the boat's motor set in neutral, and a blue and white 'Diver Down' flag displayed to warn other vessels to keep their distance.

Josh and Luke prepared themselves. They stripped to trunks, and Carla watched, disappointed when their sinewy bodies were covered by wetsuits. It was a serious business, the backup crew assisting, and finally Josh blew her a kiss before his mouth was obscured by the mouthpiece. Then he dropped head first over the side and disappeared from view, Luke with him.

Carla, who had brought her black bikini, was not about to waste the sun. She oiled herself and found a corner out of everyone's way but in a spot where she could see Josh return, bold enough to slip off the bikini top when she turned over to tan her back.

The dive went on all day. Josh and Luke surfaced and

were relieved by another pair. Josh rolled down his wetsuit to below the waist and came over to Carla.

'Did you find anything?' she asked, pushing her sunglasses up on her forehead. She was on her back now, but with the two tiny black triangles placed decorously over her breasts.

'Yep,' he said, sounding pleased. 'You'll see soon. We shall be sending some up in nets.' And he reached out to lift aside one triangle as he bent over her, wet droplets falling from his hair, his mouth lowered to suck her nipple.

The work went on, with a brief pause when the cook brought food from the galley, and then the talk was of the finds – excited talk, for it seemed they had struck lucky.

Carla left her sunbathing pitch when the first net was carefully manhandled aboard. Those receiving it gingerly untangled the objects, placing some in a bath of nitric acid to clean off fine particles and growths, while glass, wood, leather and bone were washed and then dunked in tubs of distilled water.

'There's no shortcut,' Josh explained during one of his rest periods, times that were becoming increasingly taut as he could not resist caressing her. 'Excavating is a slow process. The sand has to be sifted to minimise damage. These bits we've found so far won't look like much until they're pieced together.'

Her body quivered under his delicate touch, and her respect for him went up in leaps and bounds. He remained absolutely calm, spending hours in this painstaking work, and it was getting dark when he called a halt.

'That will do for today. Well done, all. We've made a good start, better than I anticipated. I'll take these fragments of what looks like a pottery vase to show George Pavlos, and that beautiful little ivory figure,' he went

143

on, while a crew member unbuckled the harness and took the weight of the aqualung.

Carla had been permitted to examine the statue, thrilled to know it had lain under the sea for centuries. She had shared the excitement of the divers every time a fresh object appeared in the net, and longed to go down herself.

Josh went into his cabin, and emerged in jeans and T-shirt, his wet hair loosened, just as she had hoped it would be. 'Wow, it's a relief to get out of that wetsuit,' he exclaimed.

'I know, man. It squashes your prick and balls, don't it?' Luke answered. 'But it's mighty warm, and you can take a leak in it if you have to.'

'Sleep aboard tonight,' Josh said.

'Sure, boss.'

'Set up a watch. We don't want trouble with any snoopers.'

'They'll be the ones in trouble,' Luke remarked, flexing his spadelike hands.

Carla wondered what to expect. Would Josh return her to the villa?

But when they reached the jetty, he almost raced her up the steps towards the truck. 'Where are we going?' she panted.

'To my house,' he answered, and the look on his face was like wine and fire to her. 'I've been waiting all day to fuck you.'

Chapter 8

VEHICLES HAD BEEN arriving from the airport throughout the day. Two large vans had parked round the back of the Villa Artemis, off-loading equipment. A lorry rumbled up, carrying scenery, props and costumes. The wardrobe mistress, make-up, first camera man and his minions had travelled in a couple of jeeps.

Three minibuses had disgorged support actors. Now a sleek limousine braked smoothly and the oldest and most distinguished member of the cast stepped out. He was accompanied by his secretary, the formidable Miss Willis, a gargoyle of a lady who saw it as her bounden duty to shield him from life's vicissitudes.

Leandra ignored her, descending on him with hands outstretched, her voice a throaty purr as she murmured, 'Gerald, darling ... or should I say "Sir Gerald"? Congratulations!'

'Leandra, my pet, thank you, thank you. It was a great honour and I feel myself unworthy. The Queen, so gracious, said how much she had enjoyed my last film. The flight was terrible. The bloody plane was late leaving Athens,' he responded in his famous, rolling, RADA voice, giving her a peck on either cheek. 'How the devil are you?'

'The circus is in town,' Marie remarked from her perch on the balustrade. 'Where are you going to put them all, Rutger?'

'Around and about,' he replied confidently. 'I've had caravans installed, and the villa has elastic walls. Wardrobe and catering are being housed in marquees in the garden. We've had tampon and condom machines hung in the Portaloos. A horde of extras will come streaming in tomorrow. They'll find their own accommodation – mostly locals anyway – with a few itinerants thrown in.'

'Some organisation. Rather you than me,' Marie commented, then waved to several thespians whom she included on her Christmas card list. 'It's going to be one hell of a party.'

'They can leave partying out till we've finished shooting,' he said sternly, wearing his director's head. 'I want them in rehearsal right away. We did several try-outs in London, but Robin and I have made a few alterations to the script. Now where's Gary Kenyon? The sodding leading man, and he can't even bother to get here on time.'

'I reckon that's him now,' she said, as a low, shapely Porsche glided to a stop, and an incredibly handsome man got out, long of limb and with classically perfect features.

There was that unmistakable, hungry murmur from the onlookers in response to the sheer animal magnetism that breathed through his pores. A little gaggle of starlets advanced on him, uttering welcoming squeals.

Rutger smiled darkly, and went to meet him.

Marie settled back to enjoy the show. This was not her particular end of the entertainment business, and she could take it or leave it. Rutger did not expect her to get involved, so she was free to wander about, amused by these film folk who lived on another planet, far removed from ordinary mortals.

The technicians were dressed in jeans and sweat-shirts. A blasé, hard-drinking, hard-living bunch, they lounged around the terrace, getting through innumerable cigarettes and cups of coffee. As soon as Rutger had done with them, giving orders for an early start next morning, they rushed off in search of *ouzo*.

A plethora of beautiful people remained, the minor members of the cast, some dozen in all. Though it was late by the time Rutger called a halt to the rehearsal, no one seemed tired, an undercurrent of excitement coursing through the villa like an electric charge.

Subdued lighting illumined the terrace, and bulbs lit up the pool from below water level. All the warm scents of the sun-baked earth stole over the garden, adding to the fragrance of lemon, jasmine and verbena that wafted from the ornamental hanging baskets. It seduced the mind and inflamed the senses.

Food was served outdoors. Those in the privileged position of hobnobbing with the director and his stars hung around, eating, drinking in moderation and talking – always talking. The air vibrated with gossip concerning 'the business'.

Leandra had decided that Gary should be her first course. She was wearing a fiendishly expensive outfit consisting of a tight white bustier with cloudy black chiffon frills at the half-cups supporting her breasts, which were bared to the nipples. Double flounces of the same flimsy material sprang out from the dropped waistline to reach the division of her legs. The tops of her thighs were exposed, the holdup stockings reaching half way.

Gerald Drew, who was to play Zeus in the film, had cornered Robin. The word was that he liked to roger men, the younger and prettier the better. Robin could not be called pretty, but he was overawed by Gerald, impressed by his recent elevation to the peerage, and such worship was extremely flattering. Within a short time, they had withdrawn to a shadowed section of the terrace.

'Marie!' Leandra sang out. 'Coming for a swim?' Her throat was banded by a necklace of glittering jet, and chandelier jet earrings swung against the bright fall of her silky hair.

Marie dropped down beside her at the pool's tiled edge, and after folding back her skirt fastidiously, dangled her feet in the water.

'It's tempting,' she conceded.

'Tempting? It's irresistible!' Leandra enthused, her eyes sparkling. Defying Rutger, she had been knocking back the champagne. She slid into the pool with a splash, careless of her costly outfit.

'Oh, Leandra! Your dress!' Marie exclaimed.

'So what?' Leandra said lightly. 'Clothes are to be enjoyed, not kept in glass cases. I love the effect of the wet bodice. It's gone transparent. Look, Gary!' she called as he sank to his heels, smiling down at her, giving her the full benefit of the impressive package at the front closure of his chinos.

'Get your kit off,' she ordered. 'Come in. Ever had a bonk in a pool? No? Then you haven't lived, boy.'

There was a thread of sensual awareness winding through the conversation, clear and unmistakable. Marie's body reacted to it, but not to Gary. He was too conventionally good-looking, the archetypal film star.

He took up Leandra's dare, and started to undress with all the controlled grace of an actor who started out in ballet. His body was perfectly proportioned, his curling dark hair held back by a sweatband, and he was not in the least embarrassed – indeed, he seemed to revel in displaying himself, and with good reason.

Naked, he was even more spectacular, exceptionally

well endowed, with a beautiful, curving penis and testicles that slithered against each other like plums in a velvet pouch. Everyone watching, male or female, sighed in appreciation and longed to touch, to taste, to feel that remarkable weapon and its attendant cod.

Leandra made no bones about it, going in for the kill. As soon as Gary surfaced from his impressive dive, she leapt upon him, clamping her legs round his waist and impelling him back against the tiled sides, her mouth feeding on his lips. The water sloshed as he raised her with his hands hooked under her buttocks, then brought her straight down on his ramrod-stiff organ. Leandra yelled triumphantly as it penetrated her to the womb, and the spectators cheered and took this as the cue to begin their own amatory activities.

Marie watched without a trace of envy. She was not in the mood to play with a penis tonight, and her eyes raked the rapidly pairing crowd, eventually alighting on a black actress, lean and long-legged, with firm buttocks and breasts like ripe apples. She possessed real dreadlocks, unlike Ruth's white-girl's attempt, and her night-black hair was braided into a hundred tight little plaits tipped with gold wire and multicoloured beads. She looked like a tribal queen. Marie knew that her name was Carmel Foster – sometime model, mostly TV actress. Marie had crossed glances with her at several functions in the past, and that unspoken message had flashed between them: someday we'll get it together.

Carmel, moving with the liquid grace of a cheetah, weaved between the tables, lovers, and stone urns spewing flowers, and came to rest beside her. 'Hello,' she said, in a voice like syrup running over chocolate mousse.

'Hello yourself,' Marie replied, and her bare arm pressed against the dusky one.

Carmel was tall and fine-boned. She stalked, rather

than walked, moving as if to inner music, every muscle honed. She had high cheekbones over which the skin flowed like coffee cream, slanting brown eyes, a short nose, and plum-coloured lips, full and luscious. Her breasts – crowned by pronounced nipples surrounded by sepia areolae the size of saucers – jutted through the thin, short dress she wore. As Marie edged nearer, she could smell cinnamon on Carmel's breath and sniff the warm, musky odour escaping from between her dark brown legs.

Carmel rested her fingers on Marie's knee, the almond-shaped nails painted fuchsia pink. 'Can't we go somewhere?' she asked, and her other hand came across to nestle Marie's breast in her palm.

There was only one place where Marie wanted to go, and that was her bed. She needed peace in which to enjoy Carmel, no interruptions on that journey which she intended to take through uncharted territory.

They wandered towards the house, hand in hand, unhurried, knowing their arrival in each other's arms was inevitable. Walking silently, they did not disturb Gerald and Robin whom they came across in an alcove.

The author was on his knees, his shorts removed, his bare bottom pallid compared to his back and legs. He was thrusting his buttocks backwards and holding his cheeks wide apart with both hands, offering his anus to Gerald. Positioned behind him, the older man gripped his large stiff cock and rolled a condom over the red helm and up the shaft. He then added a generous smear of lubricating jelly.

Robin's breathing quickened and he thrust his hips eagerly towards the knight's rubber-coated spear. Gerald eased the tip past the tight ring, then drove it straight in, gripping Robin's hips and holding him tight against his corpulent belly as he plundered the forbidden valley of his body.

He reached forward with one hand and rubbed Robin's erect and waving prick in time to the in-and-out thrusts of his own weapon. Their movements became more frantic, both men grunting in effort. Then Robin gave a sudden cry as milky semen shot from his cock, creaming Gerald's hand and hitting the rug on which they knelt. Gerald slammed his penis into Robin's arse, emitted a bellow that would have pulverised his audience when he gave them King Lear, and knelt there letting the final spasms of ejaculation shudder through him. Then he slumped over Robin's body, and the young man collapsed under him, both of them apparently spent.

Marie and Carmel crept away.

The bedroom became a paradise. Marie liked men, but had long ago concluded that the lover is not only the one who opens the body, but also the one who fills a space in one's heart. Women were usually gentle with other women, not like men, who seemed obsessed with penetrating and possessing.

The candlelight lent Carmel's dark skin a delicate sheen, and Marie stroked her softly, inhaling the distinctive warm aroma of her intimate parts. Naked, they quietly explored the secret nooks and crannies of their bodies. They lay voluptuously on one another, rubbing their nipples against each other's velvety skin, thrusting their pelvises and loins together so that their mounds met, sensitive vulvas touching, to be replaced by fingers and lips and tongues seeking the inner petals, pistils and cores.

Marie bent over her sultry love, relishing the smell and taste of her, exotic and strange, admiring her huge dark eyes, her ebony hair, her tiny nose, slightly flattened so that the nostrils flared, her dazzling white teeth and beautiful, rapacious lips. Slowly, she passed her hands over the dark breasts, and sucked those hard nipples into her mouth. Carmel lay on her back and spread her legs, lifting her pelvis so Marie could see every one of her female secrets.

Her cleft was enchanting, the shape of the inner lips hidden by the outer ones, and of a brown-pink colour that merged into a delicate blue-black at her anus and labial rim. Her bush was a dense, dark forest, with fronds curling between her legs, and her clitoris large and swollen with excitement, the stalk long, the head fiery – unspeakably beautiful.

She came very quickly against Marie's tongue, her juices running copiously, wetting her lover's mouth. Instantly she twisted, agile as a cat, and her own tongue fastened on Marie's love-bud, sucking and licking till she, too, spiralled into a mind-blowing climax.

They did not leave, but remained in their silken haven for a long time, repeating the experience, finding other thrilling ways in which to pleasure each other as no one else could.

When Josh and Carla stepped through the ornamental, crumbling gateway, it was like going back in time. He switched on an outside light and conducted her along a weedy path through the neglected, terraced garden to a shuttered, stone-built mansion.

'Is this a hotel?' she asked, clinging to his hand.

'No, it's mine,' he said, and taking a key from his hip-pocket he inserted it in one of the double wooden doors standing under a stone arch carved with lions' heads. 'It's Venetian,' he explained. 'They were in the islands for years, heavy dudes during the Renaissance . . . They left their architecture and influence, though the people tend to forget and call it all Turkish.'

'What do you want with a house this size?' Carla asked, as they walked into a gargantuan hall.

He shrugged, saying, 'It was going for a song. I

couldn't really refuse. I like it. It has a wonderful atmosphere. You can almost see the Venetian merchant who built it – a powerful man, maybe working for an even more powerful prince. He'd have had his own galley moored down in the harbour, the oars manned by prisoners whom he had bought to be slaves.'

'You're a dreamer,' she said, amused by this chink in his armour.

'You better believe it,' he agreed, and grinned. Then he slipped an arm round her waist and touched her lips with his other hand. She opened her mouth and sucked in his fingers, tasting the salt of the sea, the hint of tobacco, even the plastic-coated steering wheel, all the things he had touched that day, including his cock. She ran her tongue over each long, strong digit until he removed his fingers and replaced them with his lips.

His kiss was warm and deep and satisfying, and he did not stop kissing her till they had both tasted and explored, flirted and toyed with tongues and lips. While he kissed her, he stroked her breasts through the jersey cloth, skirting the nipples that were rising into hard peaks.

He removed his lips from hers and, still holding her, walked on. He switched on shaded electric lamps as he brought her straight to the bedroom, in no mood for a conducted tour. That would come later. The room was huge, with a balcony, frescoed walls, a tiled floor and an atmosphere steeped in the past. The bed was massive, a great state bed from sixteenth-century Italy. They fell into it, across it, tearing at each other's clothes.

Carla pushed his shirt open, her hands against his naked chest, the light hairs like silk, and he tugged at her T-shirt, dragging it over her head, then unzipped her shorts and eased them down. Now she wore only a tiny pair of panties, the strip between her legs wet with love-juice. She pressed her pelvis against him, arching her spine as his lips trailed from the lobe of her ear to her throat and then down to fasten on each nipple in turn.

She cried out, her hands gripping his head, holding him to her breast as if he were a suckling infant. Her nipples were engorged, and her labia swelled in sympathy, her clitoris a pouting knot of flesh. Reaching for his belt, she unbuckled it, then fumbled with the fly buttons. His jeans opened and he stood up in order to pull them off.

Opening her eyes, she watched him in the apricot glow of the antique wall lamps. She had viewed his body that day, admired and lusted after it. He was lean, with deeply etched muscles – his occupation did not encourage fat. Not very hairy either, only a sprinkling on his chest, running down to his navel and then spreading out to join the curling nest from which his erect phallus sprang.

He came back to her, bending over to caress her belly, remove her panties, and explore her depths. His heavy penis nudged her ankles as he burrowed between her legs, his saliva mixing with her juices as he licked her folds and sucked her clitoris. She moaned and writhed, her hips rising off the bed and he inserted two fingers in her vagina and moved them in a rotating motion, while flicking her nub with his thumb.

She could feel orgasm hovering, and waited for the next sensuous glide of his thumb, her breath shortening as she whispered, 'Oh, yes . . . that's perfect . . . More . . . give me a little more!'

The pulse in her core knotted, then exploded, cascading through her in a torrent. She shuddered as the spasms shook her and then he entered her, plunging in hard, and she screamed in ecstasy as her inner walls convulsed round his pulsating shaft.

He had pleasured her completely and she displayed

her gratitude by thrusting against him, kicking her legs up round his body and drawing him deeper into her darkness. He bent down so that his head was buried in her neck, slowing his movements to prolong the waves pulsing through her. She felt him shudder as he silently spent himself inside her.

He moved his weight away, rolling on his side, propping himself on one elbow and smiling at her, his hand stroking her cheek. 'You're lovely,' he said.

She almost gurgled with pleasure. This was so right: no crude turning over and snoring, as Giles had usually done. Josh, though tough, was a caring, well-mannered man who would not have dreamed of treating her so shoddily. The affair might not last – he probably showed the same consideration to all his lovers, but just for the moment, Carla was the one being pampered.

'We'll go out to eat presently,' he said.

'Must we?' she asked, yawning and stretching. 'It's nice here.'

'I could try the kitchen, I suppose,' he offered, folding the pillow against the carved and inlaid bedhead and lying back against it as he smoked a cigarette. 'I've a caretaker, a solid and trustworthy Greek lady who lives in a little house near the gate with her husband. He's supposed to do the garden, but I'm not here much. I guess he keeps the jungle at bay. She may have put something in the fridge for me. No doubt she saw the ship dock. Nothing escapes her beady eyes.'

'And what will she think when she sees the state of the bed?' Carla asked, filled with a languorous sense of well-being.

He reached out to caress her nipple. 'Nothing,' he said.

'She's used to you bringing women back here?' Jealousy pricked her. She did not like the idea that he had shared this magnificent couch with anyone else.

He laughed and sat up, then stubbed out his

cigarette. 'She minds her own business,' he said pointedly. He got up and padded over to a table with bulbous legs ending in lions' feet. He lifted the decanter standing on a silver salver and poured a little of the contents into two goblets, then returned to the bed carrying them.

'I want you to try this. Have you had Citron before?'

'No.' She shook the hair back from her face and pulled herself into a sitting position, aware of that tenderness between her legs which is the hallmark of a good screw.

Josh resumed his place on the bed, holding the goblet to the light and admiring the yellow liquid as he said, 'This is a marvellous distillation. It's a liqueur, and when you drink it you hold in your mouth the quintessence of a lemon grove . . . the pale breasts of the fruit, the dark green of the leaves, and the perfume that rises from the bruised peel.'

He *is* a dreamer and a romantic, she thought, and she savoured the liqueur and later savoured the rough, male taste of him again, both experiences unique and to be treasured. She wished that the whole perfect day could somehow be bottled, so that she might lift the stopper and take a sniff whenever she wanted.

'Where were you?' Edward said grumpily down the phone. 'I've been trying to get in touch with you since yesterday.'

'I do have a life of my own, you know,' Carla reminded him briskly. 'And, as far as I am aware, the deal is off.'

'Nonsense. Patience is all that's required, and he's come round like I knew he would.'

'Well, bully for him,' she said heavily, feeling like a woman reborn and not at all certain that she wanted to take up her pen ever again. Josh had so many more exciting options on offer.

'Look here, I'm terribly sorry,' Edward went on. 'But he really wants to see you. I think you impressed him the other night.'

'He didn't impress me,' she countered. 'Mouth-fucking Krista in front of me.'

'Oh, lord, he didn't do that, did he?' Edward groaned.

'Yes, he did. I've never been so embarrassed in my life! It's not good enough,' she complained, but with a desire to giggle.

The pompous manager sounded as if he was squirming. Let him, she thought. Let 'em all squirm. He needs me and I'm going to play hard to get.

'I can't apologise enough, Carla. He's so temperamental, unhinged at times. Ninety per cent temper and ten per cent mental. Will you reconsider? I'll make it worth your while.'

'Upping the offer? You'll have to ring Toby.'

'Can I tell him that you're thinking about it?'

'OK.'

'I'll get back to you when we've talked.'

'Right.' Carla laid down the receiver and went off to swim.

She soon grew curious about the influx of people who had appeared during her absence. Marie was walking around looking smug, her new companion a gorgeous black woman whose legs went on for ever. A harassed Ruth was trying to get some sense out of Marie and make her answer a letter from her publisher concerning a deadline.

'She's bloody cunt-struck!' she grumbled, when she bumped into Carla. 'Thinks she's a law unto herself, but they won't wait for ever. She might at least try to send them the first couple of chapters.'

Meanwhile Leandra was throwing a tantrum in the wardrobe department, and Robin was being monopolised by a large, grey-haired actor with a booming voice, who seemed to spend a lot of time avoiding his martinet of a secretary. Rutger asked Carla if she would like to be an extra, Gary Kenyon tried to chat her up, and all in all, she wasn't sure that she wanted to be incarcerated with Angelo Lorenzo when there was so much going on here.

A raise in stakes, though? That might persuade her. Toby would work out the best deal on her behalf.

The phone rang in her room as she stood there naked, oily and sun-browned after a wonderfully relaxed afternoon. 'I've spoken to Toby,' Edward said, and he sounded even more aggrieved. 'You'll get a further four thousand. How about it?'

'Will tomorrow morning suit you?'

'Not tonight?'

'I'm busy tonight,' Carla said, and clicked the amber beads round her neck. She had a date with Josh.

'And so, Miss Holt, you and I work together, eh?' Angelo said when she came to the villa next morning. He rose from a long cane chair placed in the shade on the vine-draped loggia and bowed over her hand.

'It seems that way, Mr Lorenzo,' she replied, equally formal, while thinking: this is ridiculous. I've held the man's cock in my palm, he's felt me all over, kissed me, fucked me . . . And here we are behaving like strangers.

'I know nothing about writing,' he said with an ingratiating smile, one she was sure he could turn on at will.

'And I know nothing about singing, only that I love to hear it,' she returned.

'Then that makes us equal.'

'It does.'

It was early. Josh had dropped her off before he went out to *Sea Jade*. She had showered with him in the antiquated bathroom at his mansion, but tepid water and an erratic jet had not mattered when he was there to soap her between the legs and lather her breasts, then take her standing up, her back against the slippery tiles.

They had breakfasted in a taverna, and she had not wanted to leave him. The last thing she needed was to spend the day in the company of a difficult operatic tenor. But now, sneaking glances at Angelo, she had to admit he was devastatingly attractive.

He wore a pair of tight black Armani jeans and a V-necked vest without sleeves. His skin glowed, naturally swarthy but rendered even darker by hours spent in the sun. His hair had the sheen of a raven's wing, and his eyes were peat-brown, with that luminous, melancholic softness bequeathed to those of Mediterranean birth.

Angelo lay back in his seat while a servant – not Krista, she was relieved to see, but an elderly woman – brought in coffee. Carla did not know what to say to him; she was tongue-tied just when she most wanted to make an impression, to be full of sparkling conversation. Though Josh had more than satisfied her, not once but several times over the past few hours, she was aware of a wayward throb in her womanhood when she looked at Angelo.

'How shall we start?' he said suddenly, and for a moment she imagined he referred to love-making.

She pulled herself together, stammering, 'Oh, ah, that is . . . I've never done this before.'

His smile widened and his eyes twinkled. 'Neither have I, Miss Holt. We are two virgins, no?'

Her cheeks were hot, but she managed to return his smile, 'Not quite, I think.'

'You are an author, so Edward tells me. You have had books published. This is an achievement which should make you proud,' he said, and she suddenly found herself becoming easier with him. When he chose, Angelo could charm the birds out of the trees.

'Nothing stupendous,' she hedged, and wished she had worn something more sexy, instead of opting for a long white cotton skirt and a pin-tucked camisole.

'You are too modest,' he averred, and she wondered if he was remembering just how immodest she had been in the woods.

'Let's begin, shall we?' she suggested, turning from the subject that was threatening to send her hormones into orbit.

'Where?' he asked, and moved his chair closer to hers.

'At the beginning, I suppose,' she said, having ferreted through her mind for information about what shape such a work should take. She had read several autobiographies, including a couple by singers. Could she use this format?

'Very well. I was born . . .' he began, with a dramatic gesture.

'Yes, but where?' This is not going to be easy, she thought.

'Who knows? I was brought up in an orphanage.'

'But you had the voice? Someone must have encouraged you to sing.'

'The nuns were good. I sang in the choir, then my voice broke. It was time for me to leave and find work. I had no money, no prospects, little education. This was Milan, nearly twenty years ago. Then I got a job as a waiter in a restaurant near La Scala, the opera house.'

'I have heard of it,' she said dryly.

'I used to spend all my money on seats for performances,' he said eagerly. 'It was my life – that and football, and girls, of course.'

'Football?' This was something of a disappointment.

'Sure. I love to watch Juventus play. Don't you?'

'I've never really – well, no, it doesn't float my boat,' she confessed.

'I might have been a football player,' he said with a touch of regret. 'But something happened. I met Genevra Scoville.'

'I have some of her recordings. She was a brilliant *Tosca*.'

'The role suited her,' he agreed and his good humour vanished, a dark scowl settling on his brow. 'It demands a display of passion and jealousy of which she has too much.'

'I don't understand,' Carla said, baffled. 'You're going too fast.'

He seized her hands in his and held them tightly against his chest, his voice vibrant as he said, 'Stop this play-acting, Carla. We have made love. I was disappointed when I thought you had been insincere, but then I realised that I might have misjudged you and agreed with Edward that I should tell you my story. Just for now, listen to what I have to say. We can put it in order later. I need to talk to you . . . Please.'

His touch seemed to burn through her, igniting her fire. All the wonder and rapture she had felt on that first, fatal meeting, flooded back. 'Tell me, Angelo,' she said softly.

The night was mild, and Milan throbbed with life and laughter and music, for those wealthy enough to enjoy them. Angelo was late arriving in the kitchen and the chef ranted at him, that fiery little despot who ruled the staff with a rod of iron.

Angelo did not argue. He needed to keep this job. It enabled him to live in a tiny attic room in a poor quarter of the city. He could feed himself with leftovers from the restaurant, and keep his meagre wages to buy the cheapest seats at the opera house and pay old Maestro Calvi for singing lessons.

Angelo did not intend to spend the rest of his life as

161

a waiter. He knew what he wanted to do, inspired by the sights and sounds of La Scala. He was going to be an opera singer – a great opera singer – greater even than the late lamented tenor, Mario Lanza, that Hollywood idol of the fifties whom he saw at the cinema whenever those old films were screened, and he could afford a ticket.

Maestro Calvi said he was a natural. He had faith in him, but was not soft. 'You must work, my boy,' he said. 'Work, work, work. Scales to stretch the voice. It's like any other muscle, and must be exercised. Here – musical scores. Learn them, read them. I'll help you. The Almighty has touched you with his little finger and told you to sing. Who will dare go against God?'

And then she came into the restaurant. The manager was in a ferment. 'The diva has booked a table,' he said, flapping. 'The divine Scoville! Hurry, hurry! A clean cloth, flowers, music, the finest silver . . .'

She took one look at Angelo who was waiting at table, and said, 'What do you do besides this? You can't tell me you don't have any other ambition.'

He gazed into her wide-spaced, heavily painted eyes under the dark wings of her brows, smelled her expensive French perfume, noted the elegance of her gown, sensed the sexual hunger of the body within it and said, 'I am a tenor, madame.'

He left with her, and they went back to her apartment. In the cab, he felt her hand slipping into his shirt, her long fingers seeking his nipples. His cock throbbed against her leg, and he wanted her and all she could give him, this powerful, talented, influential woman.

In the lift, she pressed against him, her arms clasping him close. He drowned in her perfume as she kissed him, her tongue winding round his as he explored that mouth from which he had heard the most heavenly notes pour forth. The glamour of Genevra blinded him, and her apartment stunned his senses: it resembled a film set, and he thought for a moment he must be dreaming.

'Later, you shall sing for me,' Genevra said. She poured wine into cut-glass flutes, lifted one to her scarlet lips and licked the rim with her tongue. 'But now, Angelo, you will make love to me.'

She dropped her blue mink coat on a gilt chair, and raised her hands to her breasts, plucking at her nipples through the silver lurex gown, watching him and smiling.

'You want me?' She reached out, feeling his cock through the shabby black trousers. He could not speak. His pulse drummed in his head, his phallus rose, so full, needy, and throbbing with seed, that he feared this might be over before he had begun.

Genevra gave a low, throaty laugh and slowly lifted her skirt. She was no longer young, but her legs were beautiful, sheathed in black silk stockings; her high heels made her ankles arch and her calves bulge. Black and gilt suspenders were clipped to her thighs and, as the skirt rode higher, Angelo could see the dark triangle of pubic hair and the heavy lips between, swollen and pink and ready for him.

Her fingers played with the thick bush, and slid into the moisture seeping from her delta. Then she advanced her hand and smeared his lips with her nectar. 'Come to bed,' she said.

'So you see, I started out as a gigolo, a kept man, Genevra Scoville's plaything. I never returned to my room or the restaurant or my dear old Maestro Calvi,' Angelo concluded, and his breathing was ragged, his body aroused by recounting this story to Carla.

'Don't say that,' she protested. 'You'd never have made it if you hadn't been talented. She opened the

163

door, that's all. Then it was up to you.'

'That's true,' he agreed, and some of the tension left him. 'An Italian audience knows the operas note for note, word for word. You can't fool them, and they soon let you know if they're displeased.'

'There you are, then,' she said, happy to have comforted him in some way.

'But there's more to tell,' he said darkly. 'This isn't the end of the story . . . Genevra has come back to torment me. She will ruin me if she can. I told you she was jealous, and this was an understatement. She still wants me, Carla, body and soul, and doesn't care what methods she uses to gain her end.'

Chapter 9

'*AND WHAT HAPPENED* after your first meeting?' Carla asked Angelo when they had stopped for a light lunch, followed by a swim. They rested on towel-draped loungers by the pool, and she kept her tanga firmly in place, risking paler stripes on her tan, but only tiny ones. The triangle of ecru cotton crochet was minis-cule.

It made her uncomfortable to think of displaying her depilated mons to Angelo. She was there on business and determined to keep it that way, though the disclo-sures he had made were arousing. She was aware of the slow, secret pulse of her body and the warm breeze caressing her naked nipples.

They were playing the game of assessment. Furtive, cautious, neither was willing to make the first move, yet both were drawn by invisible threads of sizzling attrac-tion. Her eyes went covertly to the plump finger of his phallus, clearly etched against the wet pouch, so tight she could see the ridge of his foreskin.

While in the water, she had tried to keep away from contact with his brown, muscular limbs, sticking to the shallows while he sported in the deep end. Yet it seemed that the power of his aura had caused tremors like an undersea earthquake, rippling towards her, stroking and caressing, almost as if he had touched her physically.

'You want to know more of my life?' he queried, his face turned towards her. The tinted glasses he wore gave him an oddly sinister aspect. It was impossible to read his eyes.

'It's time you got it off your chest,' she advised, attempting to be practical.

Angelo rested his head back and stared at the sky, visions and memories clouding his mind.

'And where have you studied?'

'Nowhere,' Angelo answered, trembling before that upright old woman, Madame Alboni, doyenne among teachers, and Genevra's trainer. She was renowned, a formidable lady in whose presence even the most experienced singers were reduced to students. He had just sung for her, cockily attempting 'Celeste Aida', a testing Verdi aria.

They were in a large practice room at the prestigious conservatoire where she held master classes. He was alone with her, but for Genevra and an accompanist, who was stoop-shouldered and bespectacled, and well used to singers, fledgling or otherwise.

'Don't lie,' Madame Alboni snapped imperiously, banging on the floor with her walking-stick. 'I can hear that you've studied. Your voice has been trained.'

'I've always sung like this. The only help I've had has been from Maestro Calvi, an old friend.'

'I told you Angelo was remarkable, didn't I, madame?' Genevra stated, regal in white-brimmed hat and a chiffon dress. He knew that she wore no panties under it; she had demonstrated this in the car on the way there. He had been too nervous to manage an erection, but Genevra had merely opened her legs and grabbed his hand, placing it on her damp mound. He had slipped a finger along her fleshy avenue and rubbed it, embarrassed lest the chauffeur should glance in the driving mirror and see them on the back seat, to say nothing of people looking through the windows in passing cars.

Genevra had enjoyed a noisy orgasm just before they reached their destination, pulled her skirt down, rearranged her hat, and swept Angelo in to meet her teacher. All through his rendition of the aria he had caught the pungent fragrance of Genevra's juices that lingered on his fingers.

Madame Alboni went to the door and called in a colleague, a large, bearded man who looked more like a sea-captain than a singing coach. 'Now,' she commanded Angelo. 'Sing it again.'

The upshot had been that she took him on, impressed by his natural ability, though short on praise. Genevra was torn between jealousy of his youth and talent, well aware that hers was on the wane, and the need to possess and control her young lover – and use him to give a boost to her career.

Her influence was considerable, and he was excessively ambitious. Madame Alboni gave no quarter, saying, 'We must work on breathing, to loosen your diaphragm.'

He worked like one possessed. Not only with his breath control, but also learning to relax his tongue, his lower jaw and larynx.

'Ah, darling, your mouth,' Genevra sighed when he tested this new looseness on her darkly furred crevice. 'It was fine before, but now! It's so wonderful ... You are wonderful.'

He raised his head, resting his chin on her pubic bone and looking across her voluptuous belly, 'And when am I to be launched? When will you let me sing opposite you?'

She smiled into his eyes, pulled him up to cover her with his lithe, strong body, and whispered, 'You're nearly ready. I've talked to the powers that be, and everything will be arranged. Leave it to me, my precious. We'll be a great team: La Scala, the Paris Opera, Covent Garden, and then New York. We'll take the Metropolitan by storm.'

She thrust her big breasts towards his lips and Angelo took one hard brown teat into his mouth. It tasted of perfume and her pampered skin. His cock stiffened even more, and he worked it between her legs and into the plushy depths of her vagina.

She met his thrusts with her own, and he heard her moan, her lower mouth sucking him in. He shuddered, feeling her violent contractions grasping his penis. Then he was lost, his seed bursting from him as the intensity of climax thundered through his body.

'Genevra was dictatorial, childish, vain and completely impossible, yet her talent was as huge as her sexual appetite,' Angelo said, shifting round to face the sun. The shadows had lengthened across the terrace and soon it would be evening.

'You didn't mind being bossed around by her?' Carla asked, struggling to keep awake. Though this tale was intensely stimulating, the heat made her drowsy and his voice was soporific. 'And what about her being twice your age?'

'I've never minded sleeping with mature women,' he answered frankly, taking a sip from a tumbler of iced squash. 'My analyst says it's because I never knew my mother and am unconsciously seeking her. Genevra's age enhanced her glamour, and she was very well preserved. She had the money to indulge herself. There were always beauticians, hairdressers and masseurs around, no matter where we happened to be, and we travelled world-wide.'

'So why did you break up?'

'The rot set in when I started to become successful in my own right,' he said thoughtfully. 'To begin with, all was well. She wanted to be everything to me, surrogate mother, teacher, manager and whore.'

'She was in love with you,' Carla replied, sitting up and applying more oil to her breasts and shoulders. Poor cow, she thought, an ageing prima donna infatuated with a handsome, gifted tenor young enough to be her son.

He watched her through the tinted glasses and she saw the tension on his face. He stretched out a hand towards the lotion, saying huskily. 'Let me oil your back.'

'No, thank you. That won't be necessary,' she replied, hastily tucking the bottle into her bag. Dear God, I can't let him touch me, the panicky thought rushed through her. If I do we'll be screwing, right here on the tiles.

He retreated, but she could not avoid seeing that the bough slanting across his lower belly had enlarged.

'I was flattered, ambitious. She was the answer to my prayers,' he continued, his hands in ceaseless motion, gestures accompanying his words. 'I never had to worry about money again. Of course, she needed a well-groomed escort, so we shopped. Nothing was too good for me. My clothes were superb, designed by the top fashion houses, and Italy is *numero uno* for men's wear. She bought me silk shirts, gold watches, aftershave, perfume. It gave her a thrill to run her hands over my body, feeling the texture of fine cloth, knowing she had paid for it.'

'So why do you still feel guilty?' Carla said perceptively.

He shrugged. 'Masculine pride?'

'But you brought her great happiness, surely? She had no child to spoil. You fulfilled this role, and made love to her into the bargain.'

'I did my best to please her, but she was very demanding.'

'She made you a star.'

'And I, in return, gave her another ten years of stardom.' His brows swooped into a frown. 'Without me, she would have been finished long before. Even Madame Alboni remarked on the ebullience and perfection of her performances, attributing it to love. The Italians believe in passion, and passion intermingled with music is beyond anything.'

'Music is the greatest,' Carla agreed eagerly, overjoyed to be meeting his mind, head on. 'It relaxes the body and expands the soul.'

'Yes, yes . . . I know,' he responded enthusiastically. 'It banishes fears, sadness and fatigue. I can sing for hours when I'm inspired by a great composer.'

'Just think of violins, which make one's hair stand on end.'

'Or voices. Nothing is more superb than the human voice. Genevra's was heavenly, when she was at her best.'

'It opens up the heart, makes a thousand notes burst from the centre of the universe . . . A thousand colours, a thousand images,' Carla concluded. He really is a great person. I could love this man, and sympathise with Genevra, she thought.

Then his mood changed. 'Passion like ours could not last. Hers was love, but though I admired and respected her talent, mine was not.'

'You used her.'

'We used each other. But trouble started when I became more popular than her. We toured extensively, at the start engaged because of her reputation, but later, on mine. I could draw the crowds. My records were selling, audio tapes, CDs. She was getting older. It was no longer believable for her to play the beautiful Tosca, the frail, consumptive young Mimi, and even more ludicrous when she wanted to continue singing the teenage geisha, Madame Butterfly.'

'But there are more suitable roles, surely? She could have got away with it, using stage make-up and wigs.'

He shook his head. 'Alas, these days directors demand young, slim and lovely divas and Genevra was putting on weight. I'd met Edward Connar by then, and she could no longer control me. I had my own apartment, bought my own clothes and cars, saw her only during working hours or for the occasional night of passion, but those were becoming less frequent. I had other lovers by then, and other leading ladies. There was never a shortage of women. She asked me to marry her, but I refused.'

How cruel, Carla thought, and her former suspicion of him returned. How heartless. That fading star, losing everything, her looks, her voice, the man who had made her young again.

'So you dropped her?' she said, her voice cutting.

He reacted sharply, defending himself. 'Not I – not entirely. The managers of the opera houses dropped her. Her voice was deteriorating. She could no longer sustain a performance, and was losing her high notes. She started to drink, and this didn't help.'

'And you?' You bastard, she thought inwardly, *you* were all right. Your career was on the up and up.

'I had to break with her. There was no other way. I'd been asked to make a film, playing the bandit, Ramerrez, in Puccini's cowboy opera *La Fanciulla del West*. It was to be made by an Australian film director who had already worked for the Sydney Opera House, and he demanded realism.'

'I saw it. I have the video. It's superbly done,' Carla said, recalling the Wild West spectacle, the amazing photography, the natural acting and faultless singing, and Angelo, so well cast as the bandit.

'Genevra wanted to play Minnie, the saloon owner, but they wouldn't even consider it. She asked me to turn my part down. I refused. We had a terrible quarrel and I've not seen her from that day to this. But she rang me last year.' Angelo's voice was shaking with anger.

'What did she want?' Carla held her breath, filled with vague uneasiness, and a half-realised premonition.

'She said she had given up drink and had been training again, strictly and seriously,' Angelo answered. 'She'd been on a diet, too. She suggested that I use my influence to reinstate her, thought she could sing all her old roles again. Wanted to sing with *me*.'

'How sad,' Carla commented. 'Did you feel no pity for her?'

Angelo glared at her as if she were mad. 'She's over sixty now! I told her it was ridiculous. She wouldn't listen, shouting that she had been preparing herself for a come back, but that I had to be involved. When I said no, she reviled me, threatening that if I didn't do as she wanted, she'd talk to journalists. Tell them about our affair and how I had bled her dry. Describe me as an opportunist, a man without honour who had used and abused her.'

'And you still refused?'

'Of course,' he rapped out scornfully. 'I wasn't going to give in to her blackmail. I couldn't. I had my own career to think about. Singing with her would have been a disaster. Everyone would have laughed at me.'

'This threat of hers worried you so much? Why? It's true that she helped you, but the chances are you'd have done it anyway. You have gained your reputation by your own efforts, your own glorious voice. No one can

172

take that away from you.'

He sighed heavily. 'I know, but mud sticks, and I have many rivals, many enemies, many people who envy me. I lost all heart, and fled here. An artiste pays the price by being over-sensitive. I simply could not cope with the fear that she would carry out her threat. I thought that if I removed myself from the operatic circuit she would have no hold over me.'

'But don't you see this is exactly what she wants? To stop you singing. It's such a waste! You can't allow this to happen,' Carla cried, forgetting herself and dropping to her knees beside him. 'Oh, Angelo, listen to me. We'll work something out. Please don't despair. And please, please, don't stop singing.'

He pushed up his glasses and looked into her eyes, saying, 'It means so much to you?'

'Yes, and to thousands of your admirers.'

'That's so sweet,' he whispered and took her hand in his, raising it to his lips but not quite kissing it, hovering in the air above it.

She felt his breath like a scorching wind, heating her to the marrow. Her bare nipples crimped and she wanted him to touch them, but dared make no movement. This was too poignant, too vital a moment for anything to rock it off centre.

'I'll think of some way in which you can write your story and exonerate yourself,' she said, while her breasts ached for his hands and her vulva wept silvery tears, longing for his penis.

'Stay with me,' he urged, his dark eyes aflame.

'I can't,' she said, withdrawing to her seat again.

'There is someone else,' he demanded.

'Not exactly. No commitment, but he is a friend,' she replied, thinking, oh, Josh, I need to be with you, away from this maelstrom of emotion I'm struggling to understand.

'You'll come again tomorrow,' Angelo said angrily, and she could see that he would be a bad loser.

'Not till the afternoon. I'm learning to scuba dive in the morning.'

'And tonight?' So thunderous that scowl, so intense, and furious the flashing eyes and sulky mouth. He was magnificent, and Carla almost regretted ever meeting Josh . . . But there was no doubt that Angelo was trouble with a capital T.

'Tonight Rutger Eberhardt is giving a dinner party to which I'm invited. There is a lot going on at the villa, where they're taking some of the outside shots for his new film, and later I want to make notes of everything you've told me, while it's fresh in my mind.'

'You'll be discreet? You won't repeat any of it?'

'You have my word.'

'And you won't make love with anyone tonight? Edward has told me about the orgies that take place there.'

She could feel a pleased smile tugging at the corners of her mouth. He sounded jealous. 'You, above all people, should know that it's silly to listen to gossip, Angelo,' she said, and prepared to leave.

The room was filled with a fiery light that stole between pillars and across the floor, and crept over the woman sleeping on the divan – a fairy-tale couch where she was cocooned between carved white swans' wings, now turning to rose, to burgundy, to purple.

The scene was mythical and mystical: a beautiful room in a gracious palace belonging to some high-camp civilisation lost in the mists of time. And the naked woman on the bed was the embodiment of all it had achieved, perfect in face and form.

She stirred, sighed, lifted a shapely arm, and the colours changed subtly, becoming deeper, darker, heralding the night and, more than that, the arrival of the enemy who would change her life for ever.

He entered, a tough, broad-shouldered young soldier. His eyes gleamed under the crested helm, his face was stern and streaked with dirt. He carried a short sword, the bloody blade glistening in the rays of the dying sun.

Moving over to the bed, he laid down his sword, crimson smearing the coverlet. He yanked off his helmet to reveal his sweat-soaked hair coiled across his brow and around his neck. He looked at the sleeping woman longingly, devouringly, his eyes bright with lust. One arm shot out. The light sparked off his wide damascened wrist-guard. His hand closed over her bare breast, and she woke, started, screamed.

They struggled. The sheet slipped off, revealing her rose-pink nipples, her breasts, thighs, and a quick, tantalising flash of her brownish-blonde bush. He straddled her, his white tunic riding up to display his firm, nude buttocks. His back- and breastplates gleamed in the now lurid light, symbols of his warlike occupation.

He was the conquerer and she the vanquished. He gripped her wrists, held her arms wide and with a grim laugh, took her.

Fade out.

There was a spatter of applause.

'I say, jolly good!' exclaimed Gerald, as the projector stopped whirring and someone switched on the spots. 'Wonderful simulated rape, old boy. It really looked as if you were giving her a good seeing-to.'

'Convincing, wasn't it?' Gary said, preening, an arm around Leandra's waist. 'I was trying to convey that he'd been fighting all day, taking the city, bloodlust driving him as well as the desire to shaft her.'

'And you did. Remarkable, wasn't it, Robin?'

175

'Well, yes, the acting was good, but it didn't happen like that in the book,' Robin pointed out. As Gerald's favoured catamite, he was beginning to realise that he had a certain amount of clout.

'We had to alter it. I told you why. Action, Robin. The cinema is different to the written word. I thought you understood that now,' Rutger said grittily.

'Not too much pretence, darling,' Leandra cooed, pressing her breasts against Gary. 'You had a whopping great hard on.'

'What a stonker. We had to cut some of the shots,' agreed Howard, the first cameraman, a laconic, shaven-headed Cockney, and winner of at least one Oscar.

Dinner over, Rutger had decided to treat the cast to rushes of an indoor scene taken at the London studio. They would return there to finish more interiors and then edit, but now he went into a huddle with Howard and the head of lighting about tomorrow's shoot on the beach.

All day the property department had been preparing and Howard's gang were hard at it, their language picturesque as they tested sound booms, erected a gantry and laid tracks for the cameras to run on. All this on slippery sand and in heat of ninety degrees.

The extras were issued with costumes and put through their paces. Wardrobe and make-up were in a flap. The assistant director looked as if he was about to have a full-blown nervous breakdown.

Not so Rutger. He intended to work out his stress in another way.

'Carla, dearest,' he murmured, standing so close that her breasts brushed the frills at his shirt front. 'Did you enjoy that?'

'You're a genius,' she admitted, skin tingling and clitoris stirring as it always did when he was near. 'Will it get past the censor?'

'I think so. Nothing is really seen. It's an illusion,' he murmured darkly. 'And all the more exciting because of that. I'm a conjurer with a box of magic tricks. Like you, my dear Carla, when you create your romantic characters. We beguile our audience, take them on a trip into a fantasy world, give them what they think they desire but would loathe in real life. Thus Leandra, as Princess Aegina, is ravished by Prince Iorgas, played by Gary. No woman would really like to be raped, but we provide her with the means to dream of being taken willingly – by force.'

'That's a contradiction in terms, surely?' Carla argued, yet she knew precisely what he meant.

'It is. But we make sure the rapist is desirable, don't we, darling? Thus she can allow herself to enjoy something she would never confess to wanting. It's rather similar to yourself.'

'I've never wanted to be raped!' Carla cried. She spotted Marie in the distance and tried to walk away, making frantic signals.

'Perhaps not, but can you honestly say that you didn't enjoy it when I whipped you?'

Her heart was thumping, her blood already steaming from watching the clip. She felt dizzy with wine, a tad too much sun, and the heat of a day made hotter by Angelo. For hours she had resisted the temptation of his prick, her desires fanned by the lewdness of his storytelling, for he had been nothing if not frank when describing sexual encounters with Genevra.

And Rutger was so sleek and elegantly sensual in his velvet jacket and superbly tailored trousers, his glossy dark hair flecked with silver loosened about his shoulders. His lips curled in a thin red smile and his eyes were as hard as ice-blue diamonds.

Now he had her boxed in a corner, his arm braced against the wall, cutting her off from assistance. His hand grazed across her nipples, naked beneath the Indian cotton dress. The pleasure was so acute that she drew in a sharp breath.

'You haven't answered me,' he whispered and turned his hand to cup her breast, his fingers fluttering over her aching teat. Shocks of sensation darted through her and settled in her vagina.

'No . . . no . . .' she moaned, the words forced out by her longing.

'You enjoyed me mastering you?'

'Why ask? You know that I did.'

'I wanted to hear you say it.'

She was already tumbling into the fantasy, forgetting Josh, and even Angelo. Only Rutger loomed large, the master magician who could transport her to the underworld of her own psyche.

His hand rested at the back of her waist, bringing her closer to his groin, his turgid cock like a red-hot iron burning through his clothing. His hand moved downwards, slipping into the avenue between her buttocks and pulling the fragile material taut across her tightly closed anus. He wriggled one cotton-covered finger into the tiny hole, meeting the obstruction of her muscles.

'Let go,' he murmured seductively. 'It will only hurt if you resist. Give your every orifice to me.'

She stopped clenching her bottom, and he was right. His fingertip aroused an excitingly novel sensation. Carla could not help pressing back against that invasive digit. Marie had stimulated her secret opening with a vibrator but she was still a virgin there.

Rutger continued his exploration, going lower, finding her vulva and entering this easily, though still wearing the cotton shroud. It became wet, and Carla wriggled, needing his touch on her clitoris, a slow, steady massage of its stalk and head that would bring her relief from this carnal torment.

He smiled and denied her, whispering in that sultry voice, 'Time for another lesson, I think.'

'But what about your guests?' She was still unsure, and that uncertainty and fear added another dimension to her arousal.

He raised one sharply peaked eyebrow and gave a saturnine smile. 'My guests can provide their own amusements. They're spoilt for choice: arses of both sexes, breasts and nipples, cunts and cocks, to say nothing of the wide variety of toys available.'

'You mean the whips and other things? The manacles and gags?'

'Of course.'

'They enjoy these, too?'

'Their tastes are liberal, and their horizons limitless.'

He seized her by the wrist, his touch reminding her of the silken cords that had tied her, and took her to his apartment. It was deserted. The first time she had ever been alone with him, and she did not know what to expect. He was an enigma, clever, perverse and wickedly sexy. Though she would never be sure which way his fancy would take him, at least she'd never be bored.

He closed the door and turned to her, holding her face between his palms and kissing her gently, just the tip of his tongue penetrating her lips, nothing more. His mouth was tender, perfumed with cognac. The darkened room, the glow of candles, the luxury that wrapped her like the softest fur, roused her to fever pitch. She felt trapped in a sensual web and the satisfaction of her desire was paramount.

They rocked together in a close embrace, and his tongue became a more urgent instrument of pleasure, entering the cavern of her mouth with controlled pressure. Then he left her lips and kissed her eyelids, her cheeks, her earlobes and, finally, her neck, lips sucking,

179

teeth nipping. A quick rush of goose-bumps broke out all over her, and her body quivered with pent-up longing.

'I want you,' he said. 'But not as you are used to being taken. Are you willing to try anything?'

'Yes, master,' she whispered.

'Anything at all?'

'Yes, master.'

'Stand still while I undress you,' he said, and slowly undid the tiny ball buttons that fastened the front of her camisole and continued down her skirt.

Her skirt slipped down easily, and he bent to retrieve it from the floor, pressing his face into its softness and inhaling her scent. She had the sudden urge to fold one arm across her naked breasts and cup her pubis with her hand, but he acted first.

'Hands above your head,' he said.

And she obeyed, raising her arms and clasping her hands at the back of her neck, her weight on one leg, the other hip relaxed, in an unconsciously classical pose.

He stood back, and his eyes glowed with admiration. 'My slave,' he muttered, 'my gorgeous odalisque. But I want you completely naked.' And he gripped the top of her panties, tugging so hard that the ribbon ties tore away.

Rutger held the little piece of silk in one hand, unzipped his trousers and lifted out his penis. It was half-engorged, still curled downwards, a beautiful appendage. He stroked the tip with the silken fragment, and his cock immediately swelled to full stand, dew dribbling from the slit as he continued to polish the thick stem.

Carla licked her lips, her loins heavy as she watched him masturbating with her underwear. He was watching his organ, timing its performance, stopping short of ejaculation.

She edged closer. Though she held her hands high,

her fingers twitched to hold him, and rub up and down that brown, vein-knotted stem. She longed to feel a warm flood of semen pouring into her palm, to have him utterly helpless in that fraction of a second when he was convulsing in ecstasy.

'Don't even think of touching it,' he growled threateningly, though his chest was heaving and his cock juddering.

'No, master,' she replied, dampness seeping from her cleft and spreading to her inner thighs.

He propelled her towards the bed. There he spun her round and flung her down on its springy surface, plunging an arm beneath her and arching her hips towards him. He palmed her pudenda, folded back the pouting wings with his fingers and massaged the enlarged clitoris that hung between them like a miniature penis.

A dazzling sense of freedom possessed her. She was not responsible for anything that happened to her. Rutger had taken all worry away. He would choose the time to impale her on his penis, he would select the moment when she would climax.

He did neither.

Instead she jumped violently as he slapped her buttocks with the flat of his hand. The blow shocked right through her. Before she had time to recover, his finger was rubbing her pleasure-bud, bringing her to the verge of release. He left her there, poised on the edge, and spanked her again – and again.

She did not cry out. Though each slap stung, it left her with a sense of shame coupled with wantonness. In her heart of hearts, she wanted him to use her mercilessly. But she yelled and struggled and slid to the floor. He grasped her forcibly with his free arm, hauling her to her knees and bending her body to meet his blows on her bottom and vulnerable cleft.

181

The burning sensation seemed to sear into her very core and she could feel the sap spilling from her inner recess, as orgasmic waves gathered momentum.

He kicked off his shoes and eased out of his clothes, then leaned over her again. His hands were gentle on her rump now, smoothing the flushed, blotchy skin, then opening her wide. He worked between her legs, pulling at the frantic clitoris, pinching and tweaking it till at last she spiralled into an intense orgasm.

Rutger held her quivering mound in his hand, anointed his rigid cock with the love-juice pooling at her vulva, and spread more up her crease and around her anus. She guessed his intention and, bathed in the libidinous glow of climax, hungered to feel that mighty weapon spearing her most secret depths.

He inserted two fingers. It hurt. She flinched. 'Relax,' he said in her ear, his voice sweet but commanding.

Cold air touched her vulnerable delta for an instant, then she felt the purple head of his cock rubbing against her and moaned as the hot, wet tip began to penetrate her forbidden hole. She was extremely tight and unused, and he was larger than average.

'Oh . . . oh!' she whimpered as the helm burrowed deeper.

'That's it . . . slowly . . . steadily,' he gasped. 'You've not done this before?'

'Never,' she breathed, bracing herself as he pushed harder.

Conquering the outer ring, his prick suddenly surged into her and she screamed, feeling herself expanding to take it, submerged in a welter of pain and bliss. She bucked back against him, baring her teeth, engulfing him, feeling his weapon sliding along her most intimate channel. She clenched her sphincter, holding him there, revenging herself by making it nearly impossible for him to withdraw. The crazy idea came to her that she might suck in his entire organ, snap it off at the root and keep it inside herself for ever.

Sweating and cursing, he succeeded in finding the rhythm that would bring on his crisis. He held her tightly by the hips, his coarse pubic hair chafing her buttocks, his balls tapping her cleft with every inward thrust. Crushing her beneath him, he gave full power to his lust, letting it ride him to completion.

Carla lay with her head pillowed on her arms, the hard floor pressing against her flesh, Rutger's weight pinning her down. His sweat was slippery on her skin, and his flaccid phallus left her, resting stickily between her thighs. Every delicate membrane in her loins seemed to be on fire, echoing the heat of her spanked hindquarters.

She was bemused, excited, yet sickened by her response to him. While he had carried out his possession of her most secret, private part, she would have given anything to reject his monstrous, intruding cock. But at the same time she had wanted to retain it, to experience its every last, pulsating inch. The pain had been severe, but so had the overwhelming pleasure.

Rutger sat up, stroking over her backside with his large, smooth hands, tracing round the imprints of his palms. He seemed calm and relaxed, the way men are after emptying themselves of seed. Then he rose and headed towards the bathroom, intending to shower, dress, and join his guests.

'I'll do that one day,' she said, thinking aloud, too bruised and sore to move a muscle.

He looked back over his shoulder, his eyes glinting with mocking amusement. 'And what, slave, will you do?'

'Get up and walk away when I've finished fucking someone.'

183

Chapter 10

THE POOL HAD become a scuba training centre.

'But why can't I go in the sea?' Carla complained after an hour of instruction, during which she had not set a flipper in water.

Josh said firmly, 'Now, let's try again. Pay attention. Ready? Make sure your hair is out of the way, hold the mask against your face with one hand, and pull the strap back over your head with the other. This time, we'll take it a stage further. Take hold of the snorkel, grip the mouthpiece between your teeth and slide into the water.'

An ironic cheer went up as she finned along the surface. Several of the actors were hanging around, relieving the boredom by watching her. It seemed that a large part of making a film consisted of people standing about, smoking and drinking endless cups of tea and coffee while waiting to be called.

Josh and Carla had been at it since daylight. She tried to remember his instructions as she duck dived. The snorkel tube filled. She surfaced and cleared it by tipping back her head and blowing sharply through her mouth. By noon she had progressed to scuba gear.

'Soon I may let you try it at sea,' he promised, as he

stowed the gear in canvas bags.

'From *Sea Jade*?' she asked eagerly, glad to be peeling off the clammy wetsuit.

His mouth curled in a grin and he shook his head, scattering water over her. 'First, you've got to learn to cope in an alien environment. It may be true that we originated in the briny, but we've lost our gills.'

'Oh, Josh, I'm sure I'd be fine. I so want to see the wreck,' she pleaded and, standing on tiptoe, kissed the little scar on his cheekbone. 'Did you get that diving?' she added, her heart beating faster as his arm went round her, pressing her body to his.

She could feel the shape of his penis under his wet bathing trunks. Hot as fire, it nudged her groin.

He chuckled and said, 'Nothing so glamorous, I'm afraid. I fell out of a tree when I was a kid.'

Carla broke free and towelled herself, naked save for her G-string. 'Ah, so you were a child once upon a time,' she teased. 'I thought perhaps you were a sort of Flying Dutchman, condemned to roam the seas for ever. Maybe I'm the innocent maiden willing to sacrifice her life to save your soul. It's mean of you not to share the wreck with me.'

'Not yet. As I've said, there's a risk in diving, albeit a calculated one.'

He looked so serious that she stopped what she was doing and gave him a searching stare. 'You've been in danger?'

He shrugged, his muscles moving silkily under his copper-hued skin. 'We don't take chances. That's why we dive in pairs. It usually goes like clockwork, but there have been times . . .' He stopped, and his green eyes clouded.

'What happened?' she asked, the sun burning her back but chilly fingers trailing down her spine.

He came out of his reverie and clasped her bottom,

inserting a finger into her thong. 'Oh, nothing really. It was when I first dived to the site. Imagination, of course, but I could have sworn I saw a woman down there.'

'A dead woman?' She stayed very still, absorbing this horror.

'Oh, no, nothing that was once mortal. "The Nightmare Life-in-Death was she, Who thicks man's blood with cold." D'you know Coleridge's poem, *The Ancient Mariner*?'

'He was an opium addict.'

'He was indeed, but that fits my mermaid.'

'You're putting me on, aren't you?' She had the nasty feeling that he was sincere.

'I kid you not, but have no proof. None of the film I took of her came out. Let's go. We're invited to lunch with George Pavlos. He'll tell you about the legends of the deep.'

They drove into Paxia, and then up the other side where the slopes were wooded and the white houses set back in their own terraced gardens.

'George,' Josh shouted, mounting the steps to a vine-dappled loggia.

No one answered, and with a lift of his expressive brows, Josh led Carla inside. They found George in a long cool study, one eye screwed up round a jewellers' glass as he pored over pottery shards littering the desk. 'Ah, there you are, my friend,' he bellowed, and removed the magnifying glass. It left a ring round his socket, indenting the plump flesh.

'This is Carla Holt,' Josh said, and George bowed over her hand with old-world gallantry.

'He has told me so much about you,' George gushed, beaming. 'You are most welcome to my house.'

'And the artifacts?' Josh joined him near the table.

George leaned over, resting an arm across Josh's shoulders. 'Marvellous, and so beautiful. Look at this

186

seal, for example. Touch it, Miss Holt. These are not unusual in the islands. In the old days the peasants called them milk-stones, and they were used by mothers as charms to help with breast-feeding, but really they come from past civilisations, maybe Minoan.'

Carla held the smooth disc in her hand. It was inscribed in pre-Greek script. It gave her a chill to think it had only just emerged into the daylight after centuries in the sea.

'How old?' she asked, and George's eyes twinkled at her as he replied, 'Maybe two thousand years B.C.'

'Such fine work, so much culture here, while England was still inhabited with woad-painted barbarians.'

A lusciously formed young woman entered, wearing a shirt-waisted dress and neat, medium-heeled shoes. George looked at her fondly and said, 'Desma, my dove. You already know Josh, but meet Miss Holt, the authoress.'

Desma's cool hand met Carla's and she smiled. She was olive skinned but blue-eyed, and her hair was fair. 'How nice that you could come, Miss Holt,' she said, her command of English greater than George's.

'Please call me Carla,' she insisted, amused by the way George suddenly shed years, and quickly realising that Desma was not his daughter, as she had first assumed, but his lover.

The living-room was spacious, with whitewashed walls and paved floors strewn with red and blue striped mats. Plants stood in pots on the wide windowsill and hung from baskets nailed to beams.

Desma invited them to sit on stools round the pine table, and brought in the first course. She was a confident hostess, no shy hill-girl but a university student whose studies had brought her into contact with George. The meal was superbly cooked and accompanied by red wine from the local vineyards.

'Carla wants to know about the legends,' Josh said, and recounted his experience at the wreck.

George did not laugh, just shook his leonine head and said, 'One must be careful not to offend the sea-folk. An offering may be in order, my friend. A goat, perhaps?'

'You and your demons and monsters,' Desma scoffed, and he gazed at her adoringly, obviously excited by her bossy attitude and nodding as she continued, 'Let's discuss something more entertaining. I think it would be fun to be an extra in Leandra Lafage's film.'

'I'll ask Rutger,' Carla said at once, convinced that Desma's azure eyes and high, full breasts would probably get her a speaking part.

'You must visit the museum,' George urged, as he walked Carla to the truck later. Josh was dawdling behind, examining some ancient stones that shored up a wall.

'I'd love to. Are you pleased with Josh's finds?'

'Delighted,' he said and paused, leaning his bulk against the gatepost and looking at her speculatively. 'You like him?'

'Oh, yes, I like him a lot,' she replied, and putting it into words brought home the depth of her feelings. Yes, she *did* like him, probably too much for her peace of mind.

George heaved a sigh and stared into the distance, across the harbour and out to sea. 'He's a wanderer, a roamer. I've known him for many years and he has never put down roots. Unlike myself, who lived happily with my wife and children and now, a widower, am about to marry again.'

'Desma?'

'Yes, my Desma, my jewel, the comfort of my advancing years. She brings me to life. I am performing in bed like a boy of twenty.'

'That's fine,' Carla said with a smile, wondering how Desma managed to reach orgasm with him whaling about on top of her.

'So you see, my dear young lady, it would not be wise to become too fond of Josh. The only female he loves is his ship. And the sea nymph he saw . . . she will be jealous of him, too. Perhaps harm him if he gives his heart to someone else.'

He's warning me off, Carla thought, and her spirits sank. 'It's not serious,' she replied lightly. 'Call it a holiday romance.'

A smile broke over his rubicund face. 'Good. Enjoy each other while you can. I would not like to see a lovely girl like you made unhappy.'

As if! she thought crossly. I'm never going to let a man wound me again. Yet when Josh came up to slip his arm through hers, she hurt inside, filled with lingering regrets.

'I must go,' she reminded when they were in the truck. 'I'll be late for Angelo.'

'Must you leave?' His face was turned towards her in the intimacy of the cab, raffishly handsome, and she was all too aware of his firm flesh under the ragged T-shirt and cutoffs. She longed to touch him, to hold him, to feel his body heat and lie in his arms, experiencing unity with this person who seemed already to be a part of herself.

'I suppose so,' she said without conviction.

'Phone him. Tell him you can't make it.'

'Shall I? It will be letting him down.' There's a madness in my blood, she thought. I don't care about anything but satisfying this crying need to stay with Josh and enjoy lusty, bed-rolling sex with him.

When they reached the Venetian house, she dialled Angelo's number. He answered immediately, as if he had been waiting for her call. 'You're late. Where are you?' he shouted, making her ear-drum ring.

'I've been delayed. I'm sorry, but I can't come today,' she replied, holding the phone a little away.

There was an ominous silence. 'Why? Who are you with? You promised to be here.'

'I'm shopping with Marie. She's my girlfriend.' Carla was surprised by the nimble lies that sprang to her tongue. 'We're waiting for the car to pick us up.'

'Get a cab. Come straight here.'

'It will be too late by then.'

'Work is not important. Spend the night with me.'

Oh, dear, this was so difficult! 'No, Angelo. I'll see you in the morning. Meanwhile, think about what you want me to write, find old photographs, straighten things out in your mind and we can get going. All right?'

'No, I'm not,' he snarled. 'I think I'll go out and find a whore . . . two whores . . . a party of whores!'

Is this a threat? she thought, and marvelled at his immaturity. 'That's your problem,' she returned smartly. 'Goodbye, Angelo. I'll come tomorrow.'

'Without fail?'

'Yes.'

'Your boss?' Josh enquired casually, regarding her over the edge of his wine glass.

'If you can call him that. I'm working freelance.' She was still not comfortable about lying to Angelo, not a deceiver by nature.

'How's the book going?'

'We've not started yet, only talked about it.'

'You fancy him, don't you?' His voice was thrillingly low, and she stared at his fingers curled round the crystal stem, and ran her nails lightly over the back of his hand and up his lightly furred arm.

'I fancy *you*,' she said quietly, seeing her desire reflected in his eyes.

His lips found hers and he kissed her thoroughly,

190

hungrily and with great passion. She sank into the kiss with a sigh of satisfaction. All morning she had been thirsting for the taste of his lips, the heat, their near nakedness and the stimulation of his company working on her desires like yeast. Now she opened her lips and felt his fleshy pink tongue moving sensuously in the wetness of her mouth.

Without breaking the kiss, he eased towards the door of the bedroom. There they parted for an instant, stripping rapidly. She lay on the bed and watched him, admiring every part of his body. Rays of sunlight penetrated the shutters and struck across the planes of his chest, and down to his lean, hard belly. His phallus reared up from the tangled brown pubic hair, swaying as he walked towards her.

The soft skin of her buttocks was still sore, the outer rim of her secret entrance painful, a constant reminder of her master's domination, yet she could forget this in the presence of this rugged adventurer. And when he came to her and held her tightly and slid his cock into her craving centre, she knew that this was right. Despite George's doubts, they belonged together.

Angelo was different somehow. He set out to charm her. When she arrived next morning there were no jealous scenes, no moods, and he had a file ready. Not much because, as he said, most of his documents were stored in his farmhouse in Tuscany, but there were several useful photographs and a letter or two. They worked steadily for hours. Carla had brought along her laptop, finding it easier to use than she had thought. She entered notes and took down everything he said. Edward stuck his head round the door from time to time, hopeful and encouraging. Toby phoned midday.

'How did you know I'd be here?' she asked, and the

sound of his voice calmed her as it always did, reassuring, cheerful, and affectionate.

'Edward told me.'

'So you've been keeping tabs on me?'

'Would I not? You're my favourite author. Is the work progressing?'

'Yes.'

'How long before I can see a draft?'

'It's difficult to say. We need to have material sent from Italy.'

'Tell him I'll be in London late August,' Angelo shouted from across the room.

'Did you hear that, Toby? Yes, the end of August.'

'For rehearsals with Carlo Bianza, Verdi's *Requiem*,' Angelo said, striding over to stand close to her, exuding the classy smell of *Vetiver* as he leaned his head against hers so that he could take part in the conversation.

'He's singing again? That's brilliant! You've cracked it, Carla,' Toby exclaimed down the phone, many miles away, yet sounding as if he were next door.

Angelo took the receiver from her. 'She's a wonderful girl, Mr Torrance. We make a splendid book together.'

With a heart-stopping smile, he handed it back and Carla said, a little breathlessly, 'Are you there, Toby? Yes, it looks as if I'll be coming home around the same time.'

'Excellent. Sunrise Press are nibbling, and a couple of others. It's possible we'll hold an auction for the rights. Don't worry, I made sure a percentage on sales was written into your contract. And Carla?'

'Yes, Toby.'

'I miss you like hell.'

It was late. The time had flashed by, and for every moment of that day Carla and Angelo had worked. Snacks had been brought in, and plenty of non-alcoholic beverages, but as the sun began to sink, Angelo stretched his arms till his joints cracked, grinned across at her and said, 'Now we swim.'

'I didn't bring a costume.'

He gave her a keen stare, and said, 'That doesn't matter. We shall be naked, you and I ... good friends now, as well as lovers.'

There was no answer to that.

'I'm learning to scuba dive,' she said, when after several brisk lengths she relaxed against the side of the pool.

'Yes? This is to do with your friend, no?'

She nodded, half blinded by her hair, reaching up to push it back. 'Josh Osbourne. He's a marine archaeologist.'

'This is brave, I think, but they do it for money,' Angelo observed cynically.

'He doesn't – well, not entirely. I've seen some of the things he's brought up. They're amazing, Angelo, from civilisations long gone.'

'He dazzles you, *cara*,' he murmured, and pressed his hard body close to hers under the water.

'The relics dazzle me, but yes, I admire his nerve,' she answered, aware of the rise and fall of his deep chest, the blackness of his streaming hair, and those fine, peat-dark eyes under the wet, spiky lashes.

'Carla *mia*, you have a romantic imagination,' he said, and moved in closer, till she could feel his penis stirring, pushing in between her thighs.

She eased her legs apart, accepting him, her vagina remembering his length and hardness. He raised her, and the water, too, buoyed her up so that their bodies joined seamlessly. Eyes closed, he mouthed her nipples, drawing them into sharp peaks of desire as he rocked her gently on his cock.

She pressed down, trying to find the right friction on

her clitoris but failing. She moaned in frustration and he slid a hand between them, finding that swollen point of desire and rubbing it firmly, the nubbin rendered silken smooth by water and her own honeydew. Orgasm washed over her like a tidal wave and her inner self contracted round his shaft as he, too, found his nirvana in her dark haven.

Four men, four cocks, four options.

Carla was confused.

'What do I do? Who shall I have?' she wailed, lying on Marie's bed much later that night. She had not long left Angelo, showered and climbed into a casual lounging robe.

'All of them. Is that a problem?' Marie answered, from her place in front of the vanity unit.

'This just isn't *me*!'

'No? Don't kid yourself, baby. Not the old you, perhaps, but you've changed.'

'Have I?' Carla got up and came over to look in the mirror, her hands pressed flat on the vanity's surface.

'Sure you have. It's the way you move – sort of elegant, sexy, as if you're comfortable inside your skin and ready to take on anyone in the bed stakes,' Marie said, and covered Carla's hand with hers. 'Giles would come off in his pants if he could see you now.'

Carla gave a throaty giggle, knowing that every word was true. She had gained enormously, not only financially, but in confidence and pride in herself.

'Giles? Who's he?' she asked.

Marie laughed, and twirled round on the stool, her long legs spread each side of Carla, who stood motionless, looking down at her.

'That's my girl!' Marie said; then her eyes sharpened, and she rose, taller than Carla and bigger built. She bent her head and kissed Carla on the mouth.

Carla was enveloped in the scent of Marie's exclusive perfume, and excited by the firmness of full breasts against her own. It sent a thrill through her. The kiss, too. She felt the softness of a woman's lips, and the delicate probing of a tongue, just touching her teeth and then pulling out.

'There's another option you haven't mentioned,' Marie murmured, and let her fingers drop to one of Carla's nipples, clasping the tip that immediately rose against the filmy cotton robe.

'I've never . . .'

'I know, but I've a good feeling about this. Let me teach you the subtle ways in which women can pleasure each other.'

Carla was curious and excited, the hint of naughtiness, the offer of forbidden fruit proving irresistible. As if on cue, Leandra appeared, followed by Carmel. Both women were still wearing their film costumes, Leandra's a floating, transparent Greek *chiton* girded under the breasts, and Carmel's the war-gear of a warrior queen. She was sweating under her lightweight armour, for the choreographer had been putting her and Gary through their paces in one of the stage fights.

'Christ! I need a drink,' Leandra sighed, and Marie mixed cocktails at the bedroom bar, double measures in tall glasses half full of ice shavings.

'Rutger's such a bastard!' Carmel agreed. 'God, it was hell down there today. Talk about "we'll fight them on the beaches". His mood was foul, and it was "cut, cut" all the bloody time. There was no satisfying him.'

'I've never seen the make-up team so fazed,' Leandra said, collapsing on the couch and hauling her flowing skirts back over her thighs. 'Sticks of greasepaint melting all over the place and us sweating like pigs, ruining our bases. They had fans on in the tent, but that was no damn good.'

'So it went OK?' Marie observed, smiling.

'Oh, yes. There's always high drama whatever the conditions. I'm sure Rutger got something in the can, but he wants to do it all over again in the morning.'

'Time to relax now,' Marie soothed, and she started to undress Carmel, unbuckling the breastplate and epaulettes, and removing the short, metal-plated skirt, the wide bracelets, the studded belt, the scabbard.

Leandra unwound the girdle and shook herself free of her gown. Once Marie had removed Carmel's brief black tunic and panties, both actresses were naked, their bodies and faces still heavily made-up, though Carmel's arms and legs had merely been oiled to make her coffee-coloured skin glisten.

Marie filled the circular sunken bath and dribbled in fragrant lotion, the colour streaky peacock-blue to purple, like petrol floating on a rain puddle. Leandra was the first in, giving an exuberant sigh of relief. 'Oh, that's great! I've been dreaming of water all day. There were acres of it lapping the sand, and that tyrant would-n't even let us paddle.'

Carla tingled, her groin growing heavy with desire as she watched Leandra's pink nipples peaking, her breasts gleaming, her natural tan appearing as the false one was washed away. Her face, too, in all its peerless beauty. She sponged herself thoroughly, till every trace of cosmetic had gone.

As for Carmel? She was a goddess among women, exotic and beautiful, and Carla ached to touch her upward-thrusting breasts and suck her jutting nipples. Here, in this perfumed bower dedicated to Venus, men had no place – ugly, lumpy creatures with those laugh-able appendages tacked on to their bodies like Nature's afterthought. An abomination against all that was aesthetically pleasing. She shuddered to think that she had actually enjoyed the feel of Angelo's cock within her a short while ago.

Now she feasted on the sight of Carmel's thick, curly bush, and that swelling cleft like a split peach, her centre of pleasure nestling at the top. A woman's sex was neat, discreet. Though she might be aroused to the point of climax, no one need be aware. Unlike the male, with his stiff erection shouting to the world that he was eager to mate.

Marie smiled at her, as if reading her thoughts, and said, 'Shall we join them?'

Carmel, already thigh deep, held out her long, aristocratic black fingers and said, 'Come in, sisters.'

At first they massaged one another, soothing away the stresses of the day. Carla was inexpert, but began to learn quickly as Marie used her fingers and palms to relax her shoulders and arms and Leandra worked on her back and then slid round to her loins. Carmel, meanwhile, concentrated on the soles of her feet, a particularly exquisite sensation.

By some instinct, or maybe it was through Marie, they seemed to know that Carla was a novice in the Sapphic arts. Though at first she was surprised to feel Carmel's fingers penetrating her vagina, the wonderful feeling drowned out other considerations. So slow, so gentle that touch, knowing exactly how to woo the eager clitoris into delight. Carla was lost, unaware of Marie or Leandra, her eyes closed as she inhaled the jasmine scent of the oil and the saffron essence of Carmel's body.

With her mouth, lips and teeth caressing Carla's nipples and her fingertips fondling her bud, Carmel quickly brought her to orgasm, a shattering rollercoaster that exploded into a firework display. She was so hyped up, that she had two more in quick succession, and then they left the tub, needing more space in which to carry out their discovery of each other's secrets.

Bed is always the best place, Carla thought, and within Marie's couch she dared try out her skill on Carmel. Her cheeks flamed and her heart raced as she made her lover's breasts tremble and dragged moans from her generous lips.

Carmel spread her thighs in the most graceful and elegant manner, and Carla positioned herself between those ebony limbs. She was no longer shy, fascinated as the slate-grey petals of Carmel's labia unfolded, displaying the deep pink cleft surmounted by a clitoris that was large and red and fully erect.

Carla leaned closer, smelling the hot, spicy odour of Carmel's juices, and at last venturing her lips over the swollen clit. Carmel moaned and, reaching down, held Carla's swinging breasts, rubbing the hard nipples. Carla buried her nose in Carmel's cleft, senses ravished by the potent taste of ambrosia on her tongue. She lapped at the ardent button, then subjected it to a swift sucking. Carmel cried out, rearing up to thrust against the tongue that was giving her the most excruciating pleasure as Carla brought her to her crisis.

In close embrace they lay together, joined by Marie and Leandra. They changed places at some point, and it was of no importance who pleasured whom. Far into the night, Carmel and Marie raided the kitchen and brought back a feast. They ate, drank, made love again, and then slept, black limbs twined with sun-tanned ones, a vision of satiated females that would have made men – surplus to requirements – envious and vaguely uneasy.

All sound receded, except the hissing intake of breath and the bass gurgle of expelled air bubbles. Carla descended slowly, her senses tingling.

Twelve lessons on, and Josh had consented to take her to the wreck. Following the shot line, she began to fin gently down. She looked back at the receding surface and the bottom of *Sea Jade*. Josh and Luke were with her, and she exchanged OK signals with them. Two buddies instead of one, and she knew it was on the cards that one day soon she and Luke would sleep together.

It was reassuring to have them caring for her welfare. Josh pointed to his ears and gave the OK again. OK, she signalled back – yes, her ears were fine.

Unexpectedly, the sea-bed came into view. She finned along above it. It felt like flying, and she was entranced as she glided over the rocks and weeds. Ahead, a couple of strange-shaped fish flashed off out of sight. Josh was closer than she thought. He took her hand and pointed.

She saw a lumpy mass that might have been rocks or coral. Sea grass wavered in the current, and a shoal of multicoloured fish darted in and around it. Carla opened her eyes wide and squeezed Josh's hand. He nodded and gave the OK.

It was the wreck. She stared at it almost in fright, half expecting to see the jealous mer-creature. There was nothing, only weed waving like gossamer green scarves. Josh led her closer, carefully, letting her swim round the wreck, but only where it was safe. Soon he tapped his watch, and gave the stop signal. It was time to surface. She was not tired, on a high of achievement, but he was insistent.

Going up, the floating sensation was magical, as the water got warmer, lighter, brighter. She reached the line, and Josh gave her the thumbs-up sign. Finning gently, she drifted higher, until she saw the outline of the boat against the sky.

She broke the surface in an explosion of noise. Hands reached over to haul her aboard. The regulator left her mouth, the weight belt was taken off her, and the aqualung.

'I did it,' she cried, tears welling up. 'I saw it – the wreck.'

'You did fine,' said Luke, slipping off his fins and unzipping his wetsuit.

'I want to go down again,' she declared.

'She's hooked, Josh,' Luke grinned, unbuckling his depth gauge and knife.

Josh smiled down at her as she sat on the deck, too weak in the knees to stand as yet. 'But you're a writer, aren't you?' he pointed out. 'Not a deep-sea diver.'

'I could change,' she averred, thinking, I really could, but would he want to have me with him all the time? And would I want to make that commitment? Just for now, life held a multitude of possibilities, not the least of which was her new-found fun with the girls. There was time enough for her to make up her mind, a few more weeks before she must leave Zaminos.

Meanwhile she had much to do on Angelo's book, and a great deal to find out about him, to say nothing of those occasional, darkly satisfying encounters with Rutger.

Chapter 11

THE PACKAGE ARRIVED from Tuscany, despatched under orders by one of Angelo's aides. He broke the seal and showed Carla, and she sifted through the contents.

It contained passionate notes from Genevra, indiscreet love-letters, even ill-advised fax messages that should have been censored, the agonised outpourings of a woman obsessed.

Carla read through them for an hour, seated quietly in the conservatory amid the scent of flowers and the musical sounds of a trickling fountain, and the more she read, the more she became ashamed of what she and Angelo had written so far, slanted heavily in his favour and disparaging about the soprano, covertly, of course – they had the libel laws to bear in mind.

In the end she laid the papers down, and said, 'You can't possibly use these.'

'Why?' Angelo demanded. Seated in the sun outside, he was almost too handsome in white Versace jeans, his chest bare except for the small gold chain and crucifix he usually wore.

'It's too personal, too intimate. She bares her soul.'

'So?' he said, scowling defiance, but she knew him well enough by now to recognise this smokescreen.

These letters provided an important key to the whole

book, three quarters of which she had now roughed out. An idea began to formulate in her mind, one that would surely satisfy Genevra and also make him even more of a hero to his fans.

There were several ways of snapping him out of a bad mood and making him more malleable: a superb pasta meal, a vintage wine, and sex. The last was the best, and she had no hesitation in using it.

She got up and went to work on him. The crinkled crêpe dress she wore was a simple wrap-over. It opened when she moved, showing her brown legs and the triangular point of the matching tanga that only just concealed her mons veneris.

'Angelo, you can afford to be generous,' she murmured and, standing close behind him, she slid her hands over his chest, playing with the chain and the dark fur spiralling round his pectorals. He sighed and leaned back against her, his black curls tickling her exposed breasts, the clean smell of his hair, the musky heat that rose from his body seducing her. Feeling the relaxation of tension in him, she allowed her fingertips to skim his nipples. The little points hardened immediately, and she increased the pressure, pinching them firmly.

'Carla,' he groaned. 'What is it you want of me, *mia sirena*?'

Without stopping her stimulation of his nubs, she leaned her face against the crown of his head, her heart aching with tenderness. 'I have an idea,' she ventured, hardly able to think coherently as he reached back and ran a hand up her inside thigh.

'Tell me,' he crooned, and his finger brushed delicately over the fragile fabric hiding her female treasure.

'We should take a different angle.'

'How?' He started to stroke her, pressing into the sharp line of her cleft.

It was difficult to think of anything except the yearning to have him enter her, driving and plundering, till he possessed every part of her. She felt drunk with desire, but succeeded in saying, 'Turn it into a love story. Bring out the best parts of your relationship, and there must have been some. Exaggerate, if you must, but let it appear that you and Genevra shared a passionate love, and speak of your heartbreak when, due to professional pressures, you were forced to part.'

'What?' Angelo exploded. He was on his feet in an instant, towering over her in the worst temper she had ever seen. 'You want me to lie? To pretend that I loved her? I won't do it! I'll never say that I was in love with that bitch!'

'Your public would soak it up,' she protested, her own temper reaching boiling point. All very well to try and detach from it, but he was quite impossible to work with – impossible to live with. Just downright impossible, per se.

'My public will like anything I write,' he declared loftily, resting a bare foot on the low wall and leaning an elbow on it, brooding dramatically into the distance.

'Stop posing!' she shouted. 'You're not on a photo shoot now! This is me you're talking to, and I've had enough! Your public – what's left of them, for they're a fickle bunch and soon forget – your public would rather have something other than what we've written to date.'

'Nonsense,' he grunted, and sat on the wall, his expression settling into one of deepest gloom.

'It's true. I've been worried about it. No matter how I've tried to make it look otherwise, you appear in a bad light, as a selfish, egocentric pig who was only out for himself.'

'So you'd turn me into a weak fool, her puppet, dancing to her tune! I won't do it. You won't alter a word, or I'll withdraw, forbid its publication, and stay here.'

Firing this final volley, he stalked off into the villa.

Oh, bugger it, Carla thought, though not regretting her frankness. Now what do I do? She set out to look for him.

He was not in the music-salon, and she supposed he might have gone to find Krista who, unquestioning and adoring, would soothe his dented *amour propre*. To hell with him!

Carla was seething. She was tempted to walk out, go down to the harbour and find Josh, though he was extremely busy just now, bringing up the last of the relics. In a depressed state, she fingered the amber beads. Had George Pavlos been right? Was Josh about to up anchor and leave?

It doesn't matter, she reflected philosophically. I'm due in London at the end of the month. With this book to finish? Who knows? A tiny flame sparked in her core as she wondered if Toby would be at Heathrow to meet her.

Angelo's CD collection was mainly operatic. Carla thumbed through the discs, unconsciously seeking guidance. His taste was eclectic, covering early recordings of great singers of the twenties, up to the most modern composers, avant-garde productions and new performers. He featured on several, and she found one of him singing in *Manon Lescaut* with Genevra Scoville, recorded years before. Carla rated this Puccini opera among her favourites, and felt the beginning of that slow, visceral thrill of anticipation, almost sexual in its intensity, that raised the fine down on her limbs. She recalled someone once referring to Puccini's works as musical marijuana. There was no doubt that she reached an all-time high when listening to them.

She programmed the disc to Act IV: the finale, filled with the dark fire of despairing passion, the music saturated in sombre colours as the lovers, Manon and Des

Grieux are dying of thirst in a desert near New Orleans. She settled in a comfortable armchair, lit a cigarette and surrendered herself to the dramatic music that opened the act and set the scene.

Genevra Scoville! Carla had forgotten just how good she was, her voice soaring in those difficult passages, her acting conveying loss, regret and the terrible fear of being left to die alone.

'Abandoned! I don't want to die ... Will anyone remember poor Manon?' She sang with heart-breaking intensity.

Tears rose in Carla's eyes and ran unchecked down her cheeks as Angelo's voice rang out in the lament of a man desperately trying to save his beloved. She sobbed openly as those doleful harmonies concluded the opera, with Manon dead and Des Grieux weeping over her body.

Suddenly she was aware of someone standing near the French doors. She turned, feeling a little embarrassed by her display of emotion.

'She was magnificent, wasn't she?' Angelo said very quietly, and there were tears in his eyes, too. 'No one has sung Manon like her, before or since.'

'It was because she understood,' Carla answered, her handkerchief a soggy ball in her hand. 'When she sang of being left to die alone, it was heart-wrenching. It was real for her. She felt it in her gut. She had been there ... and was reaching that point again during the recording. She knew you were going to leave her.'

'I know, I know,' he said brokenly, and came across to sit beside her, his head down, his hands clasped between his knees.

'You have the chance to make it right, Angelo,' she said, wrapping her arms round him and drawing him to her breast. 'Let's do it over. Change it. Concentrate on the romance of it. All right, so we'll have to lie about your love for her, but so what? Then send her a copy of the new draft. Dedicate it to her. I'll bet she'll be delighted and withdraw her threat.'

'But she wants to perform again!'

'Suggest a meeting. Take Edward along. See what she can do now. There are minor parts for older women, aren't there? Maybe you can persuade her to accept her age graciously. She could teach. She has so much to give to young singers.'

'You're right, most beautiful and wise Carla,' he said softly, and snuggled into her breast, caressing the underside, nuzzling at her nipple. 'And you will come with me. We shall see Genevra together.'

Carla wasn't too sure about the wisdom of this. Would the singer want to see him with a younger woman? It might not be tactful, but this wasn't Angelo's strong point; he'd had a tact bypass. They would face that hurdle when they came to it.

Meanwhile, there was Angelo, with his hot kisses and that splendid phallus rising in readiness to pleasure her.

There was a final gathering at the Villa Artemis. The shoot had been wrapped, and everyone was about to go their separate ways, to meet up again later in the film studio for indoor sequences and continuity.

Change and flux, Carla thought as she dressed. Angelo had gone to Milan to make his peace with Genevra. He had wanted her to go with him but she had refused, still sure it would not have gone down well with the soprano. Edward had been in full agreement, going along himself, Angelo's personal nanny again.

'It suits me, doesn't it, darling,' he had said to Carla the evening before their departure. 'I can just see me in a nurse's uniform and starched apron, can't you?' It was the first time he had admitted to her that he was gay, but, as he was at pains to explain, butch. Though he might fantasise about wearing women's clothes, in reality he took the active part. 'Like the actor, Sir Gerald Drew,' he added playfully. 'Though I hear that at times he likes to reverse roles. Some of us do, you know.'

Carla didn't know, but she was learning.

'Now don't you worry about a thing,' he went on, more than delighted with her achievement. 'We're taking Genevra a copy of the manuscript, and when we fly in to London, we'll see you and make any alterations. Word is already getting out,' he added, chuckling gleefully. He called over his shoulder to Angelo, 'I think this deserves champagne, don't you?'

Champagne it was, served in Baccarat crystal flutes.

'Toby is over the moon,' Edward went on, his round face all of a glow, silver hair falling over his brow, almost meeting his shaggy eyebrows. 'The auction is arranged and the publishers are wetting themselves in their eagerness to buy. They're in raptures about the title: *Love Song*. That was a stroke of genius on my part, though I say it as I shouldn't. And Angelo's present record company is planning a CD with him singing selected songs to go with it, to be released at the same time as the book. It's being hyped to the skies, my dear.'

Carla could see it all: signing sessions, Breakfast TV, late-night TV. Alicia Ashford would be dying to get her claws into Angelo.

'Don't worry, my darling. You're to be included. Angelo doesn't want your name kept out of it. You'll be famous, too,' Edward promised.

So that's one in the eye for you, Giles, she thought, permitting herself a measure of bitchy satisfaction.

Now they had gone, and Angelo had become ridiculously sentimental during their last hours together, talking about marriage, even waxing lyrical about children. Carla had taken fright. He was gorgeous, probably the sexiest man she was ever likely to bed, but she had seen the downside first hand. Could she live with that monumental ego? She doubted it. However, she had no intention of denying herself the pleasure she had with him. They would remain in close, even intimate contact. At the very least it would ensure an eternity of free tickets at all the best opera houses. And later, fate might decree that she did become Madame Lorenzo.

'Are you ready?' Ruth asked, poking her head round the door. She was dressed in a pink satin corset with suspenders stretched outside her leopard print plastic skirt. Black net stockings made her thin legs even more stork-like, legs that ended in a pair of shiny silver DMs laced to midcalf.

Dear God, Carla sighed, viewing her own more conservative outfit with distaste, I wish I had her bottle. 'Is Stefan invited?' she asked, consoling herself by admiring her solid tan made deeper still by the white chiffon slip-dress, very brief and to the point.

'Yep, and he's coming back to England. Marie has taken him on as handiman. Wicked. I never did want to stay in Greece, but he's such a babe, I couldn't bear to part with him.'

Happy Ruth, Carla thought. How wonderful to be so young. I feel as old as Methuselah at the moment. There's still a lot to do to that bloody book. All right for some, swanning off to Milan.

But she knew that what was really bugging her was Josh. He was being elusive and, though trying to be adult about it, she could not stop the hurt that quivered inside her every time she tried unsuccessfully to track him down.

The party was in full spate by the time she walked into it – had been for a while, judging by the raised voices, the gales of alcohol-induced laughter, and general air of abandon.

She saw Carmel in full dominatrix regalia, leading her lover Marie about on a chain. Marie wore black leather shorts cut so short and hoisted so high at the crotch that her hairy sex-lips protruded either side, and her nipples were exposed through slits in the laced waistcoat; Carmel alternately sucked and pinched them, then flicked Marie's bottom with a whip.

Leandra, similarly clad but in scarlet, was assisting Robin to punish Gerald, dragging him into a side room equipped with an extensive range of paddles and straps. Robin was wielding a huge dildo, forcing Gerald to bend over and then thrusting it into the peer's quivering anus.

Rutger, sardonic as ever, mingled with the cast, faultlessly attired, and lost no opportunity to seduce the actresses and female crew members, luring them to his bedchamber and indoctrinating them into the paradox of pain and pleasure. They were willing to learn, for despite his irascible temper on set, they doted on him.

The only one who refused was Desma, who had come on her own. Though Rutger had been sufficiently impressed by her face and figure to give her a line to speak, she was a level-headed young woman who knew where her true happiness lay.

Carla was glad to be left alone, feeling oddly distanced and removed from these scenes of debauchery. She had had her baptism of fire and come out of it a more integrated person. Later, she might wish to repeat it, but for the present her thoughts were with Josh.

Slipping away unnoticed, she borrowed a car from among several in Rutger's garage and drove to Paxia, finally stopping outside Josh's house. She sat there for a while, screwing up the courage to go in. Supposing he was entertaining another woman? She'd feel such a fool, having to make some feeble excuse and leave ignominiously.

There were lights on inside, and deciding that having taken the trouble to go she might as well see it through, she knocked on the massive front door.

Nothing happened for a moment; then she heard footsteps inside and her stomach lurched. The door opened to frame a large man, silhouetted against the light.

'Hi there, Carla,' said Luke, his warm, deep voice coiling round her like a caress.

She did not know whether to be disappointed or relieved. 'Is Josh in?'

'Nope. He's in cahoots with George. They're down at the museum, likely to be there a while, far as I can tell. I'm kind of holding the fort, as you might say. Got a night off from baby-sitting *Sea Jade*.

'Oh, well, if he's not here . . .' She turned to leave, but his big hand shot out and landed on her arm, holding it very gently.

'Don't go away. Come in, Carla. Have a drink.'

Who can argue with destiny? She thought, and stepped over the threshold into a new experience.

Inside music played, the sultry rhythm of salsa. Luke moved to the beat without realising, lithe, long-legged and loose in the hips. Carla knew he would be a superb dancer. She had admired him for some time, enjoying his jokes, his way of talking, his sense of humour and his genuine concern for her. Diving, she would trust him with her life, as she did Josh.

He poured her a glass of wine and sat with her on the couch, his dark skin glistening in the glow of a lamp. There was a dish of olives and some crusty bread on the low table and the television was on, pictures flickering, the sound turned down.

'How's it going? I haven't seen Josh for a while. I've been busy,' she began, watching his handsome face turned towards the TV. His profile seemed carved in ebony, with its straight nose and full lips, and that mane of tightly ringletted hair.

'So've we. Carefully stripping the wreck. It's a painstaking job. Josh won't stop till he's finished. He's a dedicated kind of guy.'

'I know.'

'You do? A lot of chicks can't hack it. They blow him out.'

'Have there been many? Chicks, I mean?'

'Some,' he returned lazily. 'But you don't want to worry about that.'

'No?'

'No. He likes you, and he wants you to be happy. He said to me before he left, "If Carla turns up, look after her, Luke. Make sure she has everything she wants."'

His hands moved to the beat, drumming on the coffee table. She was fascinated by them, long strong fingers, broad sinewy backs. She wanted to feel them on her body. Needed reassuring and comforting. Angelo had gone and it left a huge gap. She had been spending so much time with him, and now Josh wasn't there ... But he had left his buddy in charge.

'May I?' he asked suddenly, turning to her, not touching her till she said he might.

'Yes,' she answered, her breath tight in her throat.

His arm came around her and it felt familiar. He had held her sometimes to help her out of the sea, so strong that it took hardly any effort. But this was different, now his clasp was that of a man towards a woman. There was nothing platonic about it.

The music kept coming, soft South American strains that throbbed insidiously in her epicentre, rousing her blood, making her wet and lax inside. Luke ran his hand over her shoulders, her back and her breasts. Her nipples swelled under the friction of his thumb, and she sighed, resting her face against his broad chest, naked

211

through the gap in his shirt. He smelled of the sea, the boat, sandalwood.

He was beautiful as Carmel was beautiful, with smooth dark skin, rippling muscles and that innate sense of dignity and pride. Carla lay on the couch and surrendered herself to every sensation that he lavished on her. He brought her to climax with the greatest skill, using his fingers and his perfect, pointed tongue to jab so deliciously over her clitoris that she cried out as climax seized and shook her to her very foundation.

Then he eased down his baggy trousers and took out his long weapon and rubbed the purple head over her thrumming bud till another orgasm carried her to a second, shuddering release. Only then did he enter her body, when she was entirely ready for it, needing something large and solid to spasm round. Salsa pulsed in her head, matching the pounding of her blood, and Luke held her fast, his phallus driving into her, filling her, as he moved her up and down on that mighty shaft until his frenzied movements told her he was ejaculating.

He sighed, stilled, held and caressed her, and did not let her go. She slept – or maybe it was only a half-sleep, for she heard a voice saying, 'Don't move, Luke. It's OK. I share everything with my buddy.'

Josh had come in. She stared at him across Luke's shoulder and he smiled at her. 'Josh,' she murmured sleepily, worried about his reaction.

'Hello, Carla. I thought you might visit me tonight. That's why I left Luke here. I didn't want you to be lonely,' he said.

Luke rolled off her, fastening his fly, and Josh took his place, sitting with her while she came down from the heights of sexual release. And later she knew the comfort of having both men in the bed, her diving companions, her lovers, a harmonious threesome, which seemed the most natural thing in the world.

'Gosh, what a tan! You look so well!' shouted Toby across the hubbub of the arrival lounge. 'Here, let me carry that.' And he whisked Carla's bag from her shoulder. 'Hope you took lots of pics. I'm coming with you next time you fly off to exotic climes.'

'Oh, Toby, I can't begin to tell you. So much has happened,' she said breathlessly. The air was much colder, the colours less bright, the sky over Heathrow grey, not blue.

'Save it, darling. Let's get your luggage. Come on,' Toby said as he took charge.

She was glad to let him do so, more tired than she realised. He had found her a furnished flat near Hampstead Heath, ferociously expensive but, as he said, she could afford it. He drove her straight there, mothered her, refused to let her unpack or even talk about her experiences, simply tucked her into bed and removed himself.

It was not until she woke, several hours later, that he appeared with a cup of tea and listened while she recounted her adventures. He made the occasional comment, and she was perfectly frank. He learned all about Rutger and Angelo, Josh and Luke, even Carmel. After a while, she felt that what she most wanted just then was to have him in her bed, holding her, welcoming her, making love to her.

Slowly the realisation that she was really home began to sink in. She scanned the lavish bedroom, all floral wallpaper and gilt, its brass bed with barley-sugar posts hung with acres of white lace. From what she had seen so far, the furnishings were exactly what she would have chosen herself.

'Toby, you're a wizard,' she sighed.

'You like it?'

'I adore it.'

He had lost weight, and his hair was longer, falling about his shoulders; he gave it a flick after freeing it from the pony-tail. She had almost forgotten how handsome and sexy he was. And when she sat up and kissed him, his lips parted with a flattering eagerness. Her mind raced back to that moment in his office when he had brought her to orgasm, the first she had ever shared with a man.

'Have you found a lover while I've been away?' she asked, running her tongue over his lips.

'No. Saving it for you, dear,' he replied, his keen blue eyes shining with pleasure as he saw her bronzed breasts rising naked above the sheet.

'That I won't believe,' she teased, and her pulse began to race as he stroked one nipple, watching as it peaked against his finger.

'Let me show you how frustrated I am,' he whispered. He pushed back the sheet, wormed his way between her legs and burrowed into her delta like someone starved of food and sustenance.

They came together as if they had never been apart and he made love to her with the expertise of the man who loves women's minds as well as their bodies. No part of her was left in want, his kisses starting at her toes and working up, making her feel as if every inch of her was valuable and deserving of kisses. And only at the end, when he had brought her to orgasm by the slow glide of his fingers over her clitoris, did he enter her, joining her in her ecstasy.

'Did I tell you that Macbride and Lee have made an offer for *Enchanted Tapestry*?', he brought out casually when, taking a break from love-making, they lay in bed and talked.

Carla bounced up, yelling in bemused delight, 'The one Crown rejected?'

'Yes, and they want another . . . that idea about the Jane Eyre sort of governess person. Could you do it?'

'Could I not!' Carla blurted, recalling her daydream when Rutger had been masturbating her.

'Oh, and there's something else.'

'Yes?' It seemed that the room was filled with sunshine, and even a great, fat, banal rainbow. Everything was coming right at last.

'Well, how'd you like to do a bit more ghost writing? There's this guy, needs to write his life story. But this time he's a rock-singer.'

'I don't like rock,' she said, shaking her head, her hair tumbling about her face.

'We're talking telephone numbers here,' Toby replied, kissing her bare shoulder. 'He's an American, and is holed up in Bermuda.'

'I'll think about it,' she conceded, then slithered down his body, obeying the impulse to suck his penis hard – hard and deep into her throat.

Some time later, when they had prised themselves apart long enough to contemplate going out to eat, the phone rang. Carla reached a lazy hand towards the receiver, and raised it to her ear.

'Carla Holt,' she said.

'Carla! It's me, Giles!' came an instantly recognisable voice from the past.

'Hello Giles,' she replied serenely, Toby's arm round her, his hand slipped between her thighs.

'I heard you were expected back.'

'And how did you know where to find me?'

'Got your new number from Toby's secretary, told her you'd want to hear from me.'

Toby frowned and pulled a face, mouthing silently, 'She shouldn't have given it to him.'

Carla shook her head and smiled, saying down the phone, 'What do you want, Giles?'

'To see you again, of course.' He sounded surprised that she should ask.

'To take up where we left off?'

'Something like that. Look, I'm having a lot of trouble with my latest book. It's not the same without you. I need your help.'

She could picture his pleading, lost little boy expression, which had once turned her to jelly.

'I'm very busy right now,' she prevaricated, keeping him dangling.

'I appreciate that. I've been reading about you in the papers. Angelo Lorenzo's story seems set to be a best-seller.'

Let him grovel for a while longer, she thought, and said, 'Oh, yes, I think so too. It won't be out just yet, of course, but I have other irons in the fire.'

'Let's talk about them,' he responded eagerly. 'Come to dinner. I'll cook you something special. What d'you say? Will you give me the chance to apologise?'

Toby was running his lips across her shoulders, sending shivers down her spine. She touched his face tenderly as she said to Giles, 'I don't know about that. I'll have to consult my day-planner, and give it some thought.'

'Please come,' he insisted, sounding quite desperate. 'To be frank, my last book was a flop.'

'Really?' she said, cool as a mountain stream.

'Yes, and I need you if I'm going to get the next one off the ground.'

'Do you, Giles, really truly?'

'Yes, I do. Will you come back to me?'

'Giles.'

'Yes?'

'Fuck off!'

She put the phone down, not angrily, not even quickly, but with the firm, steady pressure one uses when closing a door for ever on a particularly stressful portion of one's life.

Nine months later, Carla read the reviews of *Whom the Gods Love*. It had been shown in Cannes and one eminent critic had written of it:

> That enfant terrible of the screen, Rutger Eberhardt, has done it again: *Whom the Gods Love* is wild. He had the gall to blend Homer's *Odyssey* with the *Kama Sutra* and has got away with it. It's hot, bold and outrageous. There are no half measures with Eberhardt. He is totally unscrupulous, ravishing our emotions and sensibilities. See it. You'll love it or hate it.

Carla had met Rutger several times since leaving Zaminos, renewing her acquaintance with the whip and that dark side of her, which longed to be controlled. But now she thought: poor old Robin. As the author and co-scriptwriter, there was mention of him of course, but Rutger took the lion's share. However, with the somewhat besotted Sir Gerald in his corner, Robin would not lack interested publishers and further screenplays.

She was now seated in the cabin of *Sea Jade*, off the coast of Jamaica, with several daily papers spread over the table. Josh had been following the trail of submerged pirate treasure and had asked her to go along. They had picked up where they left off – no ties, no heart-searching, just easy-going comradeship lit by passion.

She had been glad of the break after working nonstop on the rough of her new book, and then taking time out to liaise with the rock-star, fearfully attractive and totally off the wall. She knew that if she did take on his story – and there was little doubt about it, for the money offered was huge – there was a strong likelihood they would become lovers for a while. But tonight she was flying to England, where Toby would be waiting to shepherd her through the razzmatazz of Angelo's book launch.

Angelo! He was in the paper too, and she kissed the photo of him and got printers' ink on her lips. Tomorrow she might be embracing the real thing. He had been talking about marriage again, and the idea of having his babies was beginning to appeal.

'You're getting broody!' Marie had said with disgust not long ago, when they were sharing a sauna at Elysian Fields. 'Nature's trap! You won't find me falling for it.'

'Oh, I don't know,' Carmel, her live-in lover now, had put in, caressing the wet plumes on Marie's mound. 'I might do it, if I could find the right man to donate a syringe full of sperm.'

Thinking of Angelo, Carla gave a satisfied sigh, and accepted the cup of coffee Luke brought in from the galley. Life was good. She was free and had so many wonderful choices. The magical island had bestowed its blessing on her. No one would ever crush her spirit again.